MAGE BREAKER EIGHT BULLETS

MAGE BREAKER EIGHT BULLETS

SEAN R. FRAZIER

ALSO BY SEAN R. FRAZIER

The Call of Chaos (The Forgotten Years Book 1)

The Coming Storm (The Forgotten Years Book 2)

Descent into Madness (The Forgotten Years Book 3)

Ascent into Light (The Forgotten Years Book 4)

Mage Breaker (Mage Breaker Saga Book 1)

The Last Available

Published in the United States by Creative James Media.

www.creativejamesmedia.com

978-1-956183-09-2 (trade paperback)

First U.S. Edition 2024

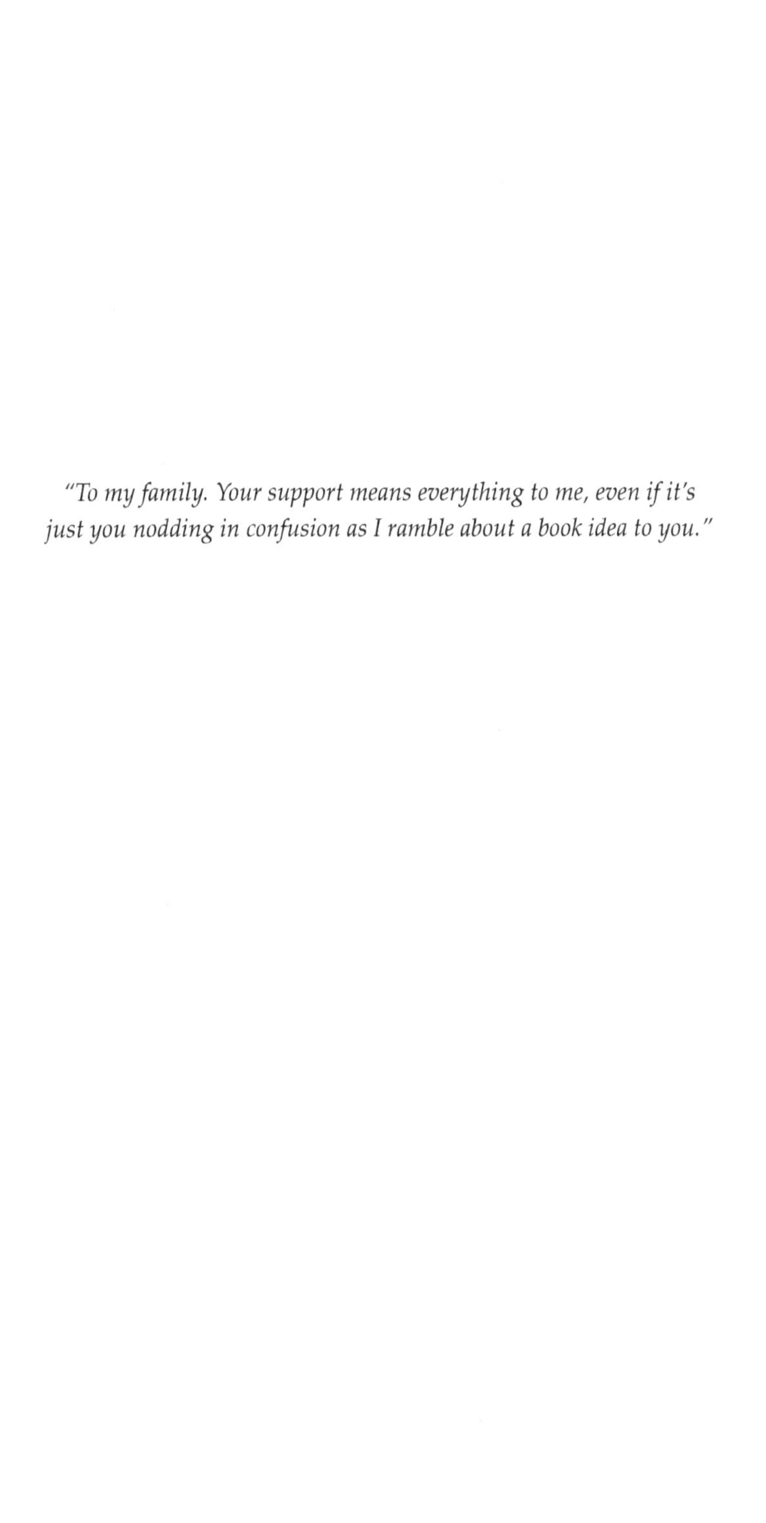

"To my family. Your support means everything to me, even if it's just you nodding in confusion as I ramble about a book idea to you."

CHAPTER
ONE

THE FAMILIAR SIRENS sounded while red lights flashed overhead in their typical irritating fashion. Shortly thereafter, as it always did, the heavy door slowly slid open, contributing even more to the annoying cacophony with its familiar melody of metal grinding on metal.

Also familiar was the cadre of guards—seven this time—standing on the other side, ready to pounce if needed. They had good reason to be on the defensive after all. Things had gone poorly several times, and it was only after three of them received broken bones that more guards were eventually added to the daily event.

That was weeks ago. Or years ago. It could've been either. When the only thing someone saw most of the time was the same four walls in a dimly lit cell, time lost all relevance.

"Ellyne Thandaral," one of the guards croaked in a deep, raspy voice. She recognized this one in particular—the guard she'd punched repeatedly in the throat. "It's time for your daily activity period."

Ellyne stared at the opposite wall, where her bed and bucket lay, just as she'd been instructed to do countless times before. Even when she finally complied with their wishes, they still insisted on reminding her, barking orders incessantly, until they were apparently satisfied with their relative safety. It brought a smile to her face every time.

"You may turn around now," the guard continued. "You know the rules. Fail to comply and—"

Though they healed over, she still recalled the bruises given to her by her last transgression. Maybe it was time to earn fresh marks.

Her snark was always lost on these brutes. And the other guards from this species she'd encountered appeared to share this same shortcoming. It may have been a language barrier, but she suspected they simply had no sense of humor.

"The Kithrak have bestowed upon you your daily limited freedom," another guard said in a much whinier voice. "Should you abuse this privilege, it will be revoked."

Ellyne slowly turned around, clasping her hands behind her back, and puffed a few strands of blond hair away from her face.

"Freedom," she laughed. "We do this every day. When are you planning to stop repeating the same garbage? I can practically lecture you guys word for word. How about, from now on, I give the speech? I've got some ideas that might add some—"

"When you comply," throat guy grunted, followed by a coughing fit. "When you comply," he continued, "maybe we'll say something else."

"And yet, here we are, doing this again and you've yet to revoke this so-called privilege."

"Exit the cell and follow us," a smaller guard commanded.

"Exit the cell and follow us," Ellyne repeated in a husky, mocking voice. She cautiously moved forward, taking in every small detail about these seven individuals. She knew very little about the Kithrak and anything she could glean was useful. She did, however, know quite a bit about their security methods, having tested them frequently. The stun batons they employed were painful and effective. The wicked blades at their sides were new, however. She scrutinized them closely as she approached.

The moment she exited her prison cell, the guards surrounded her, clutching their crackling batons and boxing her in with little room to move. It was a smart tactic, and it was proof the Kithrak learned from their mistakes, even if the process was sometimes slow.

The seven thugs led her slowly down a stark, brightly lit corridor with white walls lined with closed cells like hers. Each of her captors was heavily armored down to the purple helmets they wore, but every piece showed signs of serious neglect as if they hadn't been used often, if at all. That was surely a response to her past behavior. The thought made her grin, but it also made identifying her captors more difficult.

"I see you guys are obviously afraid of me these days," she joked, staring intently at the mismatched colors of each part of their armor. "I mean, you're all armored up and carrying such large blades—all for me. I'm flattered, really."

The guards said nothing and, instead, guided her down a corridor to the right—a corridor which looked exactly like all the others.

"Come on," she continued. "Ordinarily, there are only four of you. I appreciate the fandom but don't understand the occasion. I mean, you guys must really like me or something, right?"

Her captors remained silent. She wondered if they were making faces at her under their helmets. She would've. Maybe they had comms in their helmets and were cracking jokes about her on a private channel.

"Someone must have serious feelings about me to give me such a … robust security detail. I'm guessing all your prisoners don't get the same treatment. I'd be honored if I didn't want to punch you guys in the throat again."

The one familiar guard started to move his hand to his

throat, thought better of it, and dropped it back to his side. Ellyne smirked.

The corridor—this whole complex—seemed familiar. Sure, she'd been led down the same path every day for ... well, however long it'd been, but it felt like more than that. Maybe that was a memory from ... from before her captivity. She wished she remembered more.

The truth was, she only knew her name was Ellyne because that's what the Kithrak called her. As far as she was concerned, they could've made that up. All other knowledge she had about herself was fragmented, like so many puzzle pieces scattered about, and most of that information came from dreams which were unreliable at best.

It was better than nothing, but a trickle of memories might have been more frustrating than not remembering anything at all.

"So, the fact that I get so much attention means only one thing—you guys like me." Ellyne laughed and made exaggerated kissing sounds while mocking them with an amorous gaze. "I must be super cool or something. It does strike me as a little weird, though, since you're not human like me. I'm unsure if we can make this relationship work."

"You'd already be dead if we had our way," one of them growled. She wasn't sure which one it was, but she smirked again. It was not only fun to get under their skin, but it was also incredibly easy.

"Oh, I'm sure I would be. Big, tough Kithrak thugs in full armor with massive weapons just to keep little old me in check. Assuming the seven of you actually *could* keep me in check. Is seven the magic number?"

She laughed as one of them slugged her in the stomach, cutting her revelry short. They didn't stop marching through the hallway, so she staggered as they very nearly dragged her along with them, sputtering and gasping for air.

"What I don't understand," she grunted, finally able to

keep up with them, "is why nobody else gets an armed escort?"

"You get one hour," they told her as they stopped in front of the same door as always. One of them pushed a button and it slid open with the sound of metal grinding on metal. Then they pushed her into the yard beyond and sealed the squeaky door shut behind her.

Ellyne knew what to expect—the situation was the same every day for countless weeks. She was led out into the same courtyard for an hour of "exercise." And, every day, she scrutinized her surroundings, attempting to find something amiss—some opportunity for her to escape.

"It'd be really nice if I could remember something," she muttered. "Remembering *anything* would be nice, in fact. It doesn't have to be an important memory, either—just something new."

She was a prisoner—she'd figured that much out immediately. But why and where were questions to which she had no answers. During the time she'd been captive, however long that was, she'd gleaned very little information, and it was beginning to frustrate her.

The Kithrak were her captors, but she had no information on them. Though they may have resembled humans, they weren't actually human—that much was painfully obvious. Some of them had extra arms or extra eyes ... or both. The guards were large, hulking figures that dwarfed her size, and she knew enough to understand people didn't grow that large.

The "where" question was just as perplexing. She was being held in a secure facility but that's all she knew. Staring into the sky, the sun was in the same position it always was. Though she had no way to tell what time it was, she assumed it was an hour or so before noon.

What had been bugging her for some time now, though, was that very fact—the sun was always in the same spot.

Seasons changed and the position of the sun shifted accordingly, but not here. Was that normal?

She thought maybe they simply let her outside according to the sun's position. Perhaps they had no standard of telling time? But then, the weather would also change. It would be warmer in the summer and colder in the winter. Again, not here. There was never a shift in temperature nor did it rain.

Or had she simply not been here long enough for that to happen? Ellyne believed keeping track of the days would clarify some issues, but she didn't trust her own mind. Several times, she lost count and was forced to start over, fighting an always-present haze within her brain.

She gazed down at the soil beneath her bare feet and noticed how dirty her clothes were. The simple white shirt and pants she had been given were starting to look more a dingy yellow with brown dirt caked near her feet. Not that she cared, of course, but when she had such little variety in her life, Ellyne tried to fabricate her own excitement.

"I hope laundry day is soon," she joked. "I should always look my best for … well, the thugs who let me out to play, I guess. At least this outfit has no blood stains."

The truth was it *had* been a while since the Kithrak provided her with fresh clothes. They were hesitant enough to deliver her daily meals and never seemed to enjoy the task. It made sense they wouldn't want to replace her dirty clothes. The fact that they all avoided her whenever possible amused her.

"I promise I won't break anyone's arm if you guys drop off some fresh clothes for me!" she shouted with a smile on her face. "Though, I must admit, white's not really my color— or maybe it is. But dingy, smelly brown definitely isn't."

Her mind reeled and, suddenly, she saw herself clad in black boots, black pants, and a black jacket over a white tank top. The moment was fleeting, and she staggered backward into the wall as the image faded.

"What the hell was that?"

Ellyne reexamined herself, still clad in the same dust-covered clothes as before. Her gaze darted about, scrutinizing the courtyard she was intimately familiar with. She felt panic trying to set in and forced herself to relax.

The area was exactly twenty-two steps long and twenty-seven steps wide with patchy grass dotting the ground, struggling to survive. She sat against the trunk of the solitary maple tree that grew in the center and sighed.

"What if I'm not a prisoner? What if my brain is so broken the only option is to lock me away in a hospital to simply be forgotten and left to languish until I disappear? What if I'm the only human in a world of these ... Kithrak guys."

She closed her eyes and rested her head on the maple tree's trunk, exhaling deeply.

"These ... Kithrak call me 'Ellyne', and they're quite obviously afraid of me. But what did I do to them? Well, besides breaking the occasional nose or arm ... I mean, they feared me from the very first time they came to my cell."

That much she knew. In fact, it was about *all* she knew. Occasionally, she would have a dream, or her mind would conjure a brief illusion that felt familiar somehow, but in a strange way that seemed like a past life. Both these occurrences were rare and brief but, to her, they felt *so real*.

One such recurring vision was that of a vast city filled with technological marvels and wondrous buildings that touched the sky.

Dreams were one thing—the mind was a treasure trove of odd images and surreal plots—but, sometimes, they felt familiar, and Ellyne found that impossible to ignore. There had to be something there—some kernel of truth. Unfortunately, a feeling of familiarity was all there was. She never learned anything from these flashes of insight, but she held out hope that, one day, she might.

While most of her episodes focused on places or things,

there were occasionally people. Well, only two people, really, but they had appeared several times now. Ellyne didn't understand their significance, but one of them—a girl dressed in red—made her happy. The other—a bald man in robes—aroused inexplicable rage within her.

The Kithrak most likely knew more about her than she did, and that not only intrigued and confused, but infuriated her to no end.

"Hey!" a raspy voice called through the speakers overhead, "your time's up."

The door squeaked open.

"Proceed slowly to the door with your hands in front of you and we will lead you back to your cell. If you attack or attempt to resist, you will be punished."

"Yeah, I've heard that before."

CHAPTER
TWO

ELLYNE GAZED up at the buildings with their menagerie of multicolored lights—magnificent, illuminated tapestries reaching high into the sky that looked down upon the city streets and the people who traveled them.

The city itself held a serene beauty Ellyne never failed to overlook every time she visited. It was certainly more beautiful than her normal accommodations.

Though there was barely anyone about. The city was always quiet at night, which was how she preferred it anyway. It was easier to move around at night as opposed to the daytime hours when everyone was out, pushing and shoving on the sidewalks. It was quiet, too, and all this provided Ellyne with the benefit of operating largely unnoticed.

None of this mattered, however, because this was a dream.

She'd been here before. It always began here, with stark familiarity Ellyne couldn't quite put her finger on. But had she actually been here before—sometime in the past? Or was this feeling simply because she'd previously dreamt it? Reality and dream blended until the boundaries of both were no longer discernible.

It felt real enough—the chilly breeze, the low thrum of distant machinery, the delectable smell wafting from a restaurant somewhere close, two women making out by a dumpster in a nearby alley … and the whisper of the passenger train as it sailed past, quietly hovering above its travel platform.

As she'd done before—whether it'd been dream or reality—Ellyne slowly walked forward, in awe of the vast cityscape. Most businesses were either closed or soon would be, and the streets were largely deserted, except for an occasional vehicle quietly passing by or another person on the sidewalk hurrying to their destination.

It felt so real but, with every step she took, Ellyne became more convinced it was merely a dream. Even in this state, she remembered her bleak cell, her captors, the hour of solitary recreation each day … and her spirits sank. But, still, she felt a familiarity with this place—as if it were real and she'd truly been here. Even if it was all made up—fabricated within a mind that longed to escape—it was a respite of sorts.

It was too vivid—too detailed and she couldn't let it go. Something told her this place was *real* and whether she'd been here in the past, or whether she somehow traveled here in a dream, it held significance. It was important in some way, otherwise her brain wouldn't keep dredging it up .

It was something to cling to. It wasn't an element that offered hope or salvation, or was it? Ellyne didn't know, but she *did* understand there was more to this than a simple dream. Whatever meaning lay behind this recurring narrative, it provided the drive she needed to keep going. There was a puzzle, here, and she was determined to solve it.

Hopefully, it would lead to answers. But how many more visits would she have to make before those answers became apparent?

She passed a screen of some kind—a device she presumed broadcast messages. She saw one of them once when she fled her routine guard detail and ended up in a new area of her prison. Of course, she hadn't been able to read whatever it said, since the words were in the Kithrak language, and she'd only gotten a quick glimpse before her captors caught up with her.

This screen was dark. It was always dark. Every time she walked this way, she saw it and expected it to light up with illegible symbols but was met with the same disappointing result.

Did this city belong to the Kithrak? Was this some sort of trick?

Her captors—the Kithrak— there was no doubt they had all the information. Naturally, however, they were going to keep her in the dark. She was convinced they knew far more about her than she did which, admittedly, wouldn't take much since she knew little more than her name—if she even remembered that correctly.

Her attempts to glean little bits of information usually proved futile. The guards that interacted with her (and that was an overstatement) rarely spoke. When they *did* speak, it was usually to threaten her or insult her. Only once or twice did they ever offer up any useful information and Ellyne wasn't sure they even realized their mistakes.

The most intriguing tidbit she recalled was when one of them mentioned "magic."

Magic, of course, sounded like something dangerous, wondrous, and outside of reality, but they had once (and only once) spoken of it as if it were real. She didn't know her captors to be the lying sort or to make up stories, so she filed this interaction in the back of her mind to explore later.

Ordinarily, Ellyne would've assumed they were talking about simple card tricks or sleight of hand, but their tone and the related discussion hinted at more. She had to admit she was curious, but she also didn't like the idea.

And it was merely one of many thoughts she had while

languishing in her solitary confinement. But here, in this dream, she was free. Fleeting as that freedom might be, she savored it, though her mind wouldn't let her relax for long and she continued asking herself a barrage of questions she had no answers to.

It was peaceful, this city, and Ellyne was free. She dreaded inevitably waking and staring at the four white walls—stark reminders of her plight. If only she knew *why* she was a prisoner—what did she do to deserve such treatment? Whatever it was, she surmised her actions must've been serious.

Ellyne opened her eyes and sighed, staring at the white, featureless ceiling while still desperately clinging to the feeling of freedom from her dream. The feeling would fade as it always did, and she'd be left with nothing but despair mixed with sadness and a sprinkle of rage.

"Business as usual," she muttered, rubbing her eyes and sitting on the edge of the simple rather uncomfortable bed. She'd had worse, though … or, at least, that's what she thought she remembered. Something told her that was a bit of a memory, and she chose to believe it.

"What shall we do today?" she asked in the middle of a yawn. Something in her shoulder popped when she stretched, at first sending a brief but sharp pain down her back, but then she felt relief and moved her arm around to loosen it up. "I'm guessing we'll be doing more of the same shit we did yesterday and the day before," she mused. "And the day before and so on … and here I am, talking to myself yet again."

She waited for her usual breakfast to slide through the slot at the bottom of the door. It would inevitably be cold and barely edible. Most of the time, Ellyne couldn't determine what kind of food any of her meals truly were. She ate it because she had to, but gagging from the flavor was common and unpleasant.

Her breakfast never came. Instead, she heard the jingle of keys and the footfalls of several individuals approaching. Hers was the only occupied cell in this hallway, so she knew they were here for her.

It was highly unusual for anyone to visit her for any purpose other than letting her out to play in the yard for an hour, so Ellyne was immediately suspicious and braced herself for whatever was about to happen.

The key rattled in the lock as it turned, and the door swung open to reveal six large Kithrak. They were all armed with stun batons and clad in their usual multicolor, padded suits of armor with oversized blades at their hips.

"It's not already time for my play date outside, is it?" Ellyne quipped. "Did I oversleep or are you guys just ahead of schedule today?" She yawned but made no move to do anything. "I haven't stretched yet, so I need to do that before any rigorous physical activity. If you guys could come back in a few minutes, that'd be great."

None of the Kithrak responded. For a moment, she exchanged stares with them, unsure if she should get up or remain on her bed. One wrong move would have her drooling on the ground from a stun baton.

And if she was going to meet that punishment, she would make damned sure she earned it.

"So," she started, "are you going to tell me what I'm supposed to do? Or should I—"

"Step out of the cell," the lead Kithrak grunted. "Slowly … with your hands up."

"This is highly irregular," Ellyne argued, making herself as comfortable on the bed as she could. "It's been quite a long time since anyone interacted with me other than the usual protocols. So, what do you want with me?"

"We have come to collect you," the Kithrak continued. "That is all you need to know."

"Oh, that's cool. I'm a collector's item?"

"Go with them," a soft voice whispered.

"What?" Ellyne asked.

"I said, that is all you need to know."

"No, not you," Ellyne growled.

The guards remained silent and motionless. Ellyne figured they were a bit confused which was fine with her because she, too, was a bit confused.

"Go with them," the voice repeated.

Ellyne stared at the Kithrak who seemed to not know what to do with her. As far as she could tell, they hadn't heard the voice.

But she heard it. It was clear, lucid, and very real. And … there was a familiarity to it—something she couldn't shake. But confusion overwhelmed all other thoughts as she grappled with what was happening.

The voice in her head was very real, yes, but that didn't necessarily indicate a good situation. Good or bad—it didn't matter. The guards would get their way. The only choice she had was whether she remained conscious.

"Fine," she relented, silently mouthing the words without sound "I'll go with them."

"Yes," the Kithrak replied, "you will."

"Right. That's what I said." She held her arms aloft and slowly moved toward the group. "So where are we going?"

"Wherever we tell you to go."

"You always say the nicest things to me."

The guards led her through several familiar hallways— familiar because each one was identical to the next. The only differences were the symbols on the cell doors. With each cell she passed she wondered if it was occupied. In however long she'd been here, she'd never seen another prisoner.

It was solitary confinement within solitary confinement. If there had at one time been other prisoners, what happened to them?

"Listen closely," the voice continued. Ellyne resisted the urge to look around her. The Kithrak were still oblivious, and she wished to keep it that way. *"There will be a shiny, glowing object somewhere nearby. It's smooth and translucent, and its colors shift."*

"Who are you?" Ellyne whispered.

Several guards turned their attention to Ellyne and scowled.

"We are the Kithrak," one laughed, "your masters. Surely you already knew this."

"It's called a tyrome. I need you to find it, and I need you touch it."

"Just … touch it?"

"Touch what?" one of the guards asked, brandishing his stun baton. "You can touch *this*!"

Ellyne convulsed and dropped to her knees as he briefly prodded her with the baton. Every nerve lit up as if it were on fire.

The group of guards laughed and waited for her to struggle to her feet before continuing, still snickering quietly.

"What the hell was that for?" she asked, wiping the spittle from her chin. "At least be decent enough to buy me dinner first."

"Because I wanted to," the Kithrak laughed, his voice muffled by the helmet. Ellyne wished she could've seen his face and maybe earn another baton strike after she punched it.

"Here's a gift for you," she replied, wiping her saliva-covered hand on the Kithrak's padded armor. "When I get out of here, I'll make sure to return the favor."

The guards laughed again, slugging insults and taunts her way.

Ellyne balled her fists but did nothing. She was a formidable fighter—something she'd found out quite by accident the first time—but she had no hope against this many fully armed guards.

"You need to touch it. Touch the tyrome. This you must do—whatever it takes."

"I don't understand," Ellyne said. "What do you mean, whatever it takes?"

"What don't you understand?" one of the guards laughed. "You're never getting out of here. You'll die before you leave and, even then, we'll keep your corpse as a reminder! Maybe we'll zap it every so often just for old time's sake."

"Again, not talking to you," she growled. "Wait … a reminder of what?" she asked, being careful to whisper her words.

The guards fell silent, exchanging worried glances. Ellyne could feel the disapproval from the lead guard. She despised their helmets more than usual, so badly wishing to be able to read their faces.

"Move along, human."

"No, a reminder of what? What aren't you telling me?"

They were hiding something—something related to her. Since she had no memories from before her imprisonment, she had to assume they were talking about something from her past, and she needed to discover what it was.

"This will be your reminder!" another guard shouted, holding aloft his stun baton. "Now shut up and do as we say, or this will be far more painful than it should be."

Ellyne not only preferred to be conscious in the presence of the Kithrak, but she now felt a sudden purpose to do so. What was this tyrome and why was it so crucial she touch it?

More importantly, why did the word sound familiar?

"And who the hell is speaking to me?" she muttered.

Ellyne wanted to scream. She also wanted to start a fight, but she knew better. She had to be patient. Though patience, she'd learned almost immediately, was not one of her strengths.

"So, I'll start a fight later," she whispered to herself.

"What was that?" one of the guards asked.

"I said fine," she replied, "lead on, oh wonderful Kithrak overlords."

CHAPTER
THREE

"OW!" Ellyne shrieked. "You didn't have to throw me into the chair!"

"You shouldn't have resisted," the Kithrak responded, focusing all four of his eyes on her.

"I wasn't resisting," she insisted, "I was merely referencing your mom and how much of a—"

"Hold her." He motioned for the guards to restrain her, waving his four arms in the air. The guards obliged, holding Ellyne's arms down and keeping her confined to the hard, uncomfortable chair.

"So, what's on the agenda today, fellas? Are we having a nice lunch together?"

"*You,*" the Kithrak began, inspecting a needle, "are going to sit quietly while I draw some blood. Can you do that for me, Ellyne?"

Ellyne winced. She had that same reaction every time her name was uttered. They always said it with disdain on their lips. And, though she didn't remember much, there was something else about the way they said it—as if they weren't pronouncing it right.

It was disconcerting—the inability to remember even

one's own name, but she was pretty sure this Kithrak stooge was saying it wrong.

The first time any of them called her that—Ell-een—she hadn't recognized the name. For all she knew, they made it up and arbitrarily called her that. However, as time wore on, she not only grew accustomed to it, but felt its familiarity. But there was still something amiss.

"You didn't get enough blood the last time?" she quipped. "I'm afraid I'll need to see your medical license before we go any further. I only have so much to go around."

"I would laugh and say you're charming, but I don't ordinarily enjoy lying, even for humorous purposes."

"Oh, that makes sense," Ellyne scoffed, "because you tell me the truth so often." She squirmed a bit, pretending to attempt an escape. What she was really doing, however, was trying to get a look around the room for this … tyrome thing. She wasn't keen on listening to voices in her head, but she also had nothing better to do, having been dragged into this same room countless times.

At first, she saw no glowing, pulsing stone device but during her phony resistance, she finally caught a glimpse of something that fit the description, sitting on a display stand of sorts—as if it were an heirloom or a piece of art. It was on a counter across the room, behind the doctor or whatever this four-eyed goon was.

The two guards managed to restrain Ellyne to the point where she couldn't squirm anymore, not that she didn't continue trying.

"Have you two been working out?" she laughed. "Last time, it took four of you. I'm impressed. Been doing some arm curls?"

The guards' faces showed no sign of any emotion but irritation which, as it so often did, made Ellyne smile. At least they'd removed their helmets when they entered the room.

Not only could she read their facial expressions, but she could also punch one or two if it came to that.

"So, tell me," she said as the Kithrak with the needle approached, "why do you always need my blood? Are you vampires that are too shy to bite people? So, you take blood with a needle and make some sort of weird drink with it? I bet that's it, isn't it?"

"You think you're charming," the Kithrak responded as he plunged the needle into her arm. She wasn't sure if it was supposed to be painful or if he went out of his way to make it so. "But you're really just an obstacle."

"First of all," she said, wincing as she watched the first ampoule slowly fill, "I *know* I'm charming. And second, I'm always happy to be a thorn in your ass. I've been called worse than 'obstacle'—at least, I assume I have."

The Kithrak returned a wry smile as he switched to an empty ampoule. "This would be so much easier if I could just use magic to do it," he muttered, whispering to himself. Ellyne supposed he wasn't aware she heard him, but she paid attention far more than any of them thought and, more importantly, their overconfidence and irritation with her made them sloppy.

"You could've at least warmed up the chair for me," she continued, trying to hold their attention on her while she scrutinized the glowing rock behind on the counter. It pulsed with light and shifted colors.

After two more ampoules were full, the Kithrak withdrew the needle and threw a piece of gauze at Ellyne. She promptly grabbed it and put pressure on her arm while the Kithrak disposed of the syringe and put away some other items. They were both well-accustomed to the routine.

"That wasn't so hard, was it?" he asked, his back to her as he tidied his work area.

"Do I get a piece of candy now as a reward?"

The guards, obviously also accustomed to the routine and

believing it was over and done, released her with the assumption she would comply as they prepared to lead her back to her cell.

They assumed wrong.

Ellyne leapt from the chair and lunged for the tyromc on the counter, catching the guards by surprise. They stumbled forward, grabbing for her as she scrambled to stay ahead of them long enough to touch it. The doctor staggered backward, gasping and falling against the wall, apparently trying to avoid the fray.

One of the guards got a hand on her, grabbing her right arm and trying to pull her back. The other guard grabbed her left arm, trying desperately to restrain her. "We will have to punish you, Ellyne!" one of them grunted, obviously having difficulty holding her as she wriggled and flailed.

"This had damn well better be worth it," she growled, straining to touch the glowing object.

She somehow slipped her right arm free and elbowed the guard in the face, knocking him back past the chair and into the wall behind them. She then shifted her weight and stepped in front of the other guard, tossing him over her shoulder and onto the floor.

"You can't escape, Ellyne!" the doctor shouted.

"I don't intend to escape," she replied as she ran forward and touched the stone with the tip of her finger. "I just want to touch the pretty rock."

She suddenly found herself standing amongst the towering skyscrapers once again, as she gazed up at the night sky.

"Where am I?" she asked, gazing around the quiet city. "Is this all a dream again?" She shivered and wrapped her arms around her as a crisp breeze flitted by.

Disappointed, she sighed, feeling hopelessness creep in. She wasn't even interested in exploring the dream this time.

Something had changed. The mystic aura of the city appeared muted.

"Of course, it's a dream, Ellyne," she muttered, kicking a lamp post. "It's always a dream. In what feels like a few minutes, you'll wake up in your cell and be just as depressed as you always are when you realize you're still a prisoner. Was that whole blood draw thing even real?"

Ellyne inspected her arm, instinctively searching for the needle marks she knew wouldn't be there. She would do the same when she woke up, hoping to determine what was real and what was merely a dream.

"It's not a dream," a voice called—the same voice she heard whispering to her earlier. "Not this time, anyway."

Ellyne looked around and spotted a figure standing in the street—a black-haired woman dressed in an obnoxious red dress and boots. She couldn't have looked more out of place as she slowly approached, her piercing green eyes fixed on Ellyne.

"Well, I mean," the woman continued, "it kind of is. It's a sort of hybrid dream thing that's neither real nor a dream and it's really cool and you'll never believe—"

"Wait, who are—"

"Our time is short, Ellyne. I know you want an explanation, but I don't even have all the answers. I don't even have time to explain what I *do* know."

"Why did you need me to touch that rock thing? I'm going to be super in trouble when I wake up. Not that I care, but the only worthwhile bruises are those I've earned."

"By touching the tyrome, you connected with another tyrome and allowed this to happen." She motioned around them. "It's wonderful, isn't it?"

"That rock didn't create this, I did. I've been here countless times."

"Yes, but I haven't," the girl replied.

"Great," Ellyne scoffed, "I've let some weird girl with zero fashion sense into my dream. How exactly does that help me?"

"Because," the woman continued, "Touching that tyrome revealed your location. Now I know where you are, and I'm coming to get you."

"You? How are *you* going to break me out of a prison?"

The woman laughed. "You'll see. You don't remember, but that's okay. Your memories will eventually return but, for now, we need to take this one step at a time."

"I still don't understand how you alone are going to bust me out of a Kithrak prison," Ellyne scoffed.

"Because I'm not going to break you out. *You* are."

The ground shook and several of the buildings around them swayed. A massive shadow crept across the sky, emerging from the clouds, and coming to a stop above them.

"Shit," the woman cursed. "They're onto us. Oh, sorry for swearing but, um, we're out of time. We'll meet again, Ellyne—very soon. Until we do, you might want this."

"Huh," Ellyne chuckled, "you actually got my name right … I think."

The stranger held aloft a small dagger. She released the blade, and it floated over to Ellyne who hesitated at first but eventually grabbed it, causing it to vanish.

"Wait!" Ellyne shouted as the woman turned and walked way, headed into the fog beyond. "Who are you? Who am I?"

"Be patient," the woman's voice whispered. "I'm on the way."

The city melted into a kaleidoscope of swirling colors that formed dozens of images—the woman in red, a bald, robed man, white energy reaching into the sky, and a golden gun were just a few of the familiar things invading her mind.

She found herself back in the lab, being pulled away from the tyrome by the guards who'd leapt into action.

"You're a lot of trouble, Ellyne," the doctor scolded,

waiving a finger in front of her face. "But you always surprise me by just how much trouble you are."

"Yeah, well," she spat, "it's apparently my brand ... and the name's Ell-een-ya."

"I don't care what your name is," the Kithrak sneered.

"Well," Ellyne laughed, slowly getting up, "you should."

"And why is that, exactly?"

"Because you're going to hear it a lot when I get out of here. My name is going to keep you awake at night."

The Kithrak laughed again as the guard hoisted her to her shaky feet. "Is that so?" He moved in closer, his many eyes wandering, inspecting her. "You think you're going to escape? You have no concept of where you actually are, Ellyne. You can't possibly imagine just how difficult such an action would be."

"Your mom does."

He emphasized her mispronounced name and laughed some more, then motioned to the guards. She felt something hit the back of her head. Her vision blurred and everything went dark.

The pounding in Ellyne's head told her all she needed to know when she opened her eyes and gazed up at the all-too-familiar ceiling.

"Ow," she groaned, squinting her eyes, and running a hand through her blond hair. "I guess his mother is a sensitive subject." Her fingers eventually found the lump on the back of her head. It was impressive. She would be sure to return the favor when she escaped.

"When ..." she muttered, "yes, *when.*"

That was new. After several failed escape attempts in the past, she had long since accepted she would be captive for a long time—maybe forever. The urge to find a way out was always there, and Ellyne was constantly looking for her opportunity, but such chances were rare and always failed. Each time she tried, the Kithrak doubled down on security and fixed the problem. She hadn't seen an opportunity in a long time, having apparently spent them all.

Until now. If this woman truly *was* coming to find her, then that was worthy of renewed hope, but she had to ask herself just what could one person do for her? If Ellyne couldn't escape, how could one woman break in and then help her escape?

Or, rather, how could one individual break in and then have Ellyne liberate herself. It sounded far-fetched.

And, above all else, was it even real? It felt like a dream but, at the same time, it was different … more tangible, more real. And there was a stark familiarity about it—something more intense than her usual feelings. Sure, she still felt she had been to the city in her dreams, but she also felt she might know the woman who appeared. The woman certainly acted like she knew her, but Ellyne wasn't sure it was routine for her to hang out with not only a girl, but a girl who made such questionable fashion choices.

More than anything, right now, she wanted her memories back. Whatever the Kithrak did to her, she would make them pay. She would find out why they were keeping her here and make them restore her memories.

Then she would burn this place down.

"And how are you going to do that, Ellyne?" she laughed, trying not to cry through the pounding pain in her head. "Some … girl is going to rescue you and then you're going to set fire to this place? The two of you versus an entire prison filled with Kithrak?"

Ellyne still barely knew anything about herself, but she *did* know she could fight. She'd proven that time and again and she'd also paid for it more times than she could recall. Gone were the days when just one or two guards escorted her wherever she went. Now it was basically a small, well-armed army that kept her in check.

"They're going to need more than an army to stop me,"

she grinned. Though her situation still appeared as dire as before, she had both hope and confidence growing within her. If there truly was going to be a prison break, she resolved to be ready. "Yeah, Ellyne, but then what?" she mused.

She sat up and felt something dig into her hip.

"What the hell?" she asked, pulling the dagger from her waistband. "How did—" she gasped, inspecting the blade. "How is this even possible?"

The dagger was simple, but it was unmistakably the weapon the woman showed her in the dream—or whatever it had been. There was no denying the pure fantastic nature of the situation, and Ellyne was having trouble understanding or even just believing.

"Magic," she whispered. "The Kithrak keep mentioning it as if it's actually real."

She ran her fingers over the weapon which appeared to be fashioned from one solid piece of metal. It was cold and smooth and, after she nearly cut her finger accidentally, she discovered it was wickedly sharp. But one tiny dagger wasn't going to give her much of an advantage against however many Kithrak were in this place.

Her fingers found a bump on the dagger's small crossguard. Upon closer inspection, she determined it was a button. Several moments passed with her simply staring at the weapon with great curiosity.

"Well," she mused, "what's the worst that could happen?"

Holding the dagger at arm's length and pointing it away from her, she pushed the tiny button. The blade telescoped outward, instantly becoming the length of a sword. The crossguard also expanded, as did the hilt. She heard mechanical noises from inside the dagger as the last pieces locked into place.

As she stared, awe-stricken, she realized this, too, felt slightly familiar—as if she had not only seen this weapon before, but used it to great effect. It felt like an old friend—a friend she recognized, but whose name she didn't remember.

"Well, Ellyne from the past," she laughed, "I don't know what you got yourself into but, I gotta say, I'm really excited to find out."

CHAPTER
FOUR

WHEN SHE HEARD the Kithrak pound on her cell door, Ellyne quickly hid the dagger in her waistband of her dingy white pants. She only had two real options—slide it under her mattress or keep it on her somewhere, and she knew full well a weapon was useless if you didn't have immediate access to it when you needed it. It was a risky gamble, but what was the worst they could do to her—besides what they'd already done?

She was sure of one thing—the Kithrak wanted her alive. They could have killed her at any time, especially as retaliation for the myriad things she'd done, but they hadn't. She knew they would try everything to keep her alive, but the question was, why? Were her blood samples really that important to them?

She assumed she was being tested and observed. Her daily hour in the courtyard most likely wasn't solely for her benefit, and there were times they poked and prodded her in the lab—the blood samples, for example. She didn't understand why she was so important, but she didn't wish to stick around to discover the answer.

She was, however, acutely aware that she *was* important,

and such a fact was advantageous.

"Move to the back of the cell," the husky Kithrak voice grunted, pounding on the door again. "And keep your hands where we can see them."

Ellyne did as she was instructed, as she had countless times before. She lost track of time, but it seemed early for her hour of "free time." Either that, or she'd been unconscious for a lot longer than she suspected.

Ellyne looked down at her hip to see if the dagger produced any noticeable bulge to attract Kithrak suspicion. From her view, she couldn't see anything amiss, but the real test would come soon enough.

There was no jangling of keys or sound of a lock being turned. Instead, the door simply swung open and a hulking Kithrak entered her cell, slamming the door behind him.

"Shit," Ellyne muttered, "definitely not time for my hour of 'me' time."

This particular Kithrak was one of the largest she'd seen. He had three eyes and four thick, muscular arms. And he didn't look jovial.

"So," Ellyne said, feeling sweat on her forehead, "you're not here to discuss the finer points of knitting, are you?" She kept her right hand near her concealed weapon, ready to use it at a moment's notice. This situation was new to her, but the circumstances weren't promising.

She knew why he was here—punishment. While she was still certain she was not to die this day, a broken arm or leg might not be out of the question. The Kithrak in the lab probably ordered this retaliation, and most likely not just because of the "your mom" joke.

From what she could tell, the more arms and eyes a Kithrak had, the more important they were, and the doctor guy had plenty of each. Screwing with two-eyed, two-armed guards was inconsequential, but she'd messed with the wrong Kithrak, apparently. And this thug was likely almost as important.

"Not exactly," the beastly guard replied.

The door was shut but Ellyne believed it to still be unlocked. She might be able to get past the guard and make a break for it if she could keep moving. But she also had a weapon, now, and this Kithrak didn't know that. Surprise was on her side, and she was going to take advantage of it.

"Look," she pleaded, "When I spoke about the doc's mother, what I meant to say was that she's probably a classy lady and absolutely doesn't smell like a broken toilet."

The Kithrak ... chuckled? Ellyne had never heard anything remotely close to laughter emanate from her captors, but this particular guard found something funny? Until now, she wasn't sure Kithrak knew how to laugh.

"I'm glad you found that funny," she said, drawing her dagger and extending pressing the button, "because this is going to hurt!"

A worried look replaced the smile and the guard gasped, throwing his hands out in front of him. "No, wait a minute!" he pleaded, backing up into the door. "Hang on a second!"

Ellyne, confused, kept her blade pointed at the guard, wondering why she hadn't run him through by now. The guard, with fear all over his face, said nothing but kept his hands in front of him, waving them slightly.

"Just ... wait," he said.

"You've got ten seconds, which is ten seconds more than you deserve."

"I see you haven't changed at all," the guard laughed. "That's good."

"What?"

"And I see my spell worked! You got my present!" He pointed to the sword in Ellyne's hand. "I hadn't ever tried it before and I should have practiced but I was pretty sure it was going to work, but not *absolutely* sure but I see it worked!"

"Three seconds."

"Oh," the guard stammered, "right, I completely forgot! Hang on a sec."

The massive Kithrak shook his head a few times and mumbled some words Ellyne didn't recognize and, as he did so, his appearance shifted drastically.

Ellyne watched in awe as the once hulking guard shrunk and morphed into a much smaller woman who looked strangely familiar.

Before Ellyne could even lower her blade, the woman had her arms around her, hugging her tightly. Ellyne, still clutching her blade and absolutely confused, tried to squirm out of it, but the girl's grip was too tight. She let the hug go on for several seconds before squirming some more.

"Okay, okay," she said, having a difficult time breathing, "this is really weird, and I have no idea what's going on. You've also got a surprisingly strong bear hug going on here."

"Oh, right, sorry!" The girl released her and backed up a bit. She, like the woman in Ellyne's dream, had black hair that tumbled past her shoulders, and piercing green eyes. Unlike the woman (or girl—Ellyne wasn't sure) in her vision, this girl was wearing all black—shirt, pants, and boots.

"I forgot about ... you know, the whole memory thing. Oh, you can put your blade away and, by that, I mean *please* put your blade away. I don't really want to get stabbed today. Or tomorrow or the next day, actually. How about just ... no stabbing, okay?"

Ellyne, never taking her eyes off the girl, retracted her blade and tucked it into the waistband of her pants.

"Talk," Ellyne said.

"Well, you see ... the thing about that is, we don't have a lot of time to catch up right now. But my name's Nicole Saranuin, and we're friends!"

"Shortage of time seems to be the norm around here but, while I don't like it, I'm inclined to agree." Ellyne relaxed a little but kept her guard up as she was wont to do. "So, friends, huh?"

"Yes! Good friends!" Nicole stood nervously. "We've been through so much together and I can't wait for you to remember it all!"

"I don't mean to be rude ... what was your name again?"

"Nicole."

"Again, I don't mean to be rude, Nicole, but without even knowing a whole lot about myself, you don't exactly seem like the type of person I'd be friends with."

"I know, right?" Nicole laughed. "I know this all seems really weird and you're confused and like 'what the bleepity bleep is going on here?' but you and I are definitely best friends and hopefully you'll remember that soon enough!"

Ellyne blinked her eyes, staring at this rambling girl in her cell, unable to think of a coherent reply to this conversation.

"Me," she stammered, "friends with, what, a nineteen-year-old girl? I don't even know how old I am but I'm probably twice your age at least."

"I'm twenty-seven!" Nicole shouted, putting her hand over her mouth after she realized how loud she had just been. "I'm twenty-seven," she repeated in a whisper. "And you're ... thirty-nine, I think. Maybe forty. You never talked much about your age. Come to think of it, you never talked much about your past at all. Of course, a lot of it is printed in history books so it's largely unnecessary to hear it from you. Anyway, look, there's a lot to explain and we can't wait around until your memory comes back but maybe if you hold this it will help you remember."

The girl waved her hand in front of her and produced a gun from thin air, handing it to Ellyne who hesitated at first, but took the weapon.

She held the cold steel of a golden eight-shot revolver.

Running her fingers over it was almost like visiting an old friend. She remembered this gun and holding it in her hands felt ... right. There were a lot of memories attached to this weapon and she could almost feel them hovering on the fringes of her mind.

"I figured you needed your sidekick," Nicole said. "Well, your *other* sidekick of course ... besides me, I mean."

"I ... I remember this," Ellyne said, keeping her gaze down and scrutinizing the weapon. It felt as if she held a piece of herself in her hands.

Nicole clapped her hands together and beamed. "Good. That's a start!"

"I'd say you creating a gun out of nothing was the strangest thing I've seen today but, after your little transformation from Kithrak to human, it's only a close second."

Nicole giggled. "Well, I didn't *create* that gun," she said. "I merely brought it with me. It's yours of course. A golden gun for the Golden Gunslinger."

Ellyne paused, mulling over the words Nicole uttered. There was familiarity in that moniker. "That's me ... isn't it? The Golden Gunslinger."

"Yes, Ellyne, that's you ... and you are my friend. I wish we had time—and a nicer place—to catch up but right now we need to get out of here." Nicole poked her head out the cell door briefly before ducking back inside. "Also, uh, there's one more thing you should know. I'm not alone. I brought help."

"Whatever increases our odds of getting out of here," Ellyne replied, "is fine by me."

"Yeah," Nicole stammered, scratching her head, "so, about that ..."

A bald man in purple robes slipped into the cell and tossed a satchel at Ellyne's feet. His eyes—one green and the other blue—never strayed from her, as if he were ... afraid?"

"You son of a bitch!" Ellyne shouted, pointing her gun at the man and pulling the trigger several times.

The man flinched but no bullets fired.

"And *that* is precisely why I didn't load the gun," Nicole laughed. "I mean, I really hoped your reaction would be different, but I know you well enough to understand."

Ellyne pulled the trigger several more times. "You brought Marik with you? Give me my bullets."

"I thought you said she had no memory, Nicole!" the man growled. "Seems to me like she remembers plenty."

Ellyne clenched her jaw and winced as spittle took to the air from the man's mouth when he spoke that last word.

"Oh, you remember him though!" Nicole said excitedly. "This is progress!"

"I don't often forget those who double cross me, knock out one of my teeth, shoot me, and leave me for dead." Ellyne ran her tongue over the missing molar as instinct took over. "Now give me my ammo so I can give it to this asshole."

"You said she wouldn't remember," Marik insisted again.

"I didn't think she would! But it's a good sign she does!"

"Not from where I'm standing."

"Then we're in agreement," Ellyne added.

"We've got a lot of catching up to do," Nicole said, "but now's not the time or place for that. Our time here is short and it's running out quickly, so if you could ..." Nicole pointed to the gray satchel on the floor.

"What's this?" Ellyne asked, nudging the satchel with her foot.

"Your clothes, silly!" Nicole laughed. "You can't go walking around in those dirty ... well, whatever they are, forever. They're nasty! Do the Kithrak even have laundry facilities here?"

"Says the girl who was wearing that awful red outfit in my dream."

"I thought my old clothes might jog your memory or

something. But, as you can see, I've made upgrades!" She laughed and took a turn as if she were a fashion model. "They're a little tight, but far more functional. Now come on and change. I promise you'll feel more like yourself!"

Ellyne opened the satchel and stripped to her underwear in front of both Marik and Nicole without a shred of compunction or modesty. She slipped on a white tank top, pulled on black pants, and laced her black boots.

"You're right," she said, finishing buckling her belt, "this does feel much better than that garbage the Kithrak gave me to wear."

She slipped into her black leather jacket, slid the dagger into an inside pocket, and shoved her revolver into the holster at her hip.

"And *that* feels perfect," she continued. Then she held out her palm. "Now hand over the ammo."

"Only if you promise not to shoot Marik," Nicole replied. "He's helping us get out of here."

"I promise not to shoot Marik," Ellyne sneered, "yet."

Marik and Nicole exchanged nervous glances before Nicole waved her hand again and produced five cylinders that floated over to Ellyne who grabbed them.

"It's all we could find," Nicole continued, "so make them count."

Ellyne grabbed her weapon, flicked open the chamber, and slammed in a fresh cartridge before flicking it shut again. "Don't worry," she said, "I will."

"Now you sound like you!" Nicole cheered.

"That's what I'm afraid of," Marik grumbled.

"You should be," Ellyne said.

"OKAY," Ellyne whispered, her grip tight around her golden revolver, "so what's the plan?"

"I don't have a plan," Nicole whispered back.

"Wait, what? This is your show. You're the star, and you don't have a plan?"

"I was hoping you had a plan."

"Why would I have a plan?" Ellyne growled. "You know I *never* have an actual plan!"

"Oh, hey! You remembered that too! Good for you!" Nicole gently clapped, excitement painted on her face. "That's more progress! I mean, we still have no plan and all, but memories are good, right?"

"Can we celebrate later?" Marik asked, visibly annoyed. "Perhaps there's a better time than when we're exposed, walking down the hallways of a Kithrak prison with precious little time to figure out where we're going and what we're doing?"

"Fine, buzzkill," Nicole pouted. "So, I suppose we need a getaway vehicle of some kind, then."

"That would be optimal," Marik replied, "so, yes, a getaway vehicle. I suggest we keep heading this way." He pointed ahead of him. "Eventually, we should be able to find wherever they keep something other than prisoners."

"You don't get to suggest shit, Marik," Ellyne growled. "At this time, I'm not even fully sure yet why I hate you, but the fact I remember that much means there must be a really good reason."

"Okay, then, which way would you suggest we go?"

Ellyne looked in every direction—at each hallway that looked identical. She felt anger and fought the urge to shoot the man right there.

"Fine," she relented, "whatever. Let's just go before the Kithrak find out we're gone."

With every passage looking the same, Ellyne wondered how the Kithrak themselves navigated their own prison without getting lost. It gave her a small sense of smug satisfaction to know Marik was just as clueless as she was, though that fact didn't help their escape plan any, so her satisfaction was short-lived.

"Let's go this way," Nicole whispered, pointing down yet another white hallway lined with cell doors. Ellyne followed her lead and Marik tagged along behind them.

"I wish we could simply start blowing holes in these walls or the ceiling and blast our way out," Marik grumbled.

Ellyne, though she loathed the man, had to admit the idea was appealing.

"Me too," Nicole agreed. "But, given our circumstances, magic isn't our best option right now, and we can't go out the way we came in."

"What magic? And what circumstances?" Ellyne asked.

"The Kithrak do have a knack for security, don't they?" Marik agreed.

"Seems like it." Nicole peeked around a corner. As with every other hallway they'd traversed, the passages ahead were white, lined with cell doors, and completely devoid of any guards. "They don't even need to patrol this place. The chances of anyone finding their way out of this maze are probably slim."

"What circumstances?" Ellyne asked again.

"Well," Marik added, "given this entire situation, it's probably overkill to have guards everywhere."

"They'd probably all get lost," Nicole laughed. "I seriously don't know how the Kithrak find their way around this prison. It's like we're rats in a maze trying to sniff out the cheese at the end. Ooh! Cheese sounds really good right now, doesn't it?"

"Focus, Nicole."

"What circumstances?" Ellyne shouted.

"Keep it down!" Marik whispered angrily. "You don't want to give us away, do you?"

"Then quit babbling and tell me what's going on," she growled, pulling back her revolver's hammer, making sure Marik heard the clicking sound it made. "Or I'm going to start getting shooty."

"Ellyne," Nicole said, trying to soothe her by putting a hand on her shoulder, "I know this is all super confusing and there's a lot coming at you but trust me, you don't want to know until we get where we need to go. Once we find a vehicle to escape, we'll fill you in I promise."

"Yes," Marik interjected, "we'll babysit you later. For now, let's just keep moving and get the hell out of here."

Ellyne sensed Marik's irritation which made her want to stall even longer, but she also wanted out of the Kithrak prison, so bothering Marik would have to wait for another time. It would've helped a bit if she knew the circumstances around their past altercation and precisely *why* she hated this man so intensely.

"Fine," she relented. "Lead the way, then."

"Okay, so—"

"Not you, Marik. Her." Ellyne pointed to Nicole. "She gets to be in charge, and you get to shut up."

"Fine," Marik groused, scowling at Ellyne, "let's just get out of here, okay?"

"It's not like I have any special direction sense, but—"

Red lights flashed and a shrieking buzz blasted overhead, drowning out Nicole's words and invading Ellyne's ears.

"What the hell is that?" Ellyne yelled.

"What?" Nicole screamed.

"It's an alarm!" Marik shouted. "They've discovered our escape! We need to move, now!"

"But where?" Ellyne asked. "We've already been wandering around for too long as it is!"

Nicole waved a hand above her head and shouted something Ellyne couldn't hear. The alarms fell silent.

"Thank you!" Ellyne said. "Well, for whatever you just did. Those alarms were beginning to piss me off."

"I'm gonna try something," Nicole replied, "and see if I can't locate a vehicle. Just sit tight for a moment. I've never tried this before and I'm not sure if it's going to work, but it's exciting and, ooh! I hope it works!"

"Whatever you're going to do, Nicole," Marik said, pointing at the guards rounding the corner ahead of them, "please do it quickly."

"Actually," Ellyne laughed, "take your time." She fired a round and dropped one of the guards. "Payback is going to be fun!"

The Kithrak hesitated, then ducked around the corner for cover.

"Oh no," Ellyne mumbled in a mocking tone, "she's got a gun! How did she escape and where did she get a weapon? And who are those other two bozos? Somebody help us!" She laughed and waved her weapon in the air above her head.

"We've got more behind us!" Marik shouted.

"You know magic, right?" Ellyne asked. "Assuming it's real and whatever. Why don't you open one of these cells and find us some cover? Make yourself useful for once!"

The anger on Marik's face coaxed a wry grin out of Ellyne and she laughed in his face. It probably ate at him that not only did he have to take orders from Nicole, but Ellyne herself had better ideas than he did.

"Fine," he growled as he muttered something and moved his hands about.

Ellyne felt a sharp pain as something collided with the back of her shoulder, knocking her to the ground.

"Son of a bitch!" she swore, struggling to her feet. "What the hell was that?"

"Never mind," Marik replied, gesturing to the newly opened cell door. "Just get in!"

Ellyne ducked into the cell, rubbing her shoulder. "What took you so long?"

Marik entered the cell, followed by Nicole who appeared to be concentrating on something with her eyes closed.

Several motes of light sailed down the hall. Two collided with the open door, leaving scorched divots in the metal.

"What's that they're shooting at us?" Ellyne asked, peeking out of the cell.

"Those are spells, you skab" Marik answered.

"Spells?" Ellyne fired her gun, dropping another guard as the rest scrambled for cover. "Ugh, magic sucks."

"Now you're sounding like the Ellyne I know," Nicole laughed, opening her eyes.

Several spells whizzed down the hall. Ellyne ducked back into the cell but yelped as one struck her in the side. She collapsed for a moment, trying to stay conscious as every nerve burned as if on fire.

"I *really* hate magic!" she reiterated, slowly getting to her feet. She shook out her arms, trying to rid them of the uncomfortable tingle she felt. "I also really wish I had more bullets."

"So," Nicole said, "I know where we need to go. I used a

spell to get a general layout of this complex. It wasn't easy—magic's fighting my control—but it worked."

"Are we close?" Marik asked. "Because I'd really prefer to leave."

"Yeah, we're close, but we're going to have to fight our way out, it seems. I wish we could've evaded the guards longer."

"Fine." Ellyne peered into the hallway. Guards approached from both directions, hunkering behind metal shields. "Let's get out of here. I've had more than enough of this place to last a lifetime."

Marik and Nicole exchanged uneasy glances but said nothing.

"What?" Ellyne asked.

"This isn't going to be easy," Nicole said.

"Why not? Can't you just lob some fireballs and blow some shit up, kill a bunch of Kithrak and then we escape, right? Seems simple to me."

"There's no time to explain," Marik interrupted. "Suffice it to say, we're not able to … blow shit up and do all that at this time."

"Whatever. Sounds to me like magic isn't all that great then." Ellyne cocked the hammer back on her revolver. "You do your thing, and I'll do mine. Just stay out of my way." She leaned out from behind the door and fired three shots, dropping two guards.

"Come on, guys!" she laughed. "I'm doing all the work here! Maybe pitch in a little?"

"It's not that simple, Ellyne," Nicole said. "Magic is … difficult. It's different than before."

"Whatever." Ellyne poked out of the cell and fired her remaining three shots, killing two more guards. "I'll just keep being awesome while you guys hang out, I guess." The empty, eight-shot cartridge dropped out when she flicked open the cylinder. She quickly replaced it with a full cartridge and slapped the cylinder shut.

"That felt nice," she muttered, just before she stepped out of the cell and aimed her gun at the guards.

Before she could fire, however, she was struck by several spells from behind and collapsed to the floor, gasping for breath. Paralysis threatened to overtake her while her legs burned, and her fingers froze. She felt as if someone had stabbed her in the chest and hit her in the face—cold, hot, and tingly all simultaneously.

"Ellyne!" Nicole screamed. Her shout sounded to Ellyne as if she were underwater and her vision clouded. Just as she was getting to her feet, several more spells collided with her, knocking her onto her back.

Ellyne screamed and tried to shout but her words came out mangled and distorted.

Nicole and Marik reacted quickly, blocking incoming spells and countering with several of their own. Ellyne couldn't make out much more than that as she struggled to stand.

"Ellyne!" Nicole shouted, "get up! We need to move! Get up!"

"I'm trying," Ellyne stammered, her words slurred. "I mean, a nap in the middle of a firefight sounds divine." She fought through the pain and eventually made it to her shaky feet. "What the hell are they hitting me with?"

Nicole blocked several spells at once, reflecting two of them back at their casters. "There's no time to explain," she said, barely blocking three more.

"You keep saying that," Ellyne grunted. "Exactly how much is there to explain, anyway?"

"It's complicated," Marik added, blocking several spells and attacking with his own. Ellyne noticed, while both of them seemed to be under duress, Nicole was having an easier time in the fight. Every movement seemed natural for her while Marik appeared to require far more concentration.

"We'll tell you once we're safe!" Nicole continued. "Which, right now, we most certainly are *not*."

Several shards of light impacted near Ellyne, sending bits of the wall flying in all directions. Ellyne fired four rounds, but only one found its target as the other three rebounded off a shimmering barrier in front of one of the guards. She fired the last four, but the guard cowered behind a metal shield.

"Reloading!" Ellyne shouted, clumsily replacing the empty cartridge while still trying to shake off the various magical effects.

"Get behind me!" Nicole shouted. "Now!"

Without question, Ellyne and Marik jumped behind Nicole who conjured a shimmering barrier of her own—just in time to shelter them from the wave of fire that engulfed the area.

"I thought you said no fireballs!" Ellyne yelled. "So, what the hell was that, then?"

"I don't get to tell the guards what to do!" Marik replied.

"And it was more of a wave of fire," Nicole added. "A fireball would've—"

"It looked like a damned fireball to me!"

"Can we argue about this later?" Marik asked. "Because the guards are pinning us down here, and our options are becoming pretty limited."

Marik was right. They were running out of room and there appeared to be no shortage of guards coming at them. Every time they dropped one, there was at least one body to fill the vacancy.

"All this just for little old me!" Ellyne mused, shouting over the din of spells in the air. "I must be really important!" She fired three shots and swore under her breath as her bullets harmlessly hit the heavy Kithrak shields. "Or really powerful. But I'd certainly trade that for better circumstances."

"Sort of!" Nicole laughed, slinging several blue motes of light and hitting three guards that promptly collapsed in a torrent of electricity. "A combination of important and… well, let's just say you really pissed them off."

"It's a natural talent I have. So, anyway, how do we get past all these guards and get out of here?"

"What do you think we've been trying to do?" Marik sneered.

Several spells sailed past Ellyne, barely missing her as she ducked behind the cell door, but she was unable to dodge two that came from the other direction. Her body lit up with pain and she bit her lip to keep from screaming.

"No need to get angry, Marik." She looked directly at the man, stone-faced but still wracked with pain. The intensity of her hatred toward him was surprising, considering she barely remembered him and knew next to nothing about him. "If you'd come in with a plan, then maybe we'd already be out of here."

"Would you rather return to your cell?"

"Fine," she growled, trying to ignore the unsettling but somehow familiar burning sensation within her. "You have a point, but we really should be going."

"I think I have an idea!" Nicole exclaimed, deflecting several incoming spells and rebounding them back at their casters. "But you're not gonna like it!"

"Then why do you sound so excited, Nicole?" Ellyne asked.

"She's always excited," Marik pointed out. "It's rather annoying, actually. And she talks a lot."

"Okay," Ellyne chuckled, "I'll give you that." She fired two more shots, hitting one guard. "But if you're annoyed," she muttered, "then I'm cool with it."

"Okay," Nicole continued, "so, I need you to step out in the hallway and get hit by lots of spells!"

"Wait, what?"

Marik said nothing but laughed loudly.

"I know it sounds really weird and painful and, like, you think you're gonna die and stuff! But trust me, it's all part of the plan."

"Yes, Nicole, it sounds *exactly* like that! So, tell me why would I want to do this?"

"Once again, I don't have time to explain. But you've already been hit by a bunch of spells and you're still, like, alive right?"

"As far as I know," Ellyne retorted, "thank you for your sympathy during this trying time."

"You really don't remember, do you?"

"Remember what?" Nicole, can we just skip to the end where you tell me *why* I want to take spells to the face?"

"Is your body all tingly and warm and uncomfortable right now?"

"I have no idea—"

Marik interrupted Ellyne by pushing her into the hallway where she was immediately pelted by several spells.

"Marik!" Nicole shouted, admonishing the man, "that was rude!"

All sound drained away, and Ellyne's vision dimmed. She felt every spell hit her like they were excruciating stab wounds that not only pierced her skin but then dissipated every effect throughout her. She could feel the cold, heat, electricity, stuns, and paralysis all mixed with various other effects she couldn't identify as each sensation eventually dissolved yet still remained within her.

Her vision filled with swirling colors and radiant flashes of light, and she struggled to move, finding her limbs heavy and sluggish. She shrieked in pain, confusion, and fear as more spells hit her from both directions. Struggling desperately to stay conscious, she collapsed to one knee, gasping for breath and trying to stand. She felt as if death were near.

Yet, she was still alive. She knew very little about magic, having only recently been shown it was real, but she'd seen enough of its destructive capability just in the last few minutes. How was she still alive? These weren't stun batons or punches; these were deadly magical effects that should've killed her several times over.

Garbled voices barked at her, but she didn't understand their muffled, distorted commands. She wanted them all to shut up so she could focus on simply being able to stand. There was too much chaos around her, and her frustration level rose in accordance. She wasn't sure how many bullets she had left but she wished badly to put one in the head of every Kithrak in the vicinity.

Growling through clenched teeth, she got to her feet, gasping for air and still in pain but there was one important change—something radically different from just a few moments ago that caught her attention.

The spells had stopped.

Her hearing returned and her vision cleared. At both ends of the hall she spotted hordes of heavily armed and armored Kithrak guards staring at her, dumbfounded and … were they afraid? They glanced at one another, using metal shields as cover, unsure why Ellyne was still breathing.

Ellyne herself shared their confusion, standing dumbfounded in the corridor trying to clear her head.

"You got this!" Nicole shouted. "Now hit them!"

"With what?" Ellyne asked. "I definitely don't have enough bullets to take them all out unless you can magically produce more out of nowhere."

It was as if time had ceased, with neither side daring to make a move but obviously filled with terrible anticipation about what came next.

Everyone, that is, but Ellyne, who had no idea what would or even should come next. She assumed Nicole and Marik would've taken advantage of the lull and sprang into action.

"This isn't going as planned," Marik said. "Ellyne, if you don't act now, we're all going to be in a whole lot more danger. Get it together already and do something!"

"Act? How? What the hell are you talking about? You're the ones with the magic and spells and stuff. *You* do something!"

"I told you we were fools to trust her," Marik hissed, glaring at Nicole. "She's worthless! Her only talent is with an antique weapon!"

"Shut it, Marik!" Ellyne growled. "Or you'll get to see my antique weapon up close and personal."

"No!" he argued. "Our whole plan hinged upon *you* being able to help us escape. But you can't! You not only use an antique, you *are* an antique!"

"I said shut up, Marik!" Ellyne gripped her revolver tightly and balled her other fist, clenching her jaw and glaring at the absolutely insufferable man.

"Or what?" he laughed. "You'll call me mean names? You're pathetic, Ellyne."

She unloaded the rest of her ammunition at Marik, but the bullets harmlessly bounced off an invisible barrier surrounding him.

"That never gets old!" the bald man laughed again. "You seriously think your ancient weapon can harm me? You may not remember much but you should know me better than that. You're even more pathetic than I thought!"

Anger welled up inside Ellyne, rising from her very core and consuming her entire body. The tingling warmth permeated every part of her. At first, she felt fear, but the sensation was oddly soothing, and that fear quickly changed to anger—anger and hatred focused on one man.

"I don't need a gun, Marik," she grunted. "I'll strangle you with my bare hands if I have to, and I'll enjoy every second of it."

"You'd be dead before you took one step," the man laughed. "Admit it, Ellyne, you're insignificant. You can't use magic which makes you inferior to everyone else around you. You're nothing. Time and technology have both left you behind."

"Marik," Nicole whispered, "stop."

Her senses sharpened and she became acutely aware of everything around her. She could smell Marik's sweat and hear every breath he took. Every part of her body tingled in a harmonic thrum like a steadily ticking pendulum.

"I don't even know why we came back for you in the first place. If it were up to me—"

Ellyne heard nothing else beyond those words. She screamed in both agony and elation as raw power erupted from her body, exploding in all directions.

CHAPTER
SIX

"WHAT," Ellyne stammered through slurred words and a sluggish tongue, "what happened?" She felt arms around her, carrying her, but everything was a blur. Her boots dragged along the ground as she struggled to stand. "Who are you?" she growled. "Let go of me."

"Relax," Nicole said through labored breathing. "We're almost there. Can you walk? You're kind of heavy and Marik isn't doing his part."

"Funny," the bald man grunted while yanking Ellyne forward. "She's much heavier than she looks."

Relief washed over Ellyne when she heard Nicole's familiar voice. It was good to be back among friends. Well, with one friend, anyway. "Where are we?" she asked. "I can't feel my tongue."

"We're getting out of here," Marik said. He, too, sounded out of breath, but there was no soothing aspect to his voice. In fact, he sounded annoyed. For whatever reason, Ellyne found solace in his irritation.

"Wait," Ellyne said, resisting. "Stop a minute. I think I can walk."

"We don't have a minute," Marik grumbled. "We should keep moving."

Her vision cleared, and strength returned to her legs as Ellyne propped herself against a wall, shaking out the cobwebs. It was only then that she noticed the destruction.

Entire sections of the hallway were nothing more than rubble—walls were broken, and the ceiling threatened to collapse. Even the floor was in dire shape and looked about to crumble. The only light source was from Nicole's magic mote.

"What happened here?" Ellyne asked as several small chunks of the ceiling clattered to the floor.

"You happened," Marik replied.

"Oh, Ellyne, it was glorious!" Nicole laughed, clapping her hands. "And quite a bit more powerful than I thought it would be but it's okay because Marik and I combined our wards and shielded ourselves, but I hadn't really considered how close we would be when it happened so—"

"Okay, but what *happened*?" Ellyne asked again.

"We'll explain later," Marik said. "Right now, we don't have time to explain or just hang around a crumbling prison."

"What, Marik, are you afraid this place is going to bury us alive?"

"That would be the best outcome, and it's the least of my worries right now. Can we go now?"

"Fine," Ellyne relented, "let's get out of this hell hole." She felt strong enough to walk on her own, but the pace they kept was swift and she struggled to keep up.

"This way." Nicole pointed down a largely untouched hallway. Unlike the other passages in the prison, there were no cells lining the walls and, more importantly, there was a circular door at the end. "Through that door! Hurry!"

They sprinted, with Ellyne lagging a bit behind, struggling to move her legs properly. She only had partial control of her limbs, as if they were half asleep.

"It's probably locked," Ellyne panted. "Everything in this place is locked."

"That won't be a problem," Nicole giggled, reaching the door first. She laid her hands on the thick metal door and shut her eyes. After what seemed like an eternity, a latch popped and the door creaked open.

"Well, that's handy," Ellyne said.

"Thanks! It's a simple spell, really, and I don't think the Kithrak intended for anyone to make it this far, so they apparently didn't set any real complex wards on the door. Whether they're overconfident or just lazy, we benefit!"

Marik flourished his purple robes and his forced his way past Nicole without a word.

"Time to go," Nicole laughed, disappearing through the doorway.

Ellyne followed, ready to feel sunshine on her face and freedom in her bones. She stepped through the doorway and sighed, happy to leave this awful prison behind.

But, instead of sunlight, she found herself staring into something much different.

Instead of trees and grass, she saw darkness and stars. She couldn't be disappointed because she was too shocked.

"Wait. This damned prison is a … spacecraft?"

"She catches on quick," Marik gibed, smirking as if he'd been waiting for this moment all day.

"What the hell?" Ellyne pressed her face against the transparent surface and gazed into the void. "I … I saw the sun—in the courtyard. I felt the breeze, and I smelled the fresh air!"

"The Kithrak are the best at magic," Nicole said. "Nobody's better … well, except me of course! But I really do have to say their illusions are impressive! They obviously put a lot of effort into them."

"They tricked you, Ellyne," Marik added. "They've been

manipulating you for a long time, but we found you blah blah let's get the hell out of here already."

"Marik, every time you open your mouth, I remember just a little more about why I hate you. I'm beginning to discover lots of new and exciting reasons."

"Are you going to stand there, star struck, or are you going to move along like a good girl so we can get out of here?"

Anger roiled within her, but Ellyne suppressed it. She was stuck with the man for the time being, but it would feel liberating to finally be rid of him when her feet were firmly planted on Seralune. She almost missed the city. Karnascus might have been filled with human drones who did nothing but work and worship the government, but it was her home.

The fact she remembered enough to know what both the planet and city were named was enough to fill her with hope. But her memory was still more mystery than fact and she had a long way to go.

Also, several good, stiff drinks sounded delightful. It'd been too long since her lips had tasted the sweet tang of squama juice—another thing she was elated to recall.

"Well," she mused, "those memories are new, but welcome."

She felt a hand on her shoulder and Nicole was behind her, looking out at the void. "I know this is a lot," she whispered, "and I promise to explain it to you, but now's not the time. And before you say anything, yes, I know I've said that a lot. You just need to trust me for a little while longer. We're almost there."

Ellyne sighed. This wasn't the escape she'd expected.

"We did some major damage and this place—this prison— is deteriorating. We need to go." Marik pointed to a small ship before approaching it.

"Fine," she relented, "I was hoping to pay one last visit to a certain 'doctor', but I guess I'll have to settle for the thought of his Kithrak ass being sucked into the cold void of space."

"Now that," Nicole laughed, "sounds like the Ellyne I remember."

"I hope it eventually sounds like the Ellyne *I* remember." She followed Nicole toward the spacecraft.

"It will. I think your memories will return quicker now that you're out of there." Nicole nodded her head slightly in the direction of Marik. "He's right, though, we need to leave."

"Is it bad that I hate it when he's right?"

"Not at all," Nicole laughed. "Not in the least. I'm not too fond of it, either."

Ellyne followed Nicole and Marik down the tunnel, still marveling at everything around her. Had she been in space before? It felt like she hadn't, but she couldn't be sure. Surely, under different circumstances, it would've been wondrous.

Marik pushed some buttons on a keypad and the hatch in front of them opened, causing a brief rush of air in the tunnel.

"Mechanical systems," he scoffed, "they're so archaic. It's like we're living in the Legacy Age. I may as well be banging rocks together."

Nicole and Ellyne entered the ship, followed by Marik who sealed the door behind them.

Ellyne quickly sat in one of the four seats and copied Nicole as she strapped herself in. Marik did the same, only he sat in what appeared to be the pilot's seat.

"You guys all snug back there?" he asked, fiddling with the controls. Ellyne was certainly no expert on space navigation but, after watching him for only a few seconds, it didn't appear he knew what he was doing.

"Aye aye, captain!" Nicole laughed. She made a weird salute, but Marik kept his eyes ahead, grabbing hold of a stick by his right side.

"Good," he continued as the ship jerked forward. "Then let's get out of here."

Ellyne heard metal grinding, and something clicked loudly as they began to move. They passed through a barrier of shimmering energy and exited the prison, sailing into the darkness beyond where gravity immediately disappeared.

"Was that supposed to happen?" she asked, watching as her hair floated off her head.

"Totally weird, right?" Nicole laughed. "I don't think I could ever get used to it—not that I have a ton of experience since this is only the second time I've been in space like this. The first time was when we came to get you and it was weird then, too."

"What Nicole means to say, eventually, is yes, it's normal."

"The current state of magic is … well, it's inconsistent," Nicole explained, waving her arms in the weightless environment. She giggled as she watched them float in front of her. "There's magic in the prison back there, but there's no magic in space itself, apparently, so we have to rely on—"

"On machinery—gears and wires and the like," Marik huffed. "Just like the good ol' days or whatever people call them. Frankly, I could do without reminiscing."

Ellyne looked behind them at the prison quickly getting smaller in the distance—the only thing she really knew or remembered well. It was indeed falling apart. The structure was apparently housed in an asteroid—not just built from the rock but actually *shaped* from it, if she believed what she saw. She was surprised she'd been fooled for so long.

Several brief explosions erupted, quickly snuffed out by the vacuum of space. She thought she saw multiple bodies floating about, tumbling out of control. It was a morbid scene, but she couldn't bring herself to feel any remorse. She wondered if the doctor was one of the corpses out there, destined to float in the nothingness for eternity. The very thought brought a morbid grin to her lips. She wanted him to pay for what he'd done to her. She'd been his lab rat, but that time was over.

"And the guards can all join him," she whispered.

"What?" Nicole asked.

"Nothing," she replied, facing forward again. "So how exactly are we responsible for the complete destruction of a … space prison?"

"Nicole, here, disabled most of their protections when we came on board. She's really quite remarkable."

"Do I detect a hint of jealousy?" Nicole asked, giggling.

Marik remained silent.

The small spacecraft jolted forward. Ellyne fought the brief urge to vomit. She knew nothing about space travel, but she didn't need anyone to explain to her the fact they had just accelerated quickly.

"I guess you must be talented if Marik thinks so highly of you," Ellyne added.

"Thanks!" Nicole beamed, grinning ear to ear. "It really wasn't difficult. I mean, it took some time to figure out what they'd done and, honestly, their wards and enchantments were quite elaborate. Kithrak magic always surprises me. They use it differently than humans do. Not that it matters a whole lot but—"

"Try to focus, please," Ellyne said, hoping to be gentle but also tired of the girl's rambling. She could feel a headache forming in the back of her skull.

"Right, sorry. Anyway, most of those enchantments kept all the prison's systems running. When I messed them up, various things started malfunctioning. After that, you did the rest!"

"I'm not sure I could've removed them as fast as she did," Marik added.

"Or removed most of them at all," Nicole joked. "They were pretty complex."

Marik remained silent again.

"Wait," Ellyne interrupted, "hold up a sec. You said I did the rest. What do you mean by that?"

Nicole and Marik exchanged uneasy glances but neither said a word, as if they were each waiting for the other to speak up.

"It's ... complicated," Nicole stammered. "We have a lot we need to tell you, but it's best we don't throw it at you all at once. You've been through a lot in the past two years and—"

"TWO YEARS?" Ellyne shouted. She nearly jumped out of her chair, but the restraints kept her in place. "What the hell do you mean, two years? I was rotting in that place for two years?"

"Two years, fifteen days, eight hours—"

"Shut it, Marik!" Ellyne balled her fists. She couldn't very well grab her gun and shoot him, and such a thing would be foolish given their current whereabouts, but the urge was still there.

Marik laughed. She may not have had all her memories, but she knew that laugh well—he was enjoying her pain.

"Once we get back on Seralune, we'll fill you in," Nicole said.

"Yeah," Marik added, "and then we need to figure out what to do about—"

"Marik!" Nicole shouted. "Shut it!"

"Now you sound like me," Ellyne laughed. She brushed it off, knowing full well she wasn't going to get answers right away, but she remained curious about what they were referring to. She couldn't stop the questions from flooding her mind.

Right now, her priority was to get out of this metal container hurtling through space and back home ... wherever that actually was. She was accustomed to not having memories and, while that bothered her, she may have been more upset by their gradual return.

One thing was for sure, however, she had a nagging feeling she'd just traded one problem for another, much more serious problem.

CHAPTER
SEVEN

THE SPACECRAFT SHOOK VIOLENTLY as Marik struggled to keep control of it. He gripped the stick with both hands, desperately trying to keep it steady but it was as if the craft itself fought him at every turn. Ellyne stared out the front window, noting that the ground approached much quicker than she was comfortable with.

"Have you never landed one of these things before?" she asked, digging her fingernails into the seat's armrests. "For that matter, have you even flown one of these things before?"

"Shut it!" he yelled, continuing to struggle. "Crashing this thing and killing us all would be worth it if it would shut you up."

Ellyne smiled, though she suspected Marik was serious. The thought of him dying in a crash wasn't altogether unpleasant, but she would rather not be included in that event.

"I was really hoping magic would kick in and we wouldn't need to manually pilot this thing to the ground." He flipped a switch on the console, then pushed several buttons. "Apparently, that's not going to happen."

Saliva launched from the man's mouth as he finished his

sentence. Ellyne winced—it was a natural reaction for her by now.

"You … don't even know what those switches and buttons do, do you?" Ellyne asked.

"I was hoping at least one of them would keep us from crashing," he growled, continuing to inspect other controls on the front panel. His confused, desperate actions would've been amusing in any other situation.

"Well, you'd better figure out something fast or we're all going to be screwed really soon."

After some effort, Marik leveled the ship's course, thereby avoiding their potential deaths from a ground collision. A nearby forest, however, presented a new hazard.

"It's now or never, Marik!" Nicole shouted. "Let's just hope magic works here!"

"What do you mean by that?" Ellyne asked.

"We'll explain later."

"I'm getting really tired of that phrase."

"Well, *that's* a phrase I'm tired of hearing," Marik grunted, fighting with the flight stick. "Would you rather we all just hang out and discuss while the ship crashes in a fiery wreck? You'll never receive the explanations you so desire."

"If it takes you with it," she sneered, "then I'm fine with it."

Marik replied with something Ellyne couldn't hear well enough to understand but the anger in his voice was clear enough to convey the message. She smiled, which seemed an odd reaction given their situation.

"Nicole!" he shouted. "I need you to try and connect with the ship. It's not working for me!"

"I'm on it!"

Nicole released her harness and struggled to get into the copilot's chair as the ship bounced and rocked, slamming her into the front window.

"Could you at least *pretend* to know how to fly this thing?" she shrieked. "That hurt!"

"I … I don't even know what the hell you mean by that. Just get your ass in the seat and see if you can connect with the ship before we all die!"

After more jostling, Nicole strapped herself into the seat next to Marik who still struggled with the pilot stick. The ship continued sinking lower, now barely above the treetops. Ellyne tried not to look out the windows and instead pretended it was nothing more than a bumpy landing with some turbulence.

"Just give me a few seconds," Nicole pleaded. "I'll try to connect with the ship. Just keep us above the trees!"

"What do you think I've been trying to do all this time? I'm not simply picking my nose, here."

Ellyne mentally cycled through several snarky responses but, in this particular instance, decided to remain quiet and let the two of them keep everyone from a fiery death. There would undoubtedly be plenty of opportunities in the future to insult the man.

"Well," Ellyne mused, "at least I'm not going to die in that awful prison. Though, if we were to die now, that would make this the worst prison break ever."

Just as she braced for impact with the forest, the ship stopped. It didn't slow down first, coming to an eventual halt. Instead, it simply stopped in place. Such a maneuver should probably have caused injury, but nobody felt any adverse effects. All three sighed in relief and caught their breath with the ship hovering just slightly above the trees below.

"I assume," Ellyne gasped, "you connected with the ship or whatever?"

"I did!" the girl exclaimed. "It was literally like I was talking directly to the ship, and we communicated! I told it to stop, and it stopped! I didn't mean to instantly stop like I did but we're not dead, so I figure who cares right?"

"Right," Ellyne agreed, "yeah … so, where are we exactly?"

"Home, of course!"

The ship moved forward, though it felt as if they were still hovering in place. Ellyne wouldn't have believed they were in the air if she hadn't been able to see it herself. The ship changed direction and altitude several times, but Ellyne felt nothing.

"This is way better than your piloting, Marik," Ellyne quipped. "You'd think he didn't know what he was doing or something."

The man stared ahead and said nothing. Ellyne grinned.

"Hey, Nicole?"

"Yeah, what?"

"My arms are tingling a bit and I feel … strange—kind of the same sensation I had back at the prison before, you know." She made an explosion sound, accompanied by hand motions.

"Oh, that's not good! Just hang on for another minute or two. We're almost there."

"And don't blow us all to bits if you can avoid it," Marik added. It would be a shame for us to die like that."

"I won't," Ellyne reassured him. "I'll make sure to only blow you to bits."

"Very funny."

"It wasn't a joke."

"We're here!" Nicole exclaimed. "Everyone out!"

"Wait, we landed?" Ellyne asked. A quick glance out the window answered her question.

The hatch at the rear of the ship opened. Ellyne released her harness and stood as her right knee popped loudly. "I guess we indeed have landed," she said, gazing at a field of tall grass and stepping outside. The sun warmed her face— the *real* sun—and the fresh morning dew welcomed her. Birds sang and insects buzzed while the tall grass swayed in the gentle breeze.

Further out and up a hill, on a ridge, was the forest they'd nearly crashed into. Immediately, feelings of familiarity assaulted her as memory fragments swirled within her mind. She tried to grasp them, but they were elusive, like water through her fingers.

"Where are we?" she asked as Nicole stopped beside her. "I feel like this is a familiar place—like I've been here before."

"Welcome home, Ellyne."

'Home? But my home … my home is in a city, isn't it? I have an apartment in a city and there's a bar not far from it. This isn't my home."

"Oh good!" Nicole clapped her hands together and giggled. "More memories! Yes! In fact, we first met in your apartment in Karnascus! But this is—"

"My first home."

Ellyne walked around the ship and saw her childhood home—a simple, two-story farmhouse with a wraparound porch. "My first home, right?"

Yes, seeing this house sparked many memories—good and bad.

"I lived here with my parents. I spent most of my time in the forest over there, especially when we fought. We fought often."

"It took me quite a while to locate this place," Nicole said.

Ellyne turned away from the house and focused on the copse of trees at the top of the hill. It didn't look like much from here, but she knew a more expansive forest lay behind it. The urge to get lost in the woods was strong.

"They," Ellyne continued, "Um … they were rabid supporters of the Ilserate government, weren't they?" She paused, sorting out several entangled memories. "Yes … yes, they were—government employees, even. They disapproved of me not working for the Ilserate. They disapproved of me joining the Flocia Wars. Hell, they disapproved of literally *everything* I did."

"They're not here, Ellyne," Nicole said softly, putting a hand on her shoulder. "They're long gone. Marik checked to make sure. We don't know where they went, but they've been gone for a while. It should be safe for us to stay here."

"They believed magic was only suitable for the wealthy. They believed anyone else was uneducated and didn't deserve to have the ability—just like the Ilserate believed."

The memories rushed in like a burst dam, threatening to sweep her away in a torrent of the past. Her jaw clenched.

"The Ilserate … they lied. They betrayed me. I fought for the wrong side. I fought for the government until I discovered their true motive was to control magic. Then I allied with the Technician's Guild to keep magic away from everyone, which is when I met—"

"Well, that was a decent landing!" Marik laughed, approaching Ellyne and Nicole.

"Him," Ellyne scowled. "And then he, too, betrayed me, knocked out one of my teeth, shot me, and left me for dead!" Her tongue grazed the missing molar, and her hand went to the scar on her left shoulder.

Marik looked uneasy. "I see we're remembering things now. How unfortunate."

Ellyne drew her gun and stared down the barrel at the man she so despised.

"Whoa, now," he pleaded, his hands in front of him, "let's not be hasty. Don't forget, I helped get you out of the Kithrak prison. And, besides, you returned the favor when we last met."

"How about I do you another favor right now? Or multiple favors."

"Ellyne!" Nicole shouted, stepping between the two. "Stop!"

The gunslinger stood motionless for several seconds, her

thumb resting on the hammer, ready to pull it back. The hatred for Marik she felt within her was strong but soon, it was replaced by hatred for something else much stronger.

"Magic is the problem," she muttered, lowering her revolver, and eventually slipping it back into its holster at her hip. "Yeah, Marik, you're an asshole, but without magic, you're just a run-of-the-mill asshole."

"Yay!" Nicole cheered. "I knew you'd rekindle your hatred for magic! Though, if I'm being honest, that's never really been a good thing in my opinion but, in this instance, it means your memories are returning! And, hopefully, it means you won't try to kill Marik, because we kind of need him."

"Yeah," Marik groused, lowering his hands, "real cheery. I'm so happy for you. How's about we all get inside because the bugs out here are eating me alive."

"What, you can't just magic all the bugs away?" Ellyne jibed.

"Funny."

"I'm not sure how much you remember yet," Nicole said, "but magic doesn't work quite the same as it used to. Nobody's really sure why, but things are … well, very different now."

"Different how?"

"We'll explain—"

"Stop saying that!"

"I'm sorry, Ellyne. I know this must be super hard for you. I mean, I've had to deal with *him* for a while now, so it's not been a walk in the park for me, either." She pointed to Marik who was busy inspecting something on the ship. "Come on, laugh a little?"

Ellyne sighed. "It's just a lot right now, Nicole," she said. "But Marik might have the right idea."

"Oh really?"

"Yeah, the bugs out here are eating me alive, too. Let's get inside and see if my parents left behind anything to drink."

They walked around the ship and headed toward the house. Ellyne's mind reeled from everything that had just happened in the last few hours while trying to comprehend everything that was *going* to happen. She feared there was a lot more to come.

"Come on, Marik," she shouted. "You can have the top bunk tonight!"

CHAPTER
EIGHT

ELLYNE PUSHED on the front door. The rough, sun-bleached wood nearly impaled her hand with splinters, but the door slowly swung open without resistance.

"Sounds like some oil's in order," Marik whispered.

"The house has seen better days," Ellyne replied, "but the door was always loud and creaky. Made it really difficult to sneak out at night without alerting my parents."

"You snuck out?" Nicole laughed.

"What's so amusing about that? Yeah, I … snuck out. If you knew my parents, you probably would've, too." A wry smile crossed Ellyne's lips and she gave Nicole the side-eye.

Memories of her parents seeped into her mind, an event which pleased Ellyne. The memories themselves, however, she could've done without. "Besides, you would know all about sneaking out, wouldn't you?"

"That was different," Nicole huffed. "I was a prisoner of the government."

"We all have our different prisons, I guess."

"Wait," Marik interrupted, "you sneaked out a lot? Where on Seralune would you possibly go? It's not like there's a shopping center or arcade nearby. This house is literally out in the middle of nowhere."

Ellyne pointed behind them—at the forest up the hill. "There," she said. This was my house but that forest … that was my *home*.

"I don't understand," Marik stammered.

"I don't expect you to."

"Holy cow!" Nicole exclaimed, a little too loud for Ellyne's comfort.

Ellyne winced, resisting the urge to slap the girl. "How about not screaming in my ear?"

"Oh, sorry," Nicole giggled. "I just got excited there, for a moment."

"Excited?" Marik asked. His tone conveying boredom. "Whatever is there around here to get excited about?" he asked, gesturing wildly at the dilapidated house.

"Yes! Ellyne! You're remembering things! That's so great! At this rate, your memory will be fully back soon, I bet."

"So I am," Ellyne whispered pensively, swatting at a fly and wondering when more memories would return. "I guess seeing the ol' homestead jogged some memories. Maybe this is why the … Kithrak? Maybe this is why the Kithrak held me captive—they didn't want me to remember something."

"Probably one of many reasons," Marik sneered impatiently. "Now can we go inside, or should we keep standing out here, reminiscing about our childhoods?"

Ellyne smirked. She would've stayed outside all day if it got under Marik's skin, even if it was unpleasant for her. "Got some painful memories you'd like to share, Marik? I'd be happy to ignore you while you delve into them."

The man huffed, grunted, and pushed past them, continuing into the house.

"I guess that's a yes," she laughed. "After you." Ellyne flourished her hand toward the house's interior.

Nicole nodded, grinning, and passed Ellyne, moving into the house.

"Well," Ellyne muttered, shutting the door behind her, "this is awkward. Welcome to my childhood home, I guess?"

Images and memories flooded back like a tidal wave. The living room was mostly as Ellyne remembered it, with a large, burgundy leather couch facing the wall where a screen used to hang. The rectangular discoloration on the wall where the paint hadn't seen the sun for years was a stark reminder of what once was.

Except for the couch, a table in the corner, and a couple of overturned wooden chairs, the room was largely empty. There were no possessions or items left behind.

"Posh," Marik joked, kicking aside a bit of decayed paper. "Looks like they left some trash behind, though."

Ellyne bristled, seeing spittle launch from the man's mouth. His overly aspirated pronunciation of the letter P was a memory she would have rather not had come back. At least it could've been considerate enough to wait longer to return.

"And you're a fine addition to the pile," she sneered, glaring at the man.

"It appears they took most everything with them," he continued, oblivious to her barb. He picked up two of the chairs and righted them. "This room, at least, is cleaned out."

"Or someone else cleaned it out," Ellyne added. "I left home to fight in the Flocia Wars. That was a long time ago, and it was the last time I saw my parents. Hell, they could be dead for all I know." Ellyne sighed and sat on the couch. "I guess if I *did* know at any point, maybe that memory will return soon. It'd be a more welcome memory than some others that just recently came to the surface."

Marik sat backwards on one of the chairs by the table, adjusting his purple robes awkwardly. "So, now what?" he asked, scratching his bald head.

"I …" Ellyne stammered, sitting on the couch. "I don't

really know. You guys have way more info about what's going on than I do. You don't have a plan?"

Nicole laughed, taking a seat next to Ellyne. "If I had just five tiks for every time you told me you're not a planner, I'd be a rich woman."

"So, you guys don't actually have a plan, then?"

"To be honest," Marik said, shifting in his chair, "I'm thoroughly surprised we successfully broke you out and escaped in the first place. Of course, destroying a space prison wasn't on the original agenda. We didn't plan beyond that. I think—"

"I think," Nicole interrupted, "we need to hang tight a day or two and let Ellyne adjust. There are some things only she can tell us. When we're ready, we can return to Karnascus and see what needs to be done."

Ellyne threw Nicole a puzzled look. "Karnascus?"

"Oh yes!" Nicole shrieked, jumping up from the couch in excitement. "It's awesome! It's a huge city with all kinds of wondrous things and buildings reaching into the sky and the Metro and people on hoversticks and screens and that's where your favorite bar is and—"

"Slow down there," Ellyne said, gesturing back to the couch.

Nicole sat back down visibly trying to contain her excitement. "Anyway, it's where you live. It's … it's where I met you."

"I… don't think I remember any of that."

Nicole's face sank. "You don't remember … me? I broke into your apartment, and you threatened to kill me."

"I remember just enough to know that seems like something I'd do," Ellyne chuckled. Within, she was frustrated and keeping a happy disposition was difficult. "Sounds like good times."

Nicole smiled wearily. "The best."

"Yes," Marik sneered, "blah blah, Karnascus is great. Well, it *was*, anyway."

"Marik!" Nicole growled.

Marik, with an annoyed look on his face, fell silent and shifted his gaze to the window.

"Wait," Ellyne said, holding a hand in the air, "what do you mean, was?"

"It's been two years, Ellyne. A lot can happen in that time. I promise to explain, but it won't make any sense until you've got more of your memories back. There's no need to confuse you further—"

"Damn it, I'm not a child!" Ellyne shouted, jumping off the sofa and moving to a window. "So, stop treating me like one."

Outside, she saw the tall grasses swaying gently in the summer breeze—well, what she suspected was the summer breeze. Beyond that, the land sloped upward and gave way to the forest.

"Karnascus," she continued, still gazing out the window, "is that the city where we spoke—in my dream?"

"Yes!" Nicole shouted, clapping her hands. "I wanted to appear to you in a place that was hopefully familiar. I must say, I feel I did a pretty good job recreating it. I mean, there were some bits I had to improvise but the rest was pretty spot on."

"I wouldn't know," Ellyne whispered to herself.

"Oh," Nicole continued, "but the best part is, it wasn't actually a dream! I figured out how to create a place I could not only travel to, but also take you to! We were both *really* there, Ellyne! I mean, it wasn't easy, though, given … well, let's just say magic is still wonky and it's even weirder when you're around."

"Gee," Ellyne chuckled, "that makes me feel all warm and fuzzy. Good to know I'm screwing things up just by breathing."

"It's another thing I'll—"

"Explain to me later," Ellyne interrupted. "Yeah, I get that."

"I'm sorry."

"Why do I feel so drawn to you?" she whispered to herself, gazing at the forest in the distance. Turning from the window, Ellyne said, "It's not your fault. "Honestly, I'm not even sure I want to know any of it. It sounds complicated and frustrating. Life as a prisoner wasn't all that fun—especially getting my ass kicked—but it was much simpler than … well, all this."

"You don't mean that," Nicole countered.

"I don't know what I mean. Earlier today, I was sitting in my prison cell like I've done for countless days in the past when you two come storming in, we blow the place up, flee in a spaceship, and land here at my childhood home. It's been a busy day and I'm just trying to keep up."

"Technically," Marik laughed, "*you* blew up the prison."

Ellyne glared at the man who shrugged.

"Just being truthful," he said, backing down. "Not that it matters one way or another. The Kithrak got what they had coming to them."

"Don't you work for them?" Ellyne asked, suddenly recalling a memory.

"Well, yes … and no."

"Okay, which is it?"

"It's complicated."

"Well, uncomplicate it," Ellyne growled, feeling her hand slowly move to the golden revolver at her hip.

"I think," Nicole said, standing between the two, "we just need to calm down a bit right now. There's a lot of catching up to do but we've got time to take it slowly."

Ellyne's hand fell to her side and relaxed as she growled. "Fine," she grunted, "I'm going for a walk."

"I'll go with you!" Nicole shouted, following after her.

"I'm going alone. Stay here and babysit the child—make sure he doesn't set himself on fire or something. Or, better yet, maybe help set him on fire."

Nicole opened her mouth to argue but Ellyne cut her off before she could utter a sound.

"It's not up for debate," she said, slamming the front door behind her, leaving Nicole and Marik in the house. Sighing with her eyes closed, she leaned against the aged wood and ran a hand through her blond hair. "Well, now what?"

She needed time to think—to sort out everything that just happened combined with the memories seeping into her head. Sometimes, she wasn't even sure they were *her* memories. They felt intimately familiar yet somehow foreign —as if they were indeed hers, but she wasn't the same woman those memories belonged to.

"Fine," she groused, wading through the tall grass and swatting at insects. "But I'm not sure this is any more appealing than being stuck in a house with Marik. On second thought, no, I prefer these bloodsuckers out here to the one in there."

Every step she took urged her to return to the house, but she continued forward, arguing with herself the entire time. She felt silly, returning to a childhood haunt, but she sought clarity and something within her—something convincing— told her the forest held answers. It was a child's idea, but she followed it anyway, having nothing better to do.

Ellyne prepared for disappointment as she gazed up at the slope atop which began the tree line. She'd rolled down this hill countless times, giggling and picking bits of grass from her hair once she reached the bottom.

"Well," she said, "At the very least, this is more exercise than you've gotten in a long time, so there's that."

She chuckled and looked around. It was nice to be outside in an area that wasn't the puny courtyard from her prison. But then, she'd never really been outside at all, had she? The

Kithrak did a good job fooling her, but she believed they didn't get anything they wanted from her.

Which meant, of course, they would probably be coming for her. She could disappear altogether, leaving Nicole and Marik behind. It would be simple to enter the forest and never turn back. If the Kithrak wanted her, maybe it was for the best. And, besides, getting rid of Marik sounded divine.

"Okay," she muttered, beginning her ascent, "this had better be worth it. I don't have time to just wait around for memories or inspiration."

CHAPTER
NINE

THE SUN THREATENED to sink below the horizon behind her by the time Ellyne reached the tree line atop the hill. "This is silly," she muttered. "What is this place supposed to tell me? I'm not a little girl anymore, building forts and playing pretend. That was ages ago. But here I am, tromping around in the woods for no reason."

Try as she might to convince herself otherwise, the woods felt more like home than the house below ever did. This place was where she'd always felt like herself and not the person everyone thought she should be. Nobody would judge her here, or yell at her, or express their disappointment. Here, among the trees, she didn't have to obey anyone, please anyone, or … kill anyone.

That was a pleasing thought. The last two or so years had been full of obedience and punishment. The Kithrak wanted something from her, and they'd taken their time trying to extract it, subjecting her to tests and procedures, interrogations and studies.

As far as she knew, she'd given them nothing, and that thought alone brought a smile to her lips.

Had they discovered whatever it was they wanted, they

most likely would've killed her. It was never expressly discussed in front of her that she knew of, and she wouldn't have understood the Kithrak language if they'd let slip any information. She had Nicole and, yes, Marik to thank for her freedom.

Recalling her many attempts to escape, she chuckled. Even if she'd somehow managed to elude her captors, the realization of being in a prison built into an asteroid … well, it wouldn't have mattered how far she made it. She would've never gotten out of the prison on her own. The Kithrak knew this all along—probably the reason they never really bothered with more security than she'd encountered. She suspected she'd been the only prisoner.

But she had the last word. The Kithrak who ran the torturous experiments on her was either incinerated, blown to atoms, or sucked out into the void of deep space. That alone was enough to make her smile again.

But her thoughts eventually turned back to Marik. She loathed the man with every bit of her existence. It was a visceral hatred—one that could only come from a sordid history. The problem was, she didn't actually recall much of that history.

Not yet anyway.

But she knew enough to trust her instincts, and every feeling within her screamed not to trust him. She listened to those screams and heeded their warnings.

"I can understand why nobody wants to fill me in on him," she muttered, as if there was someone to talk to—preferring to think out loud.

She remembered the betrayal and that memory alone was enough to fuel her desire for revenge.

After all, she did try to kill him the moment he appeared in the prison. If Nicole were to tell her whatever additional reasons (and she was sure there were many) why she felt such hatred, things would probably go poorly.

Her tongue instinctively felt around at the back of her jaw on the right and prodded the hole where her molar had once been. That was one of the first memories she'd recovered—Marik's betrayal and his attempt to kill her. Her returning the favor followed shortly thereafter.

Ellyne laughed nervously as her gaze settled on the trees in front of her. "You're stalling," she whispered, flexing her fingers at her sides. "What are you afraid of? This is silly."

She sighed, giving the tree line one last look before slowly stepping into the forest.

Despite her expectations, nothing magically changed. Memories didn't flood back to her in overwhelming fashion. Instead, her foot crunched some sticks and leaves, and she took another step.

While everything had obviously grown and aged, the forest did indeed still convey a familiarity that at first tugged at her, then slowly seeped in with each step she took. Further into the forest she trudged, hopping over a fallen log and dodging some underbrush.

She soon came upon a dry creek and stopped.

"Now *this* I recognize," she smirked, hopping into the gully. "I used to play here, didn't I? Pretending I was fishing … skipping rocks in the water and watching the crawdads swim about.

They were pleasant memories, and she felt warm and safe reminiscing. But they weren't the memories she was hoping for. They did nothing to aid her in her current situation.

"Let's see," she whispered as she ascended the bank on the other side. "I used to walk along the creek for a while, didn't I?"

Slowly putting one foot in front the other, Ellyne walked along the rocky bank, being careful not to slip while also taking in as much of her surroundings as she could. It was a feeling she couldn't explain—as if her memories hovered just out of sight, mostly obscured by fog, but clearly present and ready for her to grab them if she could just stretch out far enough.

This place—this forest—was surprisingly familiar and, though Ellyne had at first thought herself silly for coming here, she now knew this is where she needed to be. None of this was she able to explain, of course, but she'd quickly become comfortable with acting on instinct since the moment she awoke in the Kithrak prison.

And, clearly, she was doing alright by that method.

Of course, there was so much more she needed to fill in the gaps. Even if her memory returned completely, she would require Nicole to offer up some information—most likely more than just a little.

Something told her reclaiming her memories was just the beginning of something larger—something she knew she wasn't going to enjoy. Even without Nicole's and Marik's odd looks and awkward behavior, she could sense it just as clearly as she could sense her memories. There was a bigger picture, and something told her it wasn't a pretty one.

"I guess I'm living in a forest until I figure shit out," she laughed, kicking a stone into the creek. It skittered off a rock and landed in a puddle with a plop. "I'll have to learn how to hunt and make clothes out of leaves and build a … house, I guess? Maybe I'll raise an army of feral wolves."

Up ahead, she noticed what could only be the remnants of one of her old forts. Simply seeing it opened her mind and memories flooded in—memories of her building it, pretending it was her house, and trying to lure a squirrel to her to make it her pet.

She stopped, staring at what was left, both amazed any of it still survived and stunned at how, though decades had passed, it felt like last week. There was little more than debris left but she recognized the fort in her mind.

She resumed her advance, in no hurry and still gazing

around her. "I guess I built them to last," she chuckled as she poked one of the old fallen logs with her finger.

It rolled out of place and broke into several pieces, revealing its dried, brittle nature.

"Or not," she laughed.

It had once been part of a shoddy wall, bound together with plants like milkweed and tanjanari vines. Those were, of course, long decayed and gone, but a few scant parts of her old fort's structure remained.

"Well," she mused, "this is possibly the silliest thing I've done. I mean, the silliest thing I *remember* doing, I guess."

Ellyne squeezed into the crowded remnants of what was once the front door and crawled inside, hitting her head on a tree branch above.

"I guess I was a lot smaller when I built it," she grumbled, massaging the top of her head as she wriggled around and finally sat. "Indeed, this felt way bigger when I was a kid."

Her old hideaway was little more than leaves and sticks piled up underneath the tree's lowest branches. Ellyne wondered if she'd glorified its stature in the past or if it truly had been a masterfully built fort.

"Okay," she muttered, "here I am. I'm sitting in one of my old forts like a fool, hanging out in the woods, so can I have my memories back now please?"

Of course, she wasn't surprised it wasn't that easy. She had to admit, however, there was a certain comfort in it—a familiarity and a warmth she hadn't felt in … maybe ever.

"Okay, so, now what? Do I close my eyes and meditate, or do I just hang out until something cool happens? Who do I have to kill to get my memories back? Whatever the Kithrak did to my memories, it should wear off soon, shouldn't it?"

She was hiding again. She had enough awareness to accept that fact. This time, instead of hiding from her parents, she was hiding from Nicole and Marik.

But she knew it went much deeper than that. She was

hiding from what was to come. She didn't even know what it was, but she was avoiding it, and this seemed like the perfect place to do so.

"Being afraid of something and not even knowing what you're afraid of," she whispered. "That's some complex mental shit, right there. My parents could try their entire lives and they'd never get close to being able to cause me this much anxiety. I'm sure they tried their best, though."

Leaves rustled nearby and Ellyne awkwardly shifted to get a look but saw nothing and hit her head on a tree branch.

"If someone wanted to fight me, this would be the absolute worst place to defend myself," she mused, rubbing the back of her head. "Couldn't build 'em any bigger, could you, Ellyne? This was foolish. Why am I even here?"

She sighed and tried to lean back against the tree, awkwardly shifting until she found the most comfortable position and tried to relax. With closed eyes, she focused on the sounds around her, trying desperately not to think about every niggling problem that plagued her.

She felt the soil beneath her, smelled its dampness mixed with the faint scent of flowers. Birds chirped overhead and leaves rustled in the breeze. She remembered how often the creek would produce the most soothing sounds as it gurgled over the rocks. Its current dry state was disappointing, but she could remember it clearly, as if it were flowing.

"Way better than a prison cell," she mused. "I'm not sure I ever got decent sleep up there."

Maybe that had been part of the Kithrak's plan—secretly deprive her of sleep so they could extract whatever information they wanted, or simply study her further. She'd been asked all kinds of strange questions while being poked with instruments and hooked up to all kinds of machines.

As far as she knew, however, they'd discovered nothing. And that thought alone brought a smile to her face. If she were being honest, however, she still didn't know why the

Kithrak held her prisoner. She couldn't remember anything, so their questions had been pointless, and their experiments always appeared to yield no results.

When she felt herself getting angry, Ellyne turned her thoughts away and once again focused on where she was instead of where she used to be. The sights, smells, and sounds consumed her mind until she became drowsy.

She felt herself slipping off to sleep, starting to dream even while she still wasn't fully in slumber. Her arms and eyelids were heavy, and her breathing slowed. The forest sounds were muted, and not even a blue wriggler's horrible shriek disturbed her as she drifted off.

ELLYNE STOOD IN AN APARTMENT. Her apartment. It was unkempt and simple, but that's the way she liked it. A girl sat on her sofa, babbling about something, but her words were muffled and incomprehensible. Nicole? What was Nicole doing in her apartment?

She ignored her and moved to the bedroom, entering instead a room full of screens and panels with buttons, levers, and blinking lights. In the center was a boy in a chair, feverishly tapping his fingers in the air, as if there was a keyboard in front of him, though she saw nothing.

He was Kithrak. She knew this somehow. Though he had dark skin and looked human, she was sure he wasn't. He was … familiar, in the way so many things were—familiar, yet unknown. She was sure she knew him somehow.

She moved toward the door on the other side of the room, unhindered and unnoticed, and passed through, finding herself in a dimly lit room with minimal furniture. It was another familiar place, but not her apartment. She wasn't sure precisely what significance this room held, but she knew bad things had happened here. People had died here. Though the room was dusty, it was orderly, and Ellyne felt the terror deeply.

She felt she knew this place intimately, but wished she hadn't. Ellyne moved quickly to exit the room.

Passing through the apartment's door, she spilled out into an empty hallway. She traversed the white corridor, passing door after door, feeling anxious and wanting to run. She knew this place well, having just recently escaped. But why was she back? What significance did it hold?

The hall eventually ended in an open, almost warehouse-like area with a strange building in the center. As she approached, she saw the girl—the same girl that was sitting on her sofa. She motioned for Ellyne to come closer before stepping inside and shutting the door.

"Nicole," Ellyne whispered. "It *is* Nicole, and this is where … where she was being held captive?"

Ellyne was wrong—this wasn't the Kithrak prison, it was Nicole's. And the boy before, in the screen-filled room, that was … Derek? That room was the hub for Karnascus's AI construct, JASN.

The puzzle pieces were fitting together!

Ellyne hurried to the door and pushed it open, hoping to be able to talk to Nicole. Instead, however, she found herself standing in front of a column of bright light that towered high into the air. Its radiance shifted color and crackled with energy, raising the hairs on Ellyne's arms and sending shivers down her spine.

She hesitated, gazing around her for an exit but finding nothing. Her footsteps echoed as her boots trod the stone ground to the edge of the plateau. She looked over the precipice, expecting to see a downward slope but, instead, was met with cloudy darkness.

"Okay, dream, so where do I go now?" she laughed. But even as the words left her mouth, she knew where the exit was. As with the other areas, she knew she'd been here, too.

She may not remember the full significance of her surroundings, but she was sure they were in her past somewhere.

She turned and approached the pillar of energy. It hummed and flowed with a sound like traffic from the Legacy Age—back when vehicles weren't powered by magic. It was a low, distant rushing sound she always found more appealing than the eerie silence of modern vehicles. The noise was comforting, and she wanted to bathe in it, to remain for a while and enjoy the moment.

"This … this is the source of magic, isn't it? Flocia itself—the Teranyne." She paused and gazed around her. There had been terrible combat here. Nicole had nearly died. Yes, the memories were true and they came back in a torrent, momentarily overwhelming her.

"I jumped in," she whispered, recalling how she charged headlong into the pillar of energy. Her next memories were of waking up in the Kithrak prison. "Why the hell did I do that? And what happened after? I know the what—well, part of it —but not the why."

The pillar's low susurrus continued, almost whispering something Ellyne couldn't understand. For several moments she stood nervously, waiting for more memories to permeate her mind but was met only with disappointment. Was there anything left to recall? Surely this wasn't everything she could remember.

"I don't know if this is a good idea or not, but it's just a dream, right?"

Ellyne started to jump into the pillar but hesitated, recalling the dream when she first met Nicole.

Except it hadn't been a dream, had it? Somehow, Nicole pulled her into a different reality or a pocket of … well, Ellyne didn't understand it, but it had been real enough for her to acquire a weapon from the girl. And this … this felt very much the same. This whole string of consciousness felt different from any dream.

She reached out her hand to touch the pillar and the energy reached back, gently touching her finger and sending a bolt of warmth through her body. Happiness saturated her and she caught herself laughing—laughing harder than she ever may have before.

She also felt power. Raw, uncontrolled power. She laughed again, unable to explain the connection. It was a kinship—a relation of some kind, as if this pillar was somehow a part of her … or she was a part of it. Whatever the result, she knew she'd found not only the exit, but so much more, even if she wasn't sure exactly what it was or its true nature.

"Okay," she finally relented, "fine. Let's do this. What could possibly go wrong?"

The multicolored energy enveloped Ellyne as she dove into the pillar. Every memory she'd ever had invaded her mind, breaking the dam and overflowing. Her childhood, her parents, the Flocia Wars, Marik, Nicole … everything instantly came back to her, and she felt whole again. It was a picture book story of her life—everything good and bad. She simultaneously felt joy in finding a friend in Nicole and shame in handing her over to the Kithrak—real memories.

She felt rage toward Marik and anger at her parents.

Through the din of the rushing energy, she heard a faint whisper.

"Welcome back, mage breaker," she thought she heard it say. It was probably another memory she'd have to sort out later, though she recognized the term "mage breaker."

It was her.

Ellyne looked around, seeing nothing but swirling, bright colors and feeling the rush of power. "Who are you?" she shouted, now floating high in the air. "Is someone there?"

Ellyne's eyes shot open, staring up at the stars through the fort's crumbled ceiling and on through the forest canopy.

"Unity."

The word clung to her mind as if someone right next to her had said it before fading into nothing, causing her to question whether she'd heard it at all.

She jumped to her feet, busting through the sticks and logs that barely held her shelter together, ignoring the pain of impact and breathing heavily.

"What … what just happened?" she gasped. "That dream was so real!"

Pausing a moment, Ellyne listened to the dormant forest. Only the crickets made a sound, now, and she reveled in the peace. No vehicles, no Kithrak or Ilserate—just crickets.

"But that wasn't actually a dream, right? Or was it? Shit, I don't know how this works."

She stumbled in the darkness, trying to find her footing as she exited the fort, toppling what little remained. She wouldn't have been able to see anything at all if it weren't for the light coming from her finger.

Her finger was glowing.

"What the hell is this?" she whispered, scrutinizing her index finger—the finger she'd used to touch the pillar in her dream state. No, when the pillar reached out to *her*. "I guess you can pretty much discount the whole dream thing, Ellyne, because this seems like it's just a tad bit more than that."

She moved her finger around in front of her, casting light wherever it pointed, completely enthralled by this development but, at the same time, disgusted.

This had to be related to magic. "Once I get back to the house," she muttered, hurrying back to the tree line, "I'll figure this out. For now, however, I'm thankful to have a light source so I don't trip over everything and break my neck."

The sun's first rays cast over the valley as she breached the tree line. Stretching and yawning, she gazed down the hill at her childhood home—still cloaked in shadow, hiding in morning's darkness for just a little while longer.

"I guess the magic forest returned your memories to you,"

she chuckled, shaking her finger in front of her. To her surprise, the light faded and disappeared. "Excellent, one hundred percent back to normal, right? No disgusting magic here. No more light-up fingers, please."

She headed down the hill, hopeful that she'd cleared the last hurdle. But how would she know if all her memories had returned? How did one remember what one couldn't remember? Her thoughts quickly shifted to next steps, trying not to dwell too long on whether she was whole again. If there were other memories locked away, they would return in due time.

"If there *are* any more memories locked away, I just hope they return before I actually need them."

As she descended the slope, Ellyne's thoughts dwelled on the future. From what Nicole said, she'd been on that damned asteroid for over two years, and now that she remembered the events leading up to her imprisonment, she wondered just what state the world was in.

"I wrested control of flocia from the Kithrak by diving into the Teranyne," she muttered to herself, navigating the tall grass, "so they no longer control magic's source. Does that mean magic is free to use now without everyone having to wear a T-helm? That would throw a decently large wrench in Marik's plans … which would be absolutely delightful."

Though, the more she thought about it, the less sure she was whether that would make things better or worse than before. She was used to the idea of everyone being able to use magic in some capacity, even if she still hated magic itself. In that respect, nothing would have changed. But, without T-helms, the populace wouldn't have to pay their dues in the form of mental donations through the helmets—that's how she thought of it, anyway.

She suddenly remembered the poor souls who neglected their T-helms … the people who were twisted by flocia and turned into savage, violent monsters.

And then she remembered the government using those monsters as their own personal attack dogs. The Ilserate certainly knew how to stoop to new levels of low. And Marik, of course, led that initiative. The man really would stoop however low he needed to just so he could climb the ladder and feel important.

"The grika," she muttered. "That's what they called them. Sorry to foil your plans for a personal monster army, Marik … but not sorry at all. I hope the Ilserate is disappointed in you. Maybe they will have fired you by now."

She suspected the Ilserate wouldn't know he helped Nicole retrieve her—if they knew of her imprisonment at all. She believed they did and, if that were the case, they were most likely quite happy about it.

Her escape, on the other hand … that would possibly frighten them. Such a thought made her smile.

When she reached the bottom of the hill, she stretched again, standing in the shadow of the area the rising sun couldn't yet reach.

Or so she assumed that was the reason she stood in shadow but, upon looking toward the sky, she discovered a different, rather large alternative explanation.

"What in all the hell is *that*?"

CHAPTER
ELEVEN

"ALRIGHT," Ellyne shouted as she slammed the door behind her, "would someone mind telling me what's going on? And do NOT tell me you'll explain later. I consider now to be 'later', so start explaining."

Nicole jumped off the couch and rushed to give Ellyne a hug, squeezing her tightly. "I'm glad you're back! I was worried! You were gone all night and, like, I know you can take care of yourself, but I still got concerned."

"She literally wouldn't stop pacing and mumbling all night," Marik added, having found something interesting about one of his fingers.

"I'm fine, Nicole. I'm fine. Please … you're crushing my spleen or whatever's in that spot."

Nicole laughed and released Ellyne but looked like she might pounce again. "I'm sorry, I was just worried you might get lost or get into trouble or hurt yourself or—"

"Nicole," Ellyne said, holding her hand up to try to calm her, "I'm fine. I was simply … revisiting some things. There's no need to worry."

Marik remained seated in a chair, looking thoroughly unconcerned with anything but one of his fingernails. Ellyne knew better. No matter how disconnected the man appeared, she knew he was paying close attention. It was true he may not have cared, but he wasn't someone to ignore something that might be important.

"Did you remember things?" Nicole asked, not skipping a beat. "What did you remember? Is it cool? Was it, like, a rush of memories coming back all at once or was it like a dream?"

Ellyne laughed, reclining on the couch. Nicole sat next to her, looking as if she might explode in a shower of bright, colorful confetti from the anticipation.

"Yes, Nicole, my memory returned. Well, I'm not entirely sure if all of it came back. I mean, how would I know what I don't know?"

"I guess you wouldn't know if you don't know," the girl giggled. "You know?"

Marik sighed. Ellyne wondered how the man had tolerated Nicole this long.

"I'm sorry," Ellyne sneered, "are we boring you? Because I really hope we are, and we can continue doing so if it annoys you."

"There really is nothing to do around here," he remarked, keeping his focus on his fingers. "I have no idea how you kept yourself entertained as a child."

"By telling people to shut the hell up," Ellyne quipped. "Anyway," she continued, turning her attention back to Nicole, "I assume that was the first step in a greater plan of some kind? Please tell me that's what it was."

Nicole shifted and nervously stared at the floor. "Um ... sort of?"

"Wait. What do you mean *sort of*? Since you busted me out of space jail, you've both acted weird—like there's some dire, sinister situation of some kind. Please tell me that I'm not the beginning and end of your grand scheme?"

"I told you it was a longshot," Marik grunted.

"Well," Nicole stammered, still averting her gaze, "we

hoped, once you regained your memories, you might have some insight or know what to do. After all, *you* basically dove headfirst into the Teranyne. We hoped it would have imparted some wisdom or something on you."

"Wait. What to do about what?"

Nicole kicked at something on the carpet and scratched at the couch.

"Nicole." Ellyne repeated. "Spill it."

Nicole slowly rose from the couch and awkwardly paced in silence around the room until finally stopping in front of Ellyne.

"You see … after you leapt into the pillar of flocia—you remember that, right?"

"Yes, I remember. Good times. Though I can't say I remember anything after that except waking up in prison."

"Well, after you did … whatever you did, magic sort of went … haywire."

"Haywire?"

"Yeah. It became unreliable and unstable. It took every bit of skill I had just to get back to Karnascus and, even then, it was almost two weeks later. Since then, things have been chaotic, to say the least."

"Downright catastrophic," Marik added, now staring out a window. "And all thanks to you. Good job."

"And we hoped by breaking you out of prison, you might have some information as to what exactly happened."

"And maybe you could actually fix it," Marik added again. Ellyne couldn't ignore the intense disdain within his words. "Because, whatever you did, you really screwed shit up."

Nicole glared at the man. For a moment, Ellyne thought a spell fight was going to break out between the two. She knew who she'd put her tiks on.

"I'm sorry, Nicole, but I don't exactly know what happened when I … when I connected with flocia. I'm still trying to figure that out, actually. But if what you say is true, then I must've done something wrong. I wish I knew what it was or how to fix it. Like I said, I jumped into the Teranyne and woke up in prison."

"The Kithrak must really not want you remembering what you did," Nicole said, the anger in her voice readily apparent.

"Looks like we broke you out of prison for nothing, then," Marik added, shifting in his chair. "I told Nicole it was a waste of time."

"Not for nothing," Nicole whispered, "I just wanted my friend back."

Ellyne grinned, feeling her eyes tear up. "Thank you," she silently mouthed.

"I figured we needed more help," Nicole continued, making sure Marik heard her, "because this guy's been just about worthless."

"Very funny," he replied, unconcerned. "You know you wouldn't have gotten far without me."

"Wait a minute!" Ellyne shrieked, jumping up from the couch. "I almost forgot. I think we should probably find somewhere else to stay, and pretty soon."

"Why? What do you mean?" Marik asked, his curiosity piqued. It was amazing how quickly the man's emotions could change.

"There's something I need you to see," Ellyne continued, hurrying to the door.

"What is it?" Nicole asked, in hot pursuit.

Ellyne opened the door and pointed up at the sky. "That."

"Oh crap!" Nicole shouted. "Oops, sorry for swearing! Marik! We need to go *now*!"

Marik appeared beside them and looked up.

"The Golgolonar! For once, Ellyne, you're right! Get in the ship! We need to go."

Marik scurried out the door with Nicole behind him.

Ellyne followed their lead, running to the ship still sitting outside the house. "Wait, what? What are you talking about? What's a … gargalor?"

"Get in the ship!" Marik repeated. "There's no time to reminisce right now! We'll explain later."

"Damn it, I *knew* you were going to say that!"

Ellyne stared up at a spacecraft so massive it blotted out the sun. A shiver ran through her as she realized she'd probably just stepped into something far worse than she'd imagined—even worse than what she'd just left.

She had a million questions swirling inside her head but tried to ignore each one as she blindly followed orders, climbing into the tiny ship, and strapping herself in.

"Do you think they noticed us?" Nicole asked, also fumbling with her seatbelt in the chair next to Ellyne.

"I'd say that's why they're hovering over the area, so yeah. Chances are, they've been waiting for the opportune time to make a move."

"What do they want?" Ellyne asked.

"Probably you," Nicole replied.

"Wait, what?"

Ellyne pressed her face against the ship's window and struggled to get a look at the massive cruiser looming overhead. It must have cast a shadow for miles. From her vantage point, she could only see a small portion and it was cloaked in shadow, so couldn't make out a lot of detail.

Not that it mattered much, but it wasn't Kithrak—at least she assumed not. The only Kithrak spacecraft she'd seen was the Sistix and this looked nothing like that.

She shivered and her heart raced. She'd hoped to make things less complicated, but the arrival of a massive spacecraft overhead blew those plans to hell.

"Hang on," Marik insisted as the ship sprang to life. "We still can't reliably use magic to fly this thing so it's going to be bumpy. If we crash, we'll have Ellyne to thank."

"Wait, me? Why? And do *not* say you'll explain later."

"I guess not *all* your memory returned," Marik chuckled. "Perfect."

Ellyne cursed the drops of spittle that flew from the infuriating man's mouth, resisting the urge to shoot him in the back right then and there. It wasn't easy, and she had to dig deep for several reasons to leave him alive.

"What's that supposed to mean?" she asked. "Nicole, what are you not telling me?"

The ship jumped into the air. Ellyne gripped the armrests and clenched her teeth. Nicole appeared serene, simply waiting until it was over to continue.

"Do you remember, back in the Kithrak prison, how you got hit with spells but shrugged them off? And then, after a while, you sort of—"

"Exploded and decimated an entire Kithrak space prison? Yes Nicole, I remember that. It was literally yesterday."

"Hang on," Marik called from the front seat.

"To what?" Ellyne shouted but her words were swallowed by a gasp as they hurtled forward and shot into the sky. "I thought you didn't know how to fly this thing!"

"I don't! But improvisation is just one of the many things I happen excel at."

"Apparently," Nicole laughed, "taking off is much easier than landing."

"So, anyway, you were saying?"

"Oh yeah! So, you're effectively immune to magic and you're able to store its power inside you and channel flocia itself into really terrible magical effects! Isn't that great?"

"Great? Great? No, it's not great! Is *that* why the Golgorakanor or whatever they're called—is that why they're after me?"

"You win the prize!" Marik shouted.

"Partially," Nicole added.

Ellyne shifted in her seat as the ship sped into the air. Marik appeared to have his hands full keeping the craft steady and level, but they hadn't crashed yet, which she took as a positive sign.

"What does that mean?"

Nicole took a few strands of black hair and twirled them around in her fingers. "Uh," she stammered uncomfortably. "Shortly after you did… whatever you did, the Golgolonar arrived. They didn't really communicate with us at first, but the Kithrak immediately scattered. Magic went haywire and combat broke out between the two. The Ilserate stepped in, and we pretty much have an actual war on our hands."

"Okay, that sounds horrible," Ellyne replied, watching out the window as various bits of scenery passed quickly by. "But what does this all have to do with me? I didn't ask the golgar things to come here and start a war."

Well," Nicole continued, giggling nervously, "everyone blames you. And, I mean, they're not wrong. You sort of screwed up everything."

"Gee, thanks."

"Oh, I'm not blaming you. It's just that—"

"It is actually entirely your fault," Marik sneered. "It really is, despite what Nicole says."

"Shut it, Marik" Ellyne growled, resisting the urge to draw her weapon.

The bald man laughed. He probably *did* blame her and was probably going to remind her every chance he got.

"Anyway," Nicole continued, "not only do they want revenge, but they also want to use you to put everything right. They believe you're not only dangerous but that you're the key… much as the Kithrak believe, actually."

"Fat chance of that," Ellyne laughed. "I don't really even know what I did in the first place! And wait, the key to what?

"Truly controlling flocia. At least that's what Marik said."

"Hey, I only heard rumors and hushed conversations within the Ilserate. Nobody's sure of anything at this point, except that the Golgolonar up there are largely in charge now."

"Hasn't our mighty government fought back?" Ellyne asked.

"Oh, certainly yes," Marik laughed. "At least, they tried. But magic is so unreliable that there really wasn't much they could do."

"And the Golgolonar apparently don't actually use magic," Nicole added. "Instead, they seem to draw on flocia directly—like you do, only at a lesser capacity, I think."

"I'm beginning to prefer being told you'll explain everything later," Ellyne sighed. Her mind was still working to process the events of yesterday, let alone an alien invasion.

"They also want to study you," Nicole continued. "So that sounds pretty fun."

"Oh, great. You mean like the Kithrak were?"

"Exactly. You've caused enough problems for not only the Kithrak and the Ilserate, but now the Golgolonar. They want to know how you do the things you do. We believe the Kithrak were keeping you concealed not only to study you, but to keep the Golgolonar from locating you."

"Well, we kind of blew that to hell," Marik added.

Ellyne hated the man, but he wasn't wrong. He was an asshole, not an idiot. But he was assuredly playing his own angle and she would never make the mistake of trusting him again. Hopefully, Nicole felt the same.

"So, I'm immune to magic?"

"Largely, yes. For the most part."

"What does that mean?" Immediately after she asked this question, Ellyne remembered what Nicole was referring to. "Wait—that time outside my apartment when—"

"When I used magic to throw you against the wall."

"Right. Also, that hurt."

"Sorry. But yes. If you were completely immune to magic,

I shouldn't have been able to affect you. You would've shrugged it off like you do spells from everyone else."

"But you're also the most powerful mage in existence, right? So maybe you're just that good, if that's even how magic works. Hell, I don't know."

"Maybe. Certainly Marik's not experienced the same effect with his skills."

Nicole winked and they both grinned, sharing a moment at the man's expense.

"If I recall correctly, it's not like we ever fully understood my abilities," Ellyne added. "It's frustrating, having so much about myself be such a mystery. Also frustrating is that ugly alien ship up there above us."

Nicole put her hand on Ellyne's. "We'll figure it out together. Like we always do."

"Yes, yes," Marik sneered, "this is all well and good—a family reunion of sorts. I'm tearing up over here listening to you two but, if you don't mind, where should we be headed?"

Nicole quietly giggled, knowing full well they'd gotten under his skin.

For the first time in a while, Ellyne felt something other than rage and hopelessness. She wasn't sure what lay ahead, even though she knew full well it would be difficult. But Nicole was right—they'd figure it out together.

"I don't know about you, but I could use a stiff drink."

"Sounds like we're going home then," Nicole said.

CHAPTER
TWELVE

ELLYNE JUMPED BACK against a building as a vehicle sped by, nearly careening out of control and kicking up a fine, post-rain mist from the street. She leaned against the wall and flipped them the middle finger as she wiped the moisture off her clothes.

Nicole stifled a laugh while Marik sighed and shook his head slightly.

"Learn to drive!" she shouted, before realizing that was a terrible idea. "I know, I know, we're supposed to be skulking through the city unnoticed. Call it a reflex."

"If the Ilserate, the Kithrak, or the Golgolonar find us—"

"Yes, Marik, you've made that abundantly clear. But that dude needs to learn how to drive. I was merely informing him of that fact. I was literally performing an important service for him."

Disapproval was written all over Marik's face as he scanned the area for patrols. "By yelling at a vehicle?" he asked. "Even if any one of the Technos or Teranynes discover you, we're dead meat."

"Well," Ellyne chuckled, "I did try to *silently* give him the finger first. I tried to be quiet, but that just wasn't doing the trick."

Nicole failed to stifle her laugh. Ellyne grinned along with her.

"Yes, yes," Marik sneered, "laugh it up. It won't be funny when we're caught and interrogated. Actually, it will probably be fun for me, because I'm sure I can talk my way out of it. You, on the other hand …"

"Buzzkill," Nicole huffed.

Once she was sure they were safe, Ellyne continued down the sidewalk. "I really wish we could've landed closer, and maybe not during the day." She recognized the area. It was good to be among familiar surroundings again. In fact, a drink at Victor's bar sounded perfect right about now—she wasn't joking when she'd said that earlier. "This is a whole lot of walking I didn't expect to do today."

"Well, you know," Nicole said, "I don't think it would be too sneaky to land a noisy ship on the rooftops somewhere."

"And where is everybody?" Ellyne asked, noticing only a fraction of the people moving about.

Ahead was a toppled building, barely more than a pile of rubble. "I remember this place," she said, stopping to inspect it. "This is where I used to go to browse music merch. I got all my Transgressors t-shirts here."

Marik made a snorting noise and chuckled. "An overrated band. Their first album was their only good album."

She kicked some bits of glass with her boot. "And now I have yet another reason to hate you."

"So … about that," Nicole said, sounding unsure. She stepped over some rubble to urge the group to continue walking. "Magic sort of went … haywire when you—"

"Yeah, we've been over that bit."

"Right. Sorry, I forgot. But you see, when that happened …"

"What she's trying to tell you," Marik interrupted, "is that lots of people died when magic failed. The Metro crashed, vehicles crashed, ships crashed, buildings crumbled—"

"Damn you, Marik!" Nicole growled, balling her fists and glaring at the man. "I was trying to break it to her gently."

Marik appeared pleased with himself. "Literally all your fault, Ellyne."

"Wait a minute," Ellyne said, suddenly finding herself on shaky legs. She reached out to a flickering light post to steady herself. "Are you saying … that *I* caused this? People died because of me?"

"*More* people died, yes." Marik added. "You're quite good at killing innocents."

"Marik, shut up!" Nicole insisted.

"When everything runs on magic," the man continued, "and magic suddenly stops working—even for a mere moment—and then continues to be unreliable for two years, yes, there are casualties. A lot of people died and there are parts of the city that suffered as well. What did you expect would happen when you disrupted a system where everything relies on magic?"

Nicole briefly waved one hand and thrust it at Marik. His body stiffened and he collapsed to the ground, unmoving.

"Not *all* magic is unreliable, and I told you to shut it," she murmured angrily. "Ellyne, I … I'm sorry. I meant to break it to you in a much gentler way, but dickhead here beat me too it. Oh, sorry for the language."

"I … let's just get to my apartment. You'll have to unfreeze the dickhead because I'm not dragging his ass all the way there. The trek's hard enough without having to drag dead weight."

She tried to keep her mind occupied, hoping to avoid the overwhelming grief of having caused such a catastrophe. She never meant to harm anyone this way. If only she could remember what she'd done, maybe she could reverse it.

Nicole waved her hand and Marik clumsily scampered to

his feet, nearly collapsing again. "You just watch yourself, girl," he warned, trying to wipe off the specs of mud from his robes. "Try that again and I'll—"

"Marik, shut up," Ellyne whispered.

"Don't tell me to—"

Nicole waved her hand again and Marik's voice disappeared. Try as he might (and he tried mightily), he couldn't make a sound.

"Thank you," Ellyne grumbled. "We should've done that a long time ago. Anyway, Marik, there's a patrol ahead so if you have something to say, now's a good time to shut it."

Marik, obviously skeptical, stepped forward to see for himself while

Two Kithrak led five bots through a street ahead, scanning the area. Though there had always been patrols at night, they were under the pretext of "keeping the peace" but Ellyne was familiar with their ulterior motives—searching for her.

Marik pointed to his mouth and Nicole reluctantly canceled her spell of silence.

"It appears the bots have gone through some upgrades," Ellyne pointed out. "They look lethal."

"They had to give them legs since magic is … well, since they can't reliably hover. And, in case they're unable to use their wands, they now have—"

"Guns." Ellyne sighed. "I kind of prefer the days when I didn't have to worry about being shot at, since I'm not immune to bullets. Wait, am I?"

Marik laughed and shook his head. "They were well into upgrading the bots' arsenal before the collapse of magic—on account of you, of course. They had to come up with some kind of a response to your abilities."

"Lovely," Ellyne sighed. "It's good to know they care. So … the collapse of magic? That's what it's called?"

Nicole kept her eyes on the patrol as they stayed put.

"Most people just call it The Collapse. Some have more colorful phrases, but yeah."

"That sounds awfully dramatic."

"So was The Collapse," Marik added.

"I'm grateful nobody calls it 'Ellyne's' Screw-up.'"

"Well, I mean, nobody knows you did it … well, except the Kithrak, the Golgolonar, and the Ilserate. Oh, probably The Teranyne Order and the Technicians' Guild also. And then maybe—"

"It was a joke, but thank you for enlightening me, Nicole."

"Oh, sorry."

"Anyway," Ellyne continued, "let's take this alley. It should allow us to avoid the patrol. Hopefully, this is the only encounter we'll have because that drink is sounding better by the minute."

Nicole nodded. Marik remained silent but followed them into the alley. It was difficult to move quietly on account of the amount of discarded garbage strewn about. Additionally, they had to step over several people sleeping among the various trash piles.

Ellyne fought back tears, knowing she was responsible for most of the city's misfortune. The Karnascus she'd left had been a gleaming jewel but, now, it was largely dark and crumbling. If only she could recall what she'd done when she communed with flocia's source, she might be able to set things right.

Even if she remembered what it was she'd done, how was she supposed to reverse it? Her memories were largely complete except for the one vital puzzle piece that was missing.

She looked down at every sleeping, shadowy figure. The signs of turmoil and destruction were everywhere and each one tore at her. She had no particular love for people in general, preferring to simply avoid them much of the time, but she never meant anyone harm. Their world was turned upside-down, and they didn't even know why.

"Looks like we evaded them," Ellyne whispered as they emerged onto the sidewalk from the alley. She glanced back at the street the group had just left and saw no signs of them. "Right, let's just get to my apartment. We're not far."

Marik pointed down the street to their right. "I think the patrols may have caught our scent."

"Shit," Ellyne spat. "They must have tracked us from my parents' house."

"It wouldn't have been difficult," Marik added, "the Golgolonar knew where we were and probably watched us speed off."

"So, the Kithrak are working with the goglolothings?"

"Sort of. They don't really have a choice. None of us do."

"Well, we do," Ellyne said, trying to make her words sound valiant but her thoughts dwelled on the destruction around them.

"A choice that could get us killed," Marik added.

"So, do they know where my apartment is?"

"I don't think so," Nicole replied, sounding sure of herself. "I threw up some wards to hide it in case they caught on, but we've been super careful and only leave the apartment when we need to. Golgolonar spies are everywhere and, though it may not look like it, they keep everyone on a short leash."

Ellyne laughed. "Stuck in my apartment with *him*, huh? That sounds worse than my imprisonment."

"Oh, Marik's not around a lot of the time."

"Some of us still have jobs," he sneered. "My position among both the Ilserate and the Kithrak has allowed me certain … freedoms."

"Like creating an army of feral humanoid monster beasts? Sounds like a pretty sweet job, there, Marik."

"Yes, well, I'm also privy to certain classified secrets which, you may be interested to know, led to your jailbreak."

Ellyne seethed internally, preferring not to think about such an annoying man being the key to her escape. If he thought she owed him a debt of any sort, he was dead wrong. The very concept made her want to vomit.

Her thoughts quickly switched to their current plight, and their options were limited--simply hide in the alley or try to cross the street unnoticed Neither was a good option and she cursed herself for allowing them to get sloppy. The alley had nowhere convenient to properly hide, and the patrol was already close enough that it might spot them.

"Looks like one Kithrak, four or five humans, and two bots," Marik remarked. "That's a hefty patrol, even for normal nighttime operations. And, here we are, in broad daylight."

"I have a feeling this is anything but normal," Ellyne replied. "We've already seen more patrol activity in the past hour than I'd normally see all day. I say we make a break for it. Nicole, can you create some kind of diversion or something?"

"I could try, but we're already really close to the patrol. They'd probably be able to detect the source of the magic, so I don't think it'd work."

"She's right," Marik concurred. "Such a process is based on very basic magic and would probably function more reliably than most spells, so the spell probably wouldn't fail, but our proximity to the patrol is indeed troublesome."

Nicole frowned, lost in thought.

"Look at you," Ellyne smirked, patting Marik on the top of the head, "being all useful and stuff. Good job, little guy."

The man looked as if he were about to destroy something which only served to fuel Ellyne's joy.

Nicole tried to hide her grin.

Marik rolled his eyes. "Yes, very funny. But the patrol is getting closer, and I don't think we can fight them with quips, humor, and degrading behavior."

"I'm not sure we'll have to fight them at all," Nicole replied. "Look, over there." She pointed to the alley further down the street between them and the Kithrak patrol.

Ellyne squinted, waiting to see whatever Nicole had seen. "What am I looking for?" she asked, continuing to stare.

Finally, she saw it—a bit of movement from the shadows, followed by some activity in another alley further down that the patrol had already passed. "Okay, so, people in the alleys," she continued, "they're probably just trying to get some sleep."

"Look closer," Nicole insisted.

"It's the Free People," Marik added.

"I'm sorry, the what?" Ellyne asked, suddenly unconcerned with the patrol.

"The Free People," a voice behind them said. All three turned and gasped, seeing a man in rags standing before them. His dark, curly hair fell to his shoulders and bushy facial hair concealed many of his features.

"The Free People," he repeated with a thick accent. "And I suggest you three stay put for the moment while we do what we need to do."

Ellyne inspected the man. What she thought were rags and tattered clothes appeared to be a disguise. Beneath them, he carried two pistols and a wand on his belt. "Clever," she said. "For a moment, I was going to question your fashion sense."

"You're the rebels!" Nicole exclaimed, clapping her hand over her mouth as if that would help stifle how loud she'd been. "I've seen news stories about you, but I thought they were just made up."

"We prefer the term 'resistance fighters' but, yeah, we're rebels. I'm Mack."

Nicole appeared riveted. "I've heard of you guys, but never thought I'd actually meet any of you."

"Oh, you've seen and met us. We're everywhere, and

we've been watching you two and now her as well. I can explain more later. For now, let's just stay here and remain quiet."

"How do I know we can trust you?" Ellyne asked. Her right hand had rested on her revolver since the man appeared behind them. She wasn't about to move it.

Mack merely pointed to a screen on a building to their left. As if on cue, it sprang to life.

"Road Work Ahead: Please Keep Left."

The message appeared for only a second or two, then the screen went dark again.

"JASN," Ellyne whispered. "Okay, so you're working with the city's AI—that's compelling evidence so I'll trust you for now. But if you make any kind of a wrong move—"

"I won't," he insisted. "My mission was to find you and get you to safety. The Free People have been eagerly awaiting this day—the day the Mage Breaker would return. Today is that day, but we obviously have some business to take care of first."

"This is all very confusing," Ellyne admitted. "You act as if I'm some sort of deity."

"It's a lot to take in," Mack continued. "And I can explain later when, you know, we're not in imminent danger. First, however…"

"Oh, she hates that phrase," Nicole said, visibly wincing.

"In this particular situation," Ellyne replied, "I'll be happy for someone to explain later—when we're out of danger. Though, yes, I'm tired of hearing it."

Mack leaned out of the alley and signaled with his hand before ducking back under cover.

"This is so exciting!" Nicole giggled.

Marik didn't appear to share her enthusiasm. Ellyne knew he wasn't keen on receiving help, and magic's unreliable nature must have bothered him every second of his existence.

While it didn't make up for all the strife she'd caused, it was a minor salve on a large wound.

"Okay," Marik grumbled, "so now what? I fail to see—"

"We let my colleagues handle it," Mack replied. "Trust me."

Marik scoffed.

They waited nervously, watching the patrol slowly make its way to the next alley, closely scrutinizing everything it passed. Ellyne was beginning to think nothing would happen when the patrol was besieged by a crowd of people. Gunfire and spellfire erupted in the street, followed by shouts and cheers. Some people even threw rocks or bricks at the Kithrak and the bots.

Mack pointed to the alley across the street. "That's our cue, my friends. Let's move. Quickly, into the alley across the street!"

Ellyne wasted no time, following the stranger closely but also keeping an eye on him in case he should betray them. It sometimes paid to accept help and settle up later if there was doubt.

"Come on," Mack said, motioning everyone forward as they skittered between buildings, "we're almost there." They crossed a street and disappeared back into another alley.

"Almost where?" Marik asked.

"Safe house."

CHAPTER
THIRTEEN

MACK LED them through the city, hurrying down several streets and ducking into and out of alleys, often having to circumvent a patrol or wait for one to pass. There were far more of them than she remembered or expected, which Ellyne didn't see as coincidence. No, they weren't merely out enforcing laws. Last time, they were hunting Nicole. This time, they were hunting *her*.

It felt no different, of course. Essentially, they'd both been hunted previously, so it's not like this was anything new. The circumstances were different, but the song was the same.

"So much for enjoying a peaceful life," she mused, wondering if things would ever return to the way they were. She hoped they would, but something told her everything had changed too much to go back. The days of hanging out at Victor's every day in between contracts were probably a thing of the past.

"We're almost there," Mack whispered, motioning for everyone to stop. "Just across this street—in that alley over there."

Ellyne's vision flashed and, for a second, everything was illuminated brighter than daytime. It was as if the city was on fire with swirling colors and flashes of light in a blinding overture of chaos only she could detect.

She squeezed her eyes shut and rubbed them as if the light would blind her. "It's too bright," she groaned.

But even with her eyes shut, she still saw the ever shifting, flowing colors as they popped and flashed until, as suddenly as it happened, it all ceased.

"What's too bright?" Nicole asked.

"You didn't see it?"

"No."

"Never mind. I think my mind is playing tricks on me."

Ellyne knew better but, since there was no obvious answer, she chose to try and explain it away. Except she wasn't buying her own lies.

"Things just got more complicated," Mack whispered, pointing to a nearby patrol.

"Crap," Ellyne muttered. "Looks like … three Kithrak, a bot and five grika."

Ellyne's skin crawled. The grika always made her uneasy with their savage howls and dripping fangs. The unfortunate subjects of Kithrak and Ilserate experiments were once human before they were twisted by uncontrolled magic and used as personal attack dogs. As disgusted as she was, she felt pangs of sorrow for them.

"Hey, Marik," Ellyne quipped, "maybe you can go out and talk to them. Maybe tell them we're friendly and not to eat us. Just remind them you're their daddy."

"Funny as always. But no thank you."

"We'll wait here until they move on," Mack continued. "There's a door on the side of the building on the right. See it? That's our safe house."

"What then?" Ellyne asked.

Mack kept his gaze on the patrol ahead of them. "One thing at a time. First, we get in. We decide our next steps once we catch our breath."

"Sounds conspicuously familiar," Nicole giggled.

"I suddenly don't feel so bad about never having a plan," Ellyne replied. "Apparently, I'm in good company."

Ellyne would've laughed, too, if things weren't so tense. Their plans really always were improvisation stuffed into a very loose framework—literally building the bridge as they crossed it. Her success during the Flocia Wars had never been attributed to good planning, at least as far as her soldiers were concerned. But they had been undyingly loyal to her just the same. The news outlets told whatever story they wanted, but Ellyne knew the truth.

"Come on," Marik growled through clenched teeth, "get this patrol out of here. Move along, boys."

"Why aren't they moving?" Nicole asked. "This doesn't seem normal."

Ellyne watched the group. The patrol appeared to be scanning the area—probably for them. Was it possible the patrol detected them somehow? "They're waiting," she said. "Maybe for reinforcements. We need to move *now*."

"You want to fight a patrol?" Mack asked.

"I've done it before. Besides, your Free People did it earlier."

"Yeah, but we attack in large groups, and we rarely win. We only enter combat strategically, and usually to divert attention. We all make it out alive or we don't engage."

"Well have a seat and watch, because I'm about to show you how it's done."

"I don't think that's a good idea," Nicole warned. "Things aren't—"

Ellyne ignored the girl and ran headlong into the patrol, her golden revolver gripped tightly in her right hand and her extended blade in her left. Whether it was the sheer thrill or the desire for revenge, Ellyne felt alive as she dove into the fray.

She was on the bot in a flash, putting three bullets into its torso at close range. The metal humanoid took aim and fired with the gun attached to its left arm, but Ellyne knocked it away, sending a hail of bullets into a nearby building and shattering a few windows.

"It's her!" one of the Kithrak shouted as he jumped back away from her. The other two followed suit as one of them began casting spells.

"No, don't!" another Kithrak shouted. It was a woman's voice, though raspy and thick with a Kithrak accent.

The bot was sluggish in its attacks and Ellyne heard the whirring and grinding of mechanics from within. She knew she had to dispatch the machine quickly before the grika overwhelmed her, and she heard them approaching from behind.

"Okay, flocia," she mumbled, "now would be a great time to … explode or whatever it is you do to me in these situations."

She felt the warm tingle within her—like a tiny spark in the darkness. It was familiar and always present, but she still felt like she had no control over it. She knew its potential for destruction and death, but she felt like it always fought her for control.

She dodged the robot's right arm as it swung, ducking under it and sliding between the automaton's legs before jumping up behind it. Without thinking about her actions, she threw a punch at its back with her left hand.

Only realizing what she'd done a split second before her fist connected with solid metal, she prepared for pain and maybe a broken hand. Instead, however, her fist glowed bright orange and her arm plunged completely through the bot's torso.

"Ha!" she screamed, pulling her arm out as the mechanical monster collapsed, sparking and whizzing as it struggled to function. "Wish I knew how I did that!"

The five feral grika jumped her, overwhelming Ellyne

immediately and bringing her to the ground as they clawed and lunged with drool-soaked jaws. Her golden revolver clattered to the ground as she lost her grip.

She shrieked and writhed as their claws tore at her skin. Vaguely humanoid, the grika weren't particularly strong but their ferocity with no regard for their own safety was unrivaled. The Ilserate had found the perfect, fearless soldiers that knew only one command—attack.

"Get off me!" she yelled lunging out with balled fists. Several times she connected with ineffectual blows, attempting to get out from under the pile.

"Hey!" someone yelled. "Come get us!"

It was Mack's voice.

"We're over here!" Nicole shouted.

The grika were single-minded in purpose, and they didn't move from the pile atop Ellyne but, for a split second, they paused and it was enough of a distraction to provide her with a way out.

And she took it.

She wasn't sure if flocia somehow bolstered her strength or if she was fueled by pain and anger, but Ellyne threw off several of the savages and rolled backwards, grabbing her gun and landing on her feet. Just as one of the grika leapt at her, she buried a bullet in it. Its corpse sailed past, skidding along the ground behind her and leaving a bloody smear on the road. Though she didn't look to make sure, she knew it was dead.

Everything that followed was a blur. Time had no influence as Ellyne fired off her remaining shots, killing her targets. She dropped the cartridge out of her gun, pulled a new one out of her jacket, slammed it in, and slapped the chamber shut in one fluid motion. She moved with purpose, as if she were dancing gracefully instead of fighting for her life.

Three more grika arrived from somewhere behind the

Kithrak and she effortlessly extinguished them. Several seconds later, the three Kithrak were also dead, leaving Ellyne standing in the middle of the street amongst a broken bot and many corpses.

She holstered her weapon, staring at the carnage. It was only one patrol, but it was a victory. She was no longer a helpless prisoner.

"That was amazing!" Nicole shouted, grabbing Ellyne in a tight hug from behind. "And bloody and disturbing but also amazing! Oh, yuck I think I stepped in grika brains or something. Gross!"

Ellyne winced, suddenly feeling at once all the grika wounds beneath Nicole's embrace. "Ow," she groaned, allowing Nicole her hug before eventually wriggling free.

"Are you okay?" Mack asked, obviously noticing the amount of blood on her clothes. The look on his face said everything.

"I will be. I'm not sure how much of this blood is even mine."

"I think quite a bit, unfortunately," Nicole replied, appearing to be fascinated with several of Ellyne's wounds. "Some of those scratches look super deep. We need to get you some bandages or something, I think."

"Yes," Marik agreed, "you're pretty torn up, but may I suggest we get to the safe house before we all play doctor? Standing out in plain sight in the middle of the street isn't really the best place to do this. Or would you like to see if another patrol can help you?"

Though his bedside manner was abysmal, Ellyne knew Marik was right—they needed to leave the scene since reinforcements would most assuredly be on the way.

"Fine," Ellyne relented, "yeah, Marik's right. We need to go."

Mack pointed ahead of them. "It's just through this alley. We can rest up, and we have medical supplies stashed inside." He hurried out of the street and into the shadowy alley.

"Do you trust this guy?" Ellyne whispered to Nicole, hanging back for a moment.

"I'm not sure we have a choice right now," the girl responded. "Besides, he can't be any worse than Marik, right?"

"I heard that," Marik grunted.

"Point taken," Ellyne grinned. "Let's go see what this safe house is all about I guess." She slowly moved further into the shadows, feeling her wounds with each movement.

"And you can tell me all about whatever it is you did," Nicole smirked.

"What do you mean?"

"Just now—during the fight."

"I didn't do anything … well, except put down a bunch of monsters. Seems pretty simple to me."

Nicole, obviously puzzled, started to speak but apparently thought better of it and, instead, pulled on Ellyne's arm to follow her into the alley.

Ellyne shrugged, which sent a wave of pain through her shoulder, and followed. During the heat of battle, she'd ignored much of the pain and blood loss, but it was catching up to her quickly.

"Let's just make it to safety and figure out everything else later. One thing at a time, as always."

"Just a second," Mack said, standing outside a metal door. He fished around in a pocket and produced a simple key "This would really be easier with magic," he chuckled.

"Yeah, sorry about that," Ellyne replied. "I hear that a lot —almost as much as the phrase 'I'll explain later.'" She shot Nicole a mischievous grin.

"You have nothing to apologize for, gunslinger."

After a few seconds fumbling with the lock, the door swung open and they hurried inside, locking it behind them.

"Welcome to the safe house," he chuckled. "Let me get the lights."

Ellyne heard the switch click, but they were still cloaked in darkness.

"Was something supposed to happen?" Nicole asked.

"Oh," Mack stammered, "yeah, sometimes it takes a few flips. These lights are still magic-based and, well, you know."

Ellyne heard the click a few more times and the lights struggled to life, dimly illuminating the room. "I love what you've done with the place," she snickered. "Very … minimalist."

The safe house consisted of one windowless room—devoid of any furniture except a bookshelf that currently held medical supplies. Though it was barren, it was clean, which meant it was often used. Ellyne wondered how many safe houses there were throughout the city, and just how big a group the Free People were.

But such things were fleeting thoughts, as she was unable to think straight. She felt her legs buckle and she slid down the wall, slumping to the ground and leaving a bloody smear behind her.

"Ellyne!" Nicole shouted, kneeling at her side. "Oh no you don't. You're not leaving us!"

But Nicole's voice was muffled and distant, and Ellyne could feel herself slipping into unconsciousness. "It's okay," she whispered, closing her eyes. "I just need to rest. I'll be fine. I'll explain later." She grinned again.

"Her wounds are pretty severe," she heard Marik say. "I fear there's nothing we can do."

The last thought that ran through Ellyne's mind was how Marik's tone sounded almost jovial, then she slipped away.

CHAPTER
FOURTEEN

ELLYNE ASCENDED THE LONG, gradual hill and stepped foot onto the plateau, her boots finding the orderly stones that paved the surface. Each footstep echoed, startling her at first. She knew this place—this was where she communed with the Teranyne over two years ago.

She was alone, left with only her thoughts and questions. So many questions.

"Why am I back here?" she asked herself. Why do my dreams keep bringing me back to this place?"

She understood the significance of it all. Here, atop this hill, she'd changed the world. She'd changed *everything*. At the same time, she'd destroyed everything. She was unaware of the consequences at the time, but she was reminded of them all too frequently as of late.

It was indeed the same place, but it was distorted somehow. The same, but not the same. A fog had descended, obscuring her vision beyond a few feet. The stones beneath her boots were dingy and crumbling. She felt the air's chill with each breath she took, yet it seemed stale.

But the most important change, of course, was the absence of the Teranyne. Flocia's source was gone. The pleasant sound of the ever-flowing column of energy was replaced by utter silence. The small dais that once contained the multicolored pillar was decayed and empty.

This place felt dead, barren, and sullen—as if a plague of corruption had taken hold.

"Hello?" Ellyne called, hearing her voice echo several times before it faded. "Why am I here? What kind of dream is this? Am I dead? I was really hoping for a more pleasant afterlife—somewhere with a beach, perhaps."

She laughed at first but then considered she quite possibly *could* have died. Marik sounded very sure of himself and, while he was one who often wished her dead, he had no clear reason to lie.

At least, not in this case.

Something about this place, despite its dark turn, felt welcoming and safe—almost as if it were home. Ellyne couldn't explain it, especially since the only time she'd physically been here she and Nicole were locked in a deadly fight with Marik, Kithrak mages, and countless grika.

"So why am I back here in a dream? There must be a significance or meaning of some sort but I'm not seeing any clues."

A low susurrus of voices responded, whispering words in a language Ellyne had never spoken, but recognized. It was the language many mages spoke when they cast spells and, while she'd never understood it before, it was clear as day to her now.

"A dream … this is not," the voices replied. "A prison, this was. Now, freedom. Through the reckoning … unity."

"What … what are you talking about? Who are you?"

"I'm Nicole, silly!"

Ellyne opened her eyes. She was in the same spot where she'd fallen, and Nicole was next to her, tears in her eyes and the biggest, goofy grin plastered across her face. "I'm so happy you're all right! I thought you'd died and, while Marik didn't seem to be broken up about it, I was afraid."

The girl squeezed her tightly and Ellyne winced, preparing for the pain of her wounds to hit her all at once beneath Nicole's hug.

"Nicole, be careful," she instinctively warned but the pain never came. To her surprise, she felt fine.

"She was literally staring at you for several hours, waiting for you to wake up," Marik snickered. "It's a bit creepy if you ask me."

Nicole frowned and glared at Marik. "Genius over there thought you were dead, but I insisted you weren't, and I was right!" The girl stuck her tongue out at Marik who appeared unconcerned.

"That's not entirely true," Marik replied, standing and dusting himself off. "I was merely *hoping* you were dead. There is a distinct difference."

"Charming as always," Ellyne sneered, slowly standing. She inspected herself. Parts of her jacket, tank top, and pants were shredded and crusted with blood, but the wounds beneath had vanished. She felt no pain and saw no scars-- no reminder of their existence. "How long was I out?"

"Only a couple of hours," Nicole insisted, also getting up and still grinning like a fool.

"How ... did someone manage to cast healing magic on me? Why am I okay?"

"I tried but healing magic is probably my worst talent. But I *did* try. It just... you know, didn't work on you. You sucked the magic up into you instead—like you always do. So, I bandaged you up as best I could and treated your cuts so they wouldn't get infected."

Ellyne felt the faint tingle within her, confirming what Nicole had said. The thought of even having her life saved by magic revolted her and, though she was thankful to Nicole for trying, she almost would've rather been left to die rather than be healed by magic.

"So, nobody knows? I'm just inexplicably fine with no injuries?"

Neither Nicole nor Marik offered an explanation, and both looked disappointed about that fact. They all shared an awkward silence while Ellyne tried to process everything.

"You're just that difficult to figure out," Marik noted. "At least, in this particular sense."

"Hey," she finally said, "where's Mack?"

"Oh, he left," Nicole replied. "He said he had a few things to attend to. I think he also thought you were going to die."

"I think we all did," Ellyne added.

"Anyway, he said he'd be back."

Ellyne wished there was at least a window to look out in case danger approached. "I don't trust him," she sighed.

"That's no surprise to me," Marik chuckled, "you don't trust anyone."

"With good reason," Ellyne snarled. "You guys have been in the know, right? So why is it we've never heard of the Free People until now?"

"Part of a resistance force is secrecy," Marik replied. "I doubt they have a marketing department to advertise their existence. I get the feeling they're a relatively recent development."

She knew Marik was right and she wanted to smack him for it. Her frustration was mounting. There were too many questions and no answers. There was also the dream she'd just had.

"What are we supposed to do now?" she asked. "We made it to the safe house. What's the next step?"

Marik wiped his index finger on the wall, inspecting it for something. "I assume Mack will connect us with the Free People and we can decide from there. At least, that's what I would suggest. We should be an integral part of the Free People."

"In the meantime," Nicole interrupted, "you have GOT to tell me how you did that!"

"Did what?"

"When you were fighting the patrol, how you did it."

"Nicole, I have no idea what you're talking about," Ellyne laughed uneasily, having a small idea to what Nicole referred.

"During the fight you … you moved faster than anything I've ever seen. You punched your fist through a bot and dodged bullets!"

Ellyne recalled the punch and just how good it felt to level a bot with her fist—she'd done it once before. But the rest didn't make any sense. "I did? I mean, I guess whatever I was doing was me somehow channeling stored flocia from absorbing magic. As always, I have zero idea how I did it."

"See," Nicole continued, "that's what I thought at first, but this was different. You were bathed in some kind of light!"

"I was?"

"Personally," Marik interjected, "I think she's hallucinating. I saw no mystical light. Sounds like bullshit to me."

Ellyne could almost taste the jealousy in Marik's voice. It must've burned him to not have the same magical prowess as Nicole and now, she herself was exhibiting magical behavior beyond his comprehension.

"It's true!" Nicole insisted. "Ellyne, it was radiant and beautiful!"

"Well, I guess there's yet another question to add to my growing list—right behind how the hell am I actually alive?"

"You're not gonna like the answer."

"What's that supposed to mean? What, you'll explain later?"

Nicole fidgeted a minute, obviously trying to formulate a

response but thinking carefully about her words. "So … I'm not really sure. There actually isn't an answer."

Ellyne inspected the many spots where the grika had torn into her. The rips in her clothing were still there, but the wounds had vanished. "Right. Because of course there's not. Why should I be surprised?"

Nicole hovered around Ellyne a moment before she grabbed her in yet another bearhug.

"And there it is. You're truly a very huggy person, you know that?"

Ellyne felt she should return the hug, but her arms were pinned in the embrace so, instead, she simply rode it out until the girl eventually released her.

Nicole dried her eyes on her black shirt, sniffed, and giggled. "I'm sorry, Ellyne, but I just don't know. We argued about what to do for you and when we were through, you'd already improved. It was like magic—"

"Except that would be impossible. We know how that turns out."

"Right," Nicole agreed. "Like I said, I'm not the greatest at using healing magic but I also didn't want my spell backfiring or exploding or whatever. I tried a couple times, and nothing happened."

"Yes," Marik chuckled sarcastically, "nobody would want that … how terrible it would be."

"Why do we keep him around again?" Ellyne asked, throwing a mean look the man's way. "Is he, like, a pet or something? Because I'd much rather have a dog. They're at least cute. But, I guess, at least Marik doesn't shed. Wait, do you shed, Marik?"

Nicole couldn't contain her laughter while Marik remained unamused, but said nothing and adjusted his purple robes, probably pretending to be concerned with a tear or stain on them.

Ellyne felt only a minor tingling sensation within her.

Whatever power she'd stored in her was exhausted during the fight. She found it difficult to admit it was a reassuring feeling, having such power to command even if she still wasn't adept at using it.

Such power came with a price, however. Sometimes it was the guilt of senseless destruction and death, and other times it was simply disdain for having used something related to magic.

It was, however, always exhausting. She wondered if the exhaustion was normal but then recalled that really nothing about it was normal.

"Okay, well, I guess there's no sense dwelling on my miraculous recovery if there are no actual explanations." There was no window in this room, and she badly wanted to look outside and see if anyone was waiting for them. Just how secure was this safe house? "So, what's our next step?"

Mack slipped inside and shut the door behind him. "You're awake!" he exclaimed. "Excellent! I went ahead and got some more medical supplies and whatever food I could find." He briefly looked down at the armload of stuff he held before dumping it on the ground for everyone to peruse.

"Thank you, Mack," Ellyne said, kneeling to sift through the various things he brought. She was willing to trust him for now, but she kept him in close observation. "I'll just take this bag of chips."

"You're welcome," he said, leaning against a wall. "I really wasn't sure any of the medical stuff would be useful, given the severity of your wounds, but I see you don't need them anyway which, I must say, is impressive."

"Yeah," Nicole laughed, inspecting a packet of crackers before tearing it open. "Ellyne does some pretty amazing things sometimes."

"Oh, I know," Mack replied. "We've heard many stories about the mage breaker, and I still can't believe I'm standing in the same room with you. I don't know how you've survived but I'm very glad you did. And what you did to that patrol was just … it was fantastic."

"Dumb luck I suspect," she responded. Such attention was awkward, and she would have preferred not to be the center of it. It was quite a contrast to the way she'd felt, once upon a time, when the legendary golden gunslinger led her soldiers heroically into battle against the Ilserate. She'd been much younger then, and much more naïve.

"Seems to be the theme most of the time," she continued, shoving a handful of chips in her mouth. "I'm pretty good at the dumb luck thing,"

"Well, either way, you certainly handed that patrol their asses. I've never seen anything like it! I'd pay good money to see something like that again. Not that I have many tiks to spend on it."

Marik sauntered over to the pile on the floor and used his foot to sift through it. Finally satisfied with what he saw, he picked up a packet of chewy fruit snacks and tore it open, retreating to lean against a wall to eat them.

"So, now that we're at the safe house, what's the plan?" Ellyne asked, finding a bag of beef jerky and devouring it. She couldn't remember ever being this hungry.

"Well," Mack sighed, "I suppose we need to consult the Oracle. Hopefully he'll know what to do and we can—"

"Wait a minute," Ellyne interrupted, nearly choking on the beef jerky, "what Oracle? What is this mystical bullshit? I've never heard of any oracle."

"I understand your skepticism, given your aversion to magic. There are a great many things even we mages don't understand. The Oracle has helped the Free People in our fight, and I am one hundred percent certain he would love to meet you."

"Sounds like a bunch of mumbo jumbo to me," Ellyne scoffed, emptying the bag of beef jerky into her mouth.

"Prophecies, oracles, and the like. Nicole, what do you know about this guy?"

"Uh, nothing really," the girl stammered through a mouth full of crackers. She waited to swallow before continuing, holding up her index finger to tell Ellyne to be patient. "I've heard him mentioned once or twice in conversations but, beyond that, nothing."

"The Oracle," Mack continued, "is known only to the Free People. We keep him a closely guarded secret and speak of him to no one. In fact, we barely mention him when in our own company. Many of the Free People don't know he exists because it's safer that way in case we're captured."

"Okay," Ellyne interrupted, "but has anyone ever actually met this guy?"

Mack paused a moment, which told Ellyne all she needed to know. "I'm really not sure," he finally said. "I know I haven't."

"So, then, how do we know where he is or how to contact him?" Ellyne scoffed. "Or how do we even know he's real?"

"He's requested to see you," Mack replied.

"This is getting pretty deep," Ellyne laughed, "but whatever. At least you have a plan so let's do whatever it is you're suggesting instead of sitting in a boring room with that toad."

She pointed to Marik who wasn't paying attention.

Mack smiled. "Excellent! He's waiting for us. But, first, let's see if magic works well enough to get there! I don't suppose you could ... somehow make magic function properly again for now, could you?"

"It doesn't work like that."

He walked to the wall opposite the door and waved his hand. A small holographic panel appeared, fading in and out of view until it finally stabilized. He tapped a button and, shortly after, a glimmering portal opened in front of him.

"Well, that was tougher than it should've been, but success nonetheless."

"Is that thing safe?" Ellyne asked. "It's not going to wink out as we're walking through it and chop us all in half?"

"I doubt that will happen," Mack chuckled, "but, then, I make no guarantees."

"You're a real confidence booster, Mack."

"After you," he said, motioning for them to proceed. "We probably shouldn't keep the Oracle waiting."

UPON EMERGING from the shining portal, Ellyne found herself in a hallway, dimly lit by various technology on the walls with flashing lights and indicators she didn't understand but also had no interest in.

Nicole and Marik filed in behind her, followed by Mack who sealed the shimmering door behind him. For a moment, they stood in near darkness until the light from the walls intensified.

"Huh," Mack mumbled. "That's new."

"What's new?" Ellyne asked.

"Er, nothing important. Come on, The Oracle is just beyond that door at the end of the hall."

"That door?" Ellyne pointed to the plain, ordinary wooden door set at the end of the hall. "I mean, no offense, but wouldn't a great, vaunted oracle have fancier accommodations? It seems a bit, I don't know, anticlimactic?"

"Ellyne," Nicole whispered, "don't piss off The Oracle. At least, not yet. Not before we've had a chance to talk."

They approached the door but before they could open it, a loud voice echoed through the chamber.

"Yes," it boomed, "don't piss off ... the Oracle."

"Great Oracle," Mack said meekly, "we bring the Mage Breaker to you in hopes you'll be able to help guide her in our struggle against our enemies! I have done as you asked."

"I see. However, bringing the Mage Breaker to the Oracle was risky. You have no idea the power and danger she represents."

"What the hell is up with this Oracle garbage?" Ellyne whispered to Nicole as The Oracle continued its monologue. "When did Karnascus become so … weird? I really do prefer the good ol' days."

"What days were those?" Nicole asked. "The days when you simply shot everything and everyone?"

"I have many fond memories."

"Are you sure nobody followed you?" the Oracle asked.

"This is all new to me," Nicole replied, whispering to Ellyne, "but let's save the shooting for later."

"Two years go by, Nicole, and you've never even heard of any of this? What were you doing all that time?"

Nicole frowned and wrinkled her face. "I was busy trying to fix magic and … find you. Which, by the way, was no easy task. Then I had to figure out how to rescue you and then there's Marik and—"

"Okay, okay I get it. You were busy. I guess the Free People would be relatively secretive anyway. You don't really advertise a rebellion I suppose. It's probably bad for business."

"Do you have something to share with the rest of the class?" the Oracle asked, its voice rattling Ellyne's teeth.

"What? I mean, no. Wait, what's going on?"

"You were interrupting me," The Oracle replied. "It's rude, and I don't like it."

"Well," Ellyne grumbled, "tough shit. I'm trying to figure things out, here, and your overly loquacious, rambling speech was boring me. Besides, what's with this crappy door?"

"What about it? The Oracle—"

"The Oracle," she replied, mocking the voice's tone, "sits in a technological bunker but resides behind a shitty wooden door that you can find literally all over the city instead of some advanced, sliding metal technological … what's another word for door?"

"Ooh!" Nicole shouted. "A hatch?"

"Yeah, a hatch."

"The Oracle's budget is tiny, and the previous door malfunctioned. The Oracle hasn't had time to fix it yet."

Nicole giggled quietly, obviously enjoying the intercourse between the two. Ellyne had to admit, it was the most fun she'd had since getting back to Seralune. Well, the most fun she'd had aside from obliterating the patrol yesterday.

"You know what?" she asked, interrupting the Oracle. "I don't really care. I nearly died yesterday, so I'm pretty sure whatever you can do to me isn't nearly so bad. I could nearly die every day and it wouldn't bother me."

She moved everyone behind her and took a fighting stance in front of the door.

"Wait," The Oracle said, "what are you doing? It's not what I think you're doing, is it?"

After one kick, the door buckled, and wooden splinters erupted in all directions. The doorknob skittered across the floor and rolled to a stop in the darkness somewhere within the dimly lit room.

"What have you done?" Mack gasped, his eyes wide. "Why would you do that?"

"I don't have time for mystical bullshit."

Ellyne peered into the room beyond. She couldn't see far but, in the darkness, she saw a myriad of various illuminated panels and blinking lights. The familiarity she felt was uncanny.

"For shit's sake," she sighed, exasperated but relieved, "Derek, is that you?"

The responding voice was not that of the Oracle but was

the familiar tone of a young man. "How did you know?" he laughed. "I changed my voice and everything."

"Why are you sitting in the dark?"

"Because magic is unreliable and difficult to use, duh. Not everything works reliably all the time."

"Come on guys," she said to the group, "it's safe. The Oracle's a friend. Hey, Derek, you'll need a new door. It seems *someone* broke the old one."

"You … you know the Oracle?" Mack asked, obviously confused and maybe a little star struck. "Ellyne Thandaral, it appears you are full of surprises."

"Well, yeah," Nicole replied. "We met him before he was the Oracle. He helped us escape the Kithrak a while back and—"

Ellyne stepped into the room slowly, shuffling her feet to avoid tripping over the remnants of the wooden door. When she was a few steps in, she felt the familiar warm, tingling sensation within her—the feeling she knew was flocia stored inside her, absorbed from the magic around her. It was a feeling that usually preceded a violent explosion.

She was about to warn her friends and tell them to leave but the sensation within her changed. Instead of warmth, it shifted and felt slightly cold. Just as she was about to tell everyone to run, the room sprang to life.

"That's better," Nicole said, gazing around the room at the various screens and panels of colored lights and buttons.

Derek, as he always did, sat in a chair at the center, surrounded by more panels and screens, furiously typing on a keyboard only he could see and swiping his fingers through the air in front of him, presumably moving more invisible things around.

"So … you are The Oracle?" Mack asked. He looked as if he was about to kneel or bow or kiss Derek's feet. "It's an honor to be in your company."

"Yep," Derek answered, never taking his eyes off whatever he was looking at. "That's me! I'm that guy."

There was an angry series of beeps followed by static.

"Oh, well," he continued, "and JASN of course. The Keeper and I work together. Sorry for leaving you out, bud. We'll discuss your harsh language later."

A growling sound followed.

"I said I was sorry! There's nothing worse than an AI that holds a grudge over such tiny things. Besides, you're not perfect either, you know."

JASN emitted several more beeps followed by a short music clip.

"Well that was rude. Simply because you derived from a piece of my brain doesn't mean I'm responsible for your deficiencies."

Derek continued doing whatever it was he was embroiled in, seemingly ignoring Ellyne. She coughed and cleared her throat to get his attention.

"Oh, right! Sorry. I'm not ignoring you. It's just … this is all new and exciting!"

"What is?" Nicole asked. "What's new and exciting?"

Marik sighed, looking bored. Ellyne knew better. It was a terrible idea to bring him here. The more he knew, the less she trusted him, which was literally zero to begin with. He was now privy to information she'd rather be kept a secret. She should've insisted he stay behind. If she'd been thinking straight, she would've.

"Oh, see all of this." Derek pointed around the brightly lit room that now felt alive. "I haven't had full power in any of my control centers since … well since magic went bonkers. So, this is extraordinary!"

"Well," Marik stated, "that's great and all, but—"

"It's not just great!" Derek laughed, furiously typing, "it's miraculous! Everything's working like it should! That's huge!"

"And if that's the case," Nicole added, "then … magic can be fixed?"

"Bingo!" Derek shouted, pumping his fist in the air. "But one thing at a time. I don't know a damn thing about why it's happening, so I can't prognosticate as to how to get it fixed permanently. But it's working, so that's a start."

Nicole appeared pleased with herself on top of her usual enthusiasm.

It was situations like this that caused Ellyne to almost forget Derek was a Kithrak and probably well older than she. But he still had a childish excitement that only Nicole could rival, and she was, what, nineteen?

"Okay, great," she said, trying to bring him back down to reality. "But what does that actually mean?"

"Stand still," was Derek's only reply. "This won't take long."

A blue light bathed Ellyne in its radiance. She squinted and put her hand over her eyes. "What the hell?"

"I said stand still! It's like you're not even listening to me!" Despite his stern words, Derek chuckled. He was enjoying this far too much. Ellyne suspected he didn't get to interact with people very often.

"So, anyway," Nicole interjected, "what exactly was the deal with that door?"

"Oh, see, automatic doors became rather … unreliable. Getting them to open and shut properly was ridiculously difficult, so I had them all replaced." He tapped at a few invisible keys and swished his hand in front of him. "Of course, now I'll have to get this one replaced … *again*. So, thanks for that."

"You're welcome," Ellyne growled, still squinting. She felt a strong urge to break something out of frustration.

Marik was busy inspecting the room. Ellyne wasn't sure what he was looking for, but her bets were it was something he could use for himself. She thought it best to watch him closely.

"So," Marik said, still gazing about, "you're the Oracle?"

Mack perked up, looking eager to hear the answer.

"More or less," Derek replied, keeping his attention on Ellyne and whatever was in front of him. "It wasn't a name I chose but when one of the Free People suggested it, I sort of went with it. I thought it sounded pretty cool."

Mack looked confused and excited at the same time. "Forgive me, Oracle—"

"There's no need to call me that. My name's Derek. And this cranky AI that's all around us is JASN, The Keeper. He runs the city—well, when magic's doing what it should, which is almost never these days. In fact, until she showed up," he pointed to Ellyne, "magic had deteriorated into its worst state yet."

"Wait," Ellyne interrupted, still trying to shield her eyes from the "magic's getting *worse?*"

Derek swiped across his vision with a perplexed look on his face. "Afraid so. It was bad enough it up and quit for a spell. That sent the entire city into chaos—"

"Yeah, I've heard that part." Ellyne felt sick. "Let's not revisit that, please."

"Right, well, when it came back everyone thought things were back to normal but, to be honest, things were probably worse."

"Worse? How? What's worse than magic disappearing? Seems like this should be better."

"If magic isn't working at all, everyone knows what to expect." The dark-skinned kid swiveled his chair around with his back to Ellyne for a moment. She couldn't see what he was doing until he turned to face her again. "But if magic is unpredictable, then everything becomes a gamble. One moment, your vehicle's operating fine and, the next moment, you die in a fiery wreck."

Nicole gasped while Marik chuckled. Mack still appeared dumbfounded—humbled to be in the presence of the Oracle.

"One day," he continued, "magic goes dark. Sure, there were major problems—I can't stress that enough. Lots of people were hurt or died and, for a while, life was pretty rough. But small traces of magic returned shortly thereafter—enough to operate a few minor systems. JASN was hobbled, but we got by."

"Thanks for that trip down memory lane," Ellyne sneered. "I get it, I screwed up."

"Yeah, you totally did. But your return has caused magic to fire up again. The moment you entered the atmosphere, there was this massive surge of magic and things sprang to life again."

"Wait, you tracked us?" Nicole asked.

"Of course I did. You guys are pretty important these days and I like to know what's going on. I just couldn't get in touch with you reliably—especially without the Ilserate, Kithrak, and Golgolonar finding out."

"I think it'd be nice if magic were reliable," Nicole added. "But we'll make do with what we've got."

"Okay," Derek continued, "all done."

Ellyne rubbed her eyes once the blue light disappeared, blinking furiously as they adjusted. "I guess… yeah, that's pretty horrible." The guilt she felt was overwhelming. Though she avoided people in general and downright loathed some of them, she never wished to kill those she didn't have a contract for.

As much as she loathed magic, there was some comfort in knowing that magic, though unreliable, had at least returned.

Several moments passed with Derek staring at whatever images he could see that nobody else could.

"So, you guys have met The Or—Derek before?" Mack asked.

"I have not," Marik responded coldly.

"Oh yes!" Nicole laughed. "He helped us escape the Ilserate a while back."

"And I helped you guys sneak into the Citadel *and* break Nicole out of their prison *and* showed you how to get into the Sistix and—"

"Okay, yeah," Ellyne interrupted, "we get it. But how did you know where I was in the Kithrak prison?"

Derek stopped typing immediately and his gaze fixed on Ellyne with intense curiosity. "Kithrak prison? You were in a Kithrak prison?"

"Yeah. I thought you would've been the one to help Nicole get me out of there."

"I hear Kithrak prisons are impossible to escape from! I didn't know you were in one. And you escaped!"

"Well, this one was built on an asteroid in space so, yeah, I'd say it was decently difficult."

Nicole giggled. "It was nothing we couldn't handle."

"If I'd known you were in a Kithrak prison in space I would've tried to get you out. Though that would've been super risky, and I don't think JASN would've had access to any of their systems."

"So how *did* you guys find me then?"

"Remember that tyrome you had? The shimmering rock thing?" Nicole reached into a pocket and produced the object which Ellyne promptly grabbed and inspected.

"There was one of these in the prison," she muttered, turning it over in her hands. "The Kithrak that experimented on me … it was in his lab."

Nicole clapped her hands together and bounced "Exactly!" she squealed. "You must have somehow connected with it without even knowing it was there. I connected with this one and was able to find you through it! I needed you to touch it to solidify the connection and, bam! Isn't magic wonderful?"

"I'll admit it was useful in that situation, and I'm glad to be out of there. I'd prefer not to rely on magic again, though."

"I'm gonna need some time," Derek said without looking up from whatever he was doing. Overhead, on several of JASN's screens, lines of indecipherable symbols and garbage scrolled quickly by. "I'm going to have JASN process the information."

"Information?" Ellyne asked. "What information?"

"The scan I just performed on you. I'm having JASN analyze it and, even already, there's some super interesting things in there."

"Exciting!" Nicole cheered. "Like what?"

Derek glared at Nicole. "Like I don't exactly know yet so you need to leave me alone so JASN and I can sort through it."

"Ugh, fine," she relented. "I guess that's our sign that we need to go, guys."

"Oh, one more thing," Derek said. "If I were you guys, I'd keep a low profile."

"As opposed to what we normally do?" Ellyne retorted.

"Okay, a *lower* profile. I wouldn't recommend getting the attention of the," he pointed upward, "the guys up there."

"The Golgolonar?" Nicole asked.

"Yeah, them."

Ellyne was about to turn and leave but stopped, her curiosity piqued. "What exactly are they?" she asked.

"Well," Derek continued, "you remember I mentioned them a while ago."

"I don't remember that," Ellyne said.

"Well, I did. They were mentioned in the Kithrak prophecy. It was supposedly foretold the mage breaker would bring about Golgolonar, as if it were an event of some sort." He tapped a few invisible keys before continuing. "Golgolonar translates roughly from the Kithrak language to yours, meaning 'reckoning.'"

"That doesn't make any sense," Marik scoffed, huffing. "Reckoning of what?"

"It appears I had the context wrong. When magic stopped, then went haywire … that's when the Golgolonar showed up. So, essentially, Ellyne did indeed draw them here—they must have sensed flocia's instability. But the reckoning, well, that must've alluded more to them taking over than anything else."

"Lovely," Ellyne snorted. "I'm famous across the cosmos."

"That's not at all what it means," Derek countered.

"Nope," Ellyne laughed, "I'm famous. The Golgolonar all want my autograph, I guess."

Marik rolled his eyes and sighed. He appeared anxious and kept eyeballing the exit. "So, we avoid attracting the Golgolonar's attention. What do you think we've been doing?"

"Fighting patrols and attracting the Golgolonar's attention," Derek growled through clenched teeth. "I've been trying to throw them off your scent, which has been no easy task—made harder by the mage breaker waltzing out into the street and decimating a patrol in broad daylight."

"That's just what celebrities do," Ellyne snickered. "My public obviously adores me."

"We can hide out in another safe house," Mack suggested, still looking more than the slightest bit confused. "We have several scattered throughout the city. That'll make it easy for us to avoid attention."

"No," Ellyne argued. "No, we're not hiding out. We're going home to my apartment."

"I don't think that's a good idea," Marik countered. "It may not be safe."

"I don't care what you think, Marik. I need my bed and my couch … and a drink or three."

"Be careful guys," Derek warned as they filed through the now doorless passage. "I don't know much about these

Golgolonar but the chatter around the Kithrak channels is … dire. Whatever's going on, the Kithrak are terrified."

"I'll alert the Free People to keep their eyes open for any suspicious activity. If the Golgolonar make a move, we'll hopefully know about it."

"Sounds good," Ellyne concurred. "Now, about those drinks."

CHAPTER
SIXTEEN

"I NEED MORE INFORMATION," Marik whispered.

"And I need you to stop talking," Ellyne replied. "Permanently would be nice."

"Why was there Kithrak language scrolling across the kid's screens back there?"

"How should I know? He's some genius coder or something. I mean, he built *and* programmed The Keeper. He knows a lot of shit. I'm sure he probably knows the Kithrak language or something."

Ellyne hated when Marik was nosy. Some people wanted knowledge for the sake of knowledge, but Marik always wanted knowledge to gain some kind of advantage, and she would rather not give him one if she could help it. Keeping him in the dark was the safest bet.

Derek was Kithrak and that fact needed to be kept from Marik. Ellyne figured the man had already settled on the correct assumption but keeping him guessing could only benefit her. Still, she knew she couldn't throw him off the scent forever. Marik was annoying and an asshole, but he wasn't stupid.

Every time Derek helped them, he risked his own skin.

She wasn't sure the Kithrak kept a close eye on him but, if they discovered his actions, it would end poorly for him. Things would probably end worse if the Golgolonar— whatever they were— found him.

"So, you're not the least bit concerned your ally has—"

"No, now get your ass up the fire escape."

Ellyne motioned to the metal ladder, resisting the urge to grab the man by his robes and force him to climb.

"Why don't we use the front door?" Mack asked, following behind Marik.

"She never uses the front door," Nicole giggled. "I asked the same question once." She followed behind Ellyne until they stood on the fire escape outside her bedroom window.

"What's the matter?" Ellyne asked, noticing Marik looking uneasy. "Are these not your preferred accommodations?"

Nicole stifled a laugh as Ellyne pulled the window up slightly until it stuck.

"I'm sure you're used to staying in much fancier places," she continued, slipping her hand through the narrow gap and feeling around the inside of the window. "But I assure you there are only a couple of rats at most running around inside."

Nicole and Mack both chuckled. Marik appeared unamused.

"I really should give them names someday."

"You know," Marik said, after letting loose a great yawn. "This would all be much quicker, much safer, and much more … elegant if you'd just use magic to secure your apartment. I can't help but feel this is all so primitive."

Ellyne felt the security bolt and pushed it aside, ignoring Marik's attempted insult. "There it is," she said, opening the window the rest of the way. "Welcome to my humble abode … which looks a lot cleaner than when I left it. Why is my apartment clean?"

"About that," Nicole muttered as she slipped inside.

"Since Marik and I were staying here occasionally, I did you the favor of cleaning the place up a bit. I didn't figure you'd mind."

Nicole using the term "a bit" was like Marik being only slightly a bit of a jerk. She hadn't seen her apartment this clean since she moved in. However, considering she'd originally been hired to dispose of the previous tenant's belongings, as well as the tenant herself, that probably wasn't saying much.

In fact, most of the furniture in the place belonged to the previous tenant and her mark. She considered it partial payment—along with free rent.

"I'm never going to be able to find anything," Ellyne mused. "It was messy, but at least I knew which pile things were in."

"Oh, don't worry," Nicole continued, "we made sure to organize everything as best we could. Well, *I* did. Marik was too busy to help. He said something about cleaning being beneath him, especially if he couldn't use magic."

Marik smirked at Ellyne and shrugged. That did indeed sound like something he would say and do.

Ellyne shut the window, locking it behind them, still marveling at the fact she could see the carpet which, now that she noticed, was worn and dirty. Maybe Nicole should have left all the clothes on the floor.

Marik looked around the bedroom with a curious glare. "Don't worry, I haven't really spent much time here. I know that would make you feel … uneasy. Besides, I still have a job to go to. Some of us must keep up appearances and, you know, be useful."

Ellyne headed into the living room, still ignoring the man's attempts at being annoying. It, too, was spotless and organized with most of her belongings tucked away and on shelves instead of on the couch or the floor.

Nicole stood beside her, a giant grin plastered on her face.

"Most of the mess was discarded clothes and garbage so it wasn't too difficult to clean up, even without magic! We probably should've burned the couch, though."

"I love this couch! Sure, it smells a little funny but it's the most comfortable thing you can sleep on!"

As if to prove her point, Ellyne relaxed on the dingy burgundy couch, closed her eyes, and let out an enormous sigh. It indeed still emitted a faint odor, but it smelled like home. The leather creaked as she got comfortable.

The events of the past two years hit her all at once—the prison, the escape, and everything that followed. Shortly thereafter, prior events flooded in. She remembered first encountering Nicole in her apartment, fighting side by side with her and ultimately handing her over to the Ilserate. Even though she corrected that mistake, she still felt shame whenever that memory surfaced.

"Is … is she asleep?" Mack whispered.

"She might be," Nicole replied. "I'd say, if she'd been drinking, then she's definitely asleep."

"I'm not asleep," Ellyne muttered, though she felt herself heading that direction, "and drinking sounds like a fantastic idea." She opened her eyes and sat up. "It's been two years since I've had a damned drink. You guys didn't clean out my stash, did you?"

"Oh, absolutely not!" Nicole exclaimed. She hurried into the kitchen and returned with a half-empty bottle of squama juice and another bottle of Hell's Elixir.

"Excellent," Ellyne replied, hands outstretched. "Gimme."

"Which one?"

Grabbing both bottles from Nicole's grasp, Ellyne laughed. "Both, obviously."

"I hope they haven't spoiled."

Ellyne took a swig of squama juice and swallowed, feeling the burn slide down her throat, and hit her stomach. It was an old, familiar feeling she'd missed. "They never spoil," she sighed contentedly. "They probably get better with age—just like gunslingers."

"I doubt they could get worse than the way they began," Mack laughed. Ellyne watched him slowly pace the living room, peering out the windows, and inspecting every inch of the place. "Are you sure we're safe here? This feels a little … exposed."

"It took a while," Nicole replied, sitting on the couch next to Ellyne, "what with magic's fickle nature, but I eventually cloaked it with enchantments and wards. Unless we're followed, we're otherwise undetectable."

"Are you sure?" Marik asked. He refused to sit down or touch anything, as if such actions were beneath him. "With magic the way it is, how can we be sure?"

"That's a good point," Mack added, finally settling into a chair but never shifting his gaze from the windows. "Is there a way to verify the wards or something?"

"Okay, so," Nicole continued, "yeah, magic is unreliable and weird and an all-around pain in the neck."

Marik rolled his eyes. "Yes, we know that already."

"So, if it's a pain in the neck for me, then it's probably even more of a pain in the neck for most other mages! I doubt they'll have the skill to see past my wards."

"I see your point," Mack laughed. I guess, if I want someone to cast reliable spells, you're probably the best option."

Marik finally relented and found a chair. He used the hem of his robes to wipe it off before he sat. "I don't think it's that simple. It sounds like a false sense of security to me."

"I think I'm gonna go with the most powerful mage on the planet on this one," Ellyne said after swallowing more squama juice. "Not that I'd ever go with your opinion, Marik. I bet some grika have better ideas than you."

"He might be right," Nicole argued. "I mean, not that I want to admit that of course, but we can never be too cautious. We have no idea what the Kithrak, the Ilserate, the Golgolonar, or even the Technicians and Teranyne Order are up to. They may have knowledge we don't."

"These wards," Mack interrupted, "are amazing, Nicole." He was scanning the room, his mouth agape.

It occurred to Ellyne the man wasn't simply inspecting the apartment when he was walking around. She forgot that normal magic-using people could see lingering spells to varying degrees whereas she could not.

"Thanks! They're not the most complex magic but they keep trying to unravel themselves and I must refresh them from time to time. It's simple but often takes a bit of time, especially when magic misbehaves, but—"

"These … Golgolo things…" Ellyne knew Nicole probably wouldn't stop talking unless someone barged into the conversation. "What are they? Derek didn't seem to know a lot about them."

"Marik would know more than I do," Nicole said, looking at the purple-robed bald man.

"Oh?" Ellyne asked. "Why's that?"

"Because I still work for the Kithrak and the Ilserate as not only a liaison but also on special projects—security, for one."

Ellyne laughed and downed more squama juice. "Oh really? I figured you would've been fired after your massive failure at the Teranyne column of flocia source or whatever it was."

"Yes, that was … particularly difficult to come back from." Marik nervously dry washed his hands. Ellyne could tell she'd gotten under his skin and just that very observation made her happy. "It took a lot of ass-kissing and maneuvering but I did manage to keep my post even if they are watching me much more closely than before. In fact, I even got a promotion."

"Look at you, failing up. Isn't that usually how sycophants like you rise through the ranks?"

"Cute," he sneered. "But where would you be now without my help and stature?"

She didn't want to admit it, but the man had a point. "My question still stands—what are these … Golgolonards or whatever?"

"Another space-faring race. They arrived several months after The Collapse when magic ceased to be. We were just starting to rebuild and get used to the unreliable nature of flocia when their massive ships appeared in the skies."

"Like the one above my home."

"Correct." Marik leaned forward, propping his elbows on his knees. "They're dangerous—more dangerous than we know. My clearance within the Kithrak isn't high enough to give me access to any information on them but I've overheard enough hushed conversations to understand the same thing Derek said—they're deeply concerned."

"And the Ilserate?"

"The Ilserate," he continued, "is just as worried. There appears to be no more covert competition between our government and the Kithrak. They're genuinely working together to decide what to do about the Golgolonar. From what I gather, however, it's not going well."

"So, what are they—these Garglelolonar?"

"They're reptilian," Mack replied. "They vary in form. Some have leathery wings, maybe multiple arms, a tail, two heads … they're just as random as the Kithrak seem to be. They keep to themselves, though, and they've only made one or two public appearances."

"Lovely," Ellyne mused. "Another bunch of alien rejects wanting … wait, why the hell are they here?"

"We don't know," Mack continued. "But their invasion took only a few weeks. The Ilserate and Kithrak put up a fight but, with magic the way it is, the Golgolonar had a distinct advantage. I suspect some of the highest Kithrak castes know far more about them and their motives, but they aren't revealing any information."

"So … I caused yet another disaster by royally screwing up the source of flocia by allowing the Golgolonar to swoop in and take over. I'm not gonna lie, but even I'm beginning to hate me."

Nicole put her hand on Ellyne's. "Ellyne, this isn't your fault. There's no instruction manual for anything that's happened in the past two years."

"Actually, it sort of is." Marik laughed, but the look on his face held a different emotion.

Ellyne knew he was serious. He wasn't simply trying to get under her skin this time though he still did so.

"By essentially removing magic from the equation, both humans and Kithrak became largely defenseless. It's not so surprising another alien race would possibly be waiting for their moment to jump. We have such little knowledge of existence beyond Seralune."

"It makes you wonder what else is out there," Mack added. "But what else are the Kithrak hiding? Why were we all not made aware of this threat before they showed up?

Ellyne suddenly felt ill. On top of everything else she'd learned and re-learned recently this was possibly the worst development yet.

"So, we just went from one enemy to another," she mumbled. "And if we beat these … lizard things? What then? What's next? If the Kithrak know of these things, then we need to somehow pull that information out of them. They're supposed to be stewards of magic, but they treat us like children and keep us in the dark."

"It's all about control," Marik replied, "and they appear to have lost control."

Mack picked at something on the chair with his fingernail, looking sullen. "I think we must beat them first. That's our current problem."

Ellyne stood, unsure of what to say or do. This wasn't a problem she could simply unload ammunition at. "So how do we do that? The Golgolonar are the main threat but let's not forget the Kithrak and the Ilserate. They may be joining forces but, in this case, the enemy of our enemy is *not* our friend."

"I don't know," Marik replied, staring at the carpet. "We don't even know what they want or really even what combat power they command. We only know they're far more powerful than we are. And, as you can see just by looking up, their ships are massive."

"But things are different now!" Nicole insisted. "Ellyne's back!"

"Fat bit of good that does us," Marik scoffed. "Ellyne's back to, what, screw up more things and cause a bigger disaster?"

Ellyne glared at him even though she secretly agreed. "Nicole, I think this is far bigger than just one person."

"No, it's not!" Nicole argued, jumping up from the couch. "You freed us from the Kithrak! They're afraid of you, Ellyne. Surely the Golgolonar know who you are even if it's just by word of mouth or reputation."

"Yeah, I freed us from the Kithrak ... and apparently delivered us right in the claws of the Gloggo whatever the hell they are! Great job, me! Besides, I didn't do it alone last time."

"And you won't do it alone this time, either."

Ellyne moved to the window and watched as the night sky set in. The city was darker than it used to be—because of her. Different areas lit up randomly then faded, only to be replaced by other illuminated areas. Those that remained bathed in light were probably utilizing Legacy Age technology that didn't run on magic. They would be powered from a generator somewhere, running on fuel.

The skies were clear and there were no vehicles winding through the streets. Karnascus felt ... dormant. No, that wasn't accurate. Karnascus felt dead.

"You wanted magic destroyed," she muttered under her breath. "You nearly got your wish, but you couldn't even do *that* right … and you're fortunate you didn't. I guess. Hell, I don't even know."

"I hope," Mack whispered, "once word spreads that the golden gunslinger is back, the Free People might gain more momentum. Maybe the reemergence of a famed war hero will lift their spirits and we can gain more recruits. Also, maybe, the Kithrak and Golgolonar will feel a little pressure … perhaps even fear. I see this as a good thing all around, though."

Ellyne knew he was trying to avoid her picking up the conversation, but she heard every word. They were putting a lot of faith in her, which made her feel all the more uneasy. She'd never felt she lived up to the hype around her, even if she knew she'd done some incredible things. To put one on such a high pedestal was … it was an illusion. It always would be.

"The golden gunslinger is a dead icon," Marik argued, also keeping his voice low. "The Mage Breaker is who they need now. But, either way, I don't think she's got it in her. I told you this was a gamble. She's not a leader, despite what history says."

"I can be both," Ellyne growled, still facing the window. "If you want to turn me into a martyr, then why not just go all out? Build me up as high as you want, I guess."

Maybe it was her own stubborn ways, or maybe it was the alcohol finally hitting her system, but she felt compelled to act. She wasn't about to let Marik besmirch her, even if she truly did believe he was correct in his assessment.

"What do you mean?" Marik asked.

Turning from the window, she took a long drink from the bottle of squama juice. "I mean," she said, slamming it down on a small table next to the couch, "why not make me larger than life?"

"That'll paint a target on your head," Nicole warned.

"That's the point, though, isn't it? Give our allies some hope and give our enemies something to fear, right? You can't simply half-ass this."

She could see they were obviously confused. Marik, in particular, appeared dumbfounded, which wasn't surprising since the man had never in his life sacrificed anything for anyone but himself.

Ellyne leaned on the back of the couch to steady herself as the alcohol ran its course. She hadn't kept track of how much she'd drank but it was probably a lot in a little time. There were no regrets.

"Bring the fight to us," she continued. "Let's draw these bastards out and see what they want. If they believe I'm a threat then they'll come after me, right? At least, that much, I'm used to."

"How is that going to solve anything?" Marik asked. His skeptical demeanor made her skin crawl. He was probably mad he hadn't come up with this plan first.

"Well," she sneered, glaring daggers at the man, "we're going to capture one of them. Then we can figure out what we're dealing with."

"She's obviously had too much to drink," Marik scoffed, laughing and shaking his head.

"What makes you say that?" Ellyne asked, feeling pleasantly calm for the first time in a long time.

"Because, if you knew what you were saying, you wouldn't be saying it. Do you know how dangerous what you're suggesting is? Just one Golgolonar can destroy an entire Kithrak patrol, and you think *we* are going to have a chance at capturing one of them? I understand you think you're really powerful or whatever, but you don't know what I know. The Golgolonar are beyond your comprehension."

"With the support of the most powerful mage," she looked at Nicole, "combined with the Free People and … you I suppose. Yes! But I'm not going to ask anyone else to risk their lives if these lizards are that dangerous."

"You can't do this alone," Nicole argued. "Marik's normally full of hot air but, from everything I've heard, he's probably right."

"I think maybe I can. You saw how I dismantled that patrol, right?"

"And it almost killed you," Mack added.

"But it didn't! I survived and I think I can use whatever abilities I've got, surprise one of them, and grab it. Guys, I've got to try. I'm the reason we're all in this mess. And, besides, I didn't really know what I was doing, and I *still* decimated the patrol."

"Do you know what you're doing now?" Marik asked, snorting.

"Shut it, Marik. I'm learning."

The room was silent for a moment as everyone was obviously pondering Ellyne's idea. She'd certainly hoped for more enthusiasm and was already beginning to rethink her plan. Sober Ellyne may have suggested this same plan, but possibly without as much enthusiasm.

"I'm with you!" Nicole said. She looked absolutely giddy with excitement. "I think it can work! Besides, our options are limited right now, and we can't just sit on our hands, waiting for someone else to make the next move."

Mack shook his head. "I cannot commit the Free People to something like this. I will, however, alert them to what you are planning in case that bolsters morale. We're just not equipped for this kind of a fight. We will support you any way we can, but an outright confrontation isn't likely for us."

"I understand, Mack. Any help is appreciated but we need to keep everyone safe." Ellyne was disappointed, but not surprised. He was simply doing what he thought was best. The Free People weren't an army … yet.

"Ugh," Marik groaned. "Fine, whatever. This is suicide, though."

"Don't worry your pretty little hairless head," Ellyne laughed. "I'm the one risking my ass. You'll be perfectly safe."

"Tell us what you need," Nicole said, grinning wildly.

"I need time to think," Ellyne replied. "And ammunition."

"THIS IS A BAD IDEA," Marik whispered.

"Why didn't you say so earlier?" Nicole asked.

"I *did* say so earlier. But nobody ever listens to me."

"There's probably a reason for that," Nicole giggled.

"Quiet, you two."

Ellyne walked to the edge of the alley and peeked out. The streets and sidewalks were busy with the standard, daily hustle of people hurrying from one place to another as they probably had so many times before. The only difference now was more foot traffic and less vehicles and hoversticks.

"I guess, without reliable magic, many people get more exercise," Ellyne mused. "I thought the streets would be emptier by now. Shouldn't they all be at work?"

"It takes many people longer to get to their destinations," Marik replied. "As far as I can tell, the more adept one is at magic, the more reliable it is for them. But, as you can see, even my incredible skill can't command it effectively."

Ellyne snorted, trying not to laugh too loudly. "Sure, that's obviously got to be the reason."

Nicole giggled.

"Yes, you're very clever," Marik sneered. "Are you clever

enough to have figured out an actual plan for this ... Golgolonar trap? Is that what you're calling it?"

"Be patient. I'm working on it."

"Considering we're about to start a fight, shouldn't you have it all figured out by now?"

"That's not the way I operate."

"Clearly," Marik scoffed.

"Listen, I'm relatively new here so cut me some slack. Life in prison was much simpler and a bit more pleasant without having to deal with you. But I also came back to this shit show and I'm still getting used to it."

"Fine."

"Indeed. Look, we just need to lure one out from ... wherever they are." Ellyne looked up at the hulking spacecraft floating high above the city. She saw several more dotting the landscape beyond. "I guess from up there?"

"Okay, listen," Marik said. "I've heard several Kithrak mention them, and I *think* they're attracted to flocia. So, a massive surge would probably draw at least one of them out."

"That would've been nice to know earlier. Were you planning on keeping that a secret?"

Marik replied only by shrugging, but also looking pleased with himself. Ellyne wasn't sure she should even begin to trust him, but there was no harm in testing his theory.

"So, what?" she asked. "We just have Nicole blast a few powerful spells into the air and they come running?"

"No, it's not that simple, but that would most assuredly attract the Kithrak which we *don't* want."

"Okay, then what?"

Marik sighed. "I know you understand nothing about magic and flocia, so I'll put it in simple terms. Magic is a *product* of flocia. Flocia is the fuel—the source of magic. The Golgolonar don't use magic—of that much we're certain. But they can detect flocia itself."

"I'm still not sure I follow you."

"What he means, Ellyne, is … If you want to attract the Golgolonar, you're going to have to do one of your … whatever it is you do. But make it big. Like, *really* big"

"Yes, that," Marik agreed, pointing to Nicole. "It's like I'm trying to teach a five-year-old. I can draw you a picture if you'd like—perhaps in purple marker with labels and stickers?"

"So, I need to do something with flocia?" she asked, completely ignoring Marik and his snide comments. "That doesn't sound too bad … except I have no idea how to control it or even how to properly use it."

"Well," Marik continued, "this *was* your idea after all. If I recall, I raised such a concern when you were formulating your plan."

"Thanks for the reminder."

"You can do this, Ellyne," Nicole cheered. "Channel flocia to attract the Golgolonar, then we'll capture one and get whatever info we can!"

"Since when do you guys trust my plans?"

"It's a good plan, Ellyne. I just know it'll work!"

"It's barely a plan," Marik added.

"I was drinking. You should never listen to my plans while I'm drinking. They suck even worse than when I'm sober."

"Ellyne, you're always drinking!" Nicole laughed.

Ellyne wished the area would empty out. There was no sense endangering the people in the vicinity, but she figured they'd scatter the moment there was trouble. "Okay, I'll give you that. I'm surprised you don't drink, having to put up with Marik all the time."

"Marik and I will back you up. There's nothing to worry about. We've pulled off more miraculous things."

"This is a bad plan," the man muttered, gripping the hem of his robes.

"You mean a bad *barely* plan," Ellyne snorted.

"Whatever it is," Marik replied, "it's terrible."

"Shush," Ellyne and Nicole said in unison.

Ellyne closed her eyes and relaxed, feeling the spark within her, ever-present yet buried deep down. She knew she could access it but never reliably. It always surfaced at the worst possible times.

Or the best.

The truth was, she couldn't prepare for this situation. Unfortunately, her abilities only seemed to surface under the duress of combat and, right now, she simply needed to misbehave.

"Okay, but look," she said, "you guys stay hidden unless I need you. This is likely to get ugly really fast and there's no sense in us all getting caught up in it. Try to keep people out of the area and away from danger."

Nicole and Marik both nodded, Marik looking as if he were barely paying attention.

"Except you, Marik. You're certainly welcome to strut out there at any time and have your face blasted off or something."

"Charming, as usual," he sneered.

She knew him, and she knew he could take any opportunity to fulfill his own desires. Unfortunately, she had to trust him ... for now. She hated the thought, but they needed every able body they could get, and he at least fit that description.

Ellyne nodded and cautiously walked into the open street, dodging people along the way. "Okay, flocia," she whispered as she entered the street, "I need you to work with me. No random explosions or whatever—just you and me, working together."

No vehicles traveled the road and pedestrians took advantage of this fact by crowding the street. Ellyne had to steady herself as several people bumped into her, muttering rudely. They quietly passed one another, miserably starting their days without reliable magic—Ellyne's fault, of course. She might have felt sorry for them if she hadn't been concerned with her own situation.

"And … go!" she muttered, stretching her arms above her.

The expected blast of energy, however, didn't happen. She tried again, thrusting her fingers to the sky above and reached the same result. Several people looked at her and shook their heads, probably assuming she was trying to use magic and failing like the rest of them.

She was certainly failing, but not in the way they assumed.

Dropping her hands to her sides, she closed her eyes, took a deep breath, and tried to relax. She could still feel it—the well of power within her—but, as always, she knew nothing about tapping into it. Previously, she'd only been able to produce destructive effects by accidentally absorbing too much magic or channeling flocia without a thought.

And those times were all under duress in the heat of combat. But here she was, placidly standing in the middle of the street looking like a fool. She could feel Marik's gaze on her, probably pointing and laughing and saying something he thought was witty.

Maybe she should try to hit him with a blast of flocia just to prime the pump.

"Well, this is a bad omen," she laughed, "but at least I had a plan this time instead of winging it yet again—even if that plan failed."

"Move it, lady," a man growled as he pushed past her.

She took another deep breath and closed her eyes, this time letting her arms dangle and relax. There was nobody to ask for help. Mages didn't channel flocia directly and such a thing was believed to be impossible until she proved them wrong. Being a maverick had always given her a sense of pride but, in this situation, it was supremely annoying.

Several people brushed past her, one of them muttering something about people with no sense standing in the middle of the street.

The throng of people wasn't helping her state of mind.

"Just … focus or something," she whispered, attempting to ignore her surroundings while searching herself for the tingly spark within. Somehow, she'd gotten accustomed to the sensation without realizing. It was as natural as wearing clothes or breathing, and not something she thought about.

Until now.

There it was—ever present but only detectable when she searched for it. She felt its warmth and thought for a moment she could hear it—the same sound she'd heard just seconds before she jumped into flocia's source—the multicolored column of energy mages called the Teranyne.

She reached out, attempting to grab hold of the sensation, but it resisted and threatened to recede deeper within her. It was a strange struggle because, while it felt like a physical action, it was all in her head. But it felt *so real.*

She breathed deep again, trying to relax.

"I just need you to cooperate," she whispered. "Just this once, work with me. No accidents or failures. Just you and me, working together to blow some crap up."

Everything fell away and it was just Ellyne and the sensation. Nicole, Marik, the people crowding the streets … it was as if they all disappeared, leaving just her.

In front of her, floating above, Ellyne saw an ever-changing, shapeless void, crackling with energy and shifting colors. It looked like a tiny blob of paint, hovering just out of reach.

She reached out to touch it and it recoiled, retreating mere inches out of her grasp. "Okay, little fella," she said, "you just tell me how to do this and we'll work together. I have a feeling you're just as invested in the outcome as I am … whatever you are. We need each other, don't we?"

The blob continued hovering just out of reach. She lowered her hand and it followed, approaching closer until it was a mere few inches from her face. The familiar sound of distant, mechanical traffic saturated her ears again, as she waited to see what happened.

She was not ready for the rush of hot energy that pervaded her body as the blob collided with her chest and spread through her. She gasped for air and struggled to remain standing, watching multicolored light invade every part of her body and dissipate.

The sensation was brief, and she recovered quickly, feeling reinvigorated and energized. But there was more. Far more.

She felt power. It filled her up and she clenched her fists, grinning at the mere thought of the abilities she now commanded. She was unstoppable.

The well of pure, brilliant energy was deep—possibly endless. For a moment, Ellyne reveled in it, truly understanding what mages probably felt before she realized even they had no idea. Spells and wands … these didn't even scratch the surface of what was possible with flocia.

It was intoxicating.

"Thank you," she whispered a few seconds before energy erupted from her, painting the sky above a bright yellow hue. The rush of power was almost refreshing this time. Instead of the painful blasts she'd experienced previously, this almost felt pleasurable. She reveled in the sensation before the energy stopped and dissipated above her, and she floated gently to the ground.

The ground. She looked down at her feet. "Was I floating or something? When did I leave the street?"

Stunned and confused, Ellyne looked around her at the crowd which had at some point withdrawn and given her plenty of room. Never had she experienced such a quiet, still Karnascus during daylight hours. Nobody moved or spoke— not even Nicole and Marik who remained in the alley staring at Ellyne, dumbfounded. She could see them, their faces mired in awe and confusion.

She stared back and shrugged, wanting to laugh. Though there was no humor in the situation, she wasn't sure what else to do. Had she just discovered new powers? Or had she simply been able to reliably control them for once? The questions piled up and, as usual, she was left with few answers.

She couldn't contain her laughter, and it felt good. "Come and get it!" she yelled, still cackling. "That should be plenty of flocia to attract at least one of you, right? Do you guys need a personal invitation or what?"

Was this even close to what using magic was like? The power was … unimaginable.

She heard several gasps from the bystanders, along with low murmurs and concerned whispers. Surely, they knew what the outcome would be—the same outcome she hoped and waited for. She also figured nobody had ever seen such a display of power, and that she now had a target painted on her back, but she would address that later. Either everyone would want a piece of her, or no one.

Now all she could do was wait and hope these new aliens got the message.

She didn't wait long.

WHEN THE HULKING, scaly creature landed behind Ellyne, she didn't jump or scream. After all, this was what she wanted—what she'd begged for.

She got her wish.

"Took you long enough," she whispered, turning around to face her foe. "Oh, and you are a large one, aren't you? Kind of ugly and … are you slimy or not? You look a bit like you're glistening or something, but I can't tell."

Beneath her cool exterior, Ellyne shook inside. There was real fear, but she was determined to keep it concealed. The only thing she'd heard about these guys was that they were powerful, but nobody knew enough to give specifics. She was about to find out, she supposed.

The monster flexed its leathery, bat-like wings and grinned, showing off several rows of drool-covered, sharp teeth and a forked tongue that quivered. It flexed its arms, causing every taut muscle to bulge.

She winced, catching a whiff of its breath which resembled rotten eggs.

"We've been searching for you," it growled in a low, guttural tone. "You've been particularly difficult to locate."

The street cleared out, now empty except for a few curious but frightened onlookers.

"Well … here I am. You found me, I guess."

It raised a taloned fist and smirked. "Indeed."

"So, like, now what? Do we go back and forth with witty banter, or should we just get right to it and fight each other? I'm not really sure what the etiquette for meeting a new alien species is."

Ellyne could feel the Golgolonar's eyes moving over every inch of her, inspecting her. She returned the creature's gaze, still trying to accept this thing was probably ten feet tall and … it had a tail!

It sniffed the air for a moment. "Ah," it said, "you reek of it—flocia."

"You don't like that?"

"On the contrary, morsel," it laughed, "it smells absolutely delicious!"

"Okay, I'm not gonna lie, that's … a bit creepy." Her right hand slowly found the strap on her gun's holster and loosened it. "But, I suppose, as far as pick-up lines go, I've heard worse. But don't worry—"

Ellyne jumped to the side, landing on the street but successfully dodging the blast of flame jetting from the creature's mouth. The remaining observers screamed and fled chaotically as she rolled to her feet.

"Okay," she muttered, "you breathe fire. That's … unexpected, but also really cool."

The Golgolonar appeared proud of himself, chuckling and confident, but never taking his eyes off her.

"So, I'm fighting dragons now. Space dragons … okay then, cool … this is fine. Certainly, this isn't totally weird or anything."

She glanced at Nicole and Marik who were still hiding in the alley. Nicole shrugged, her eyes wide.

In one fluid motion, Ellyne's golden revolver was in her hand, and she fired off three rounds. But her adversary merely laughed as the bullets ricocheted off its thick scales.

"Uh," she stammered, "mind if I try the other five?"

"You annoy me," it growled. She felt the three claws of its hand tear into her shoulder. The force of the impact knocked her into the air, and she collided with a lamp post. Her gun clattered to the street and slid away from her.

She should have been dazed or unconscious or even broken. With the force of that blow, she was supposed to be lying in a heap, clinging to life, and bleeding out. But, instead, she got to her feet, expecting to experience unimaginable pain but feeling almost nothing.

"Huh," she mused, "how about that?"

The lamp post, however, was twisted and bent. She shrugged off her jacket and inspected her shoulder, watching as the wound slowly closed itself.

"And that. I could get used to this."

What was usually a spark within her burned with intensity.

Her opponent appeared as surprised as she, but with different emotions, as was evident by the look on its scaly face.

"That could've hurt, asshole," she laughed. She'd intended to sound angry but couldn't hold back. "And you've just destroyed city property. The Ilserate will be so angry with you. That's, like, at least a few hundred tiks to replace a lamp post."

"You talk too much," it growled.

"Really? Normally I keep to myself and let the girl do all the blabbing. I guess, it's just—"

She didn't finish her sentence and, instead, she pulled her weapon to her and fired the remaining five bullets.

For a moment, the two stared at each other, each unsure of

what to do. The Golgolonar winced. It was brief and almost unnoticeable but then she saw a tiny trickle of purple blood coming from its side.

"Okay good, your scales aren't *that* strong," she muttered, barely having time to drop another cartridge into her gun before the lizard lunged at her.

She deftly dodged, sensing a flocia-powered burst of superhuman speed and reflexes, leaving the brute confused as it nearly collided with a building. It stopped short and turned around with a quizzical look on its scaly face.

"I could *really* get used to this," she muttered, watching her enemy's confusion. "I wonder what else I can do."

She barely had time to finish her thoughts. The creature cautiously lumbered toward her, pressing its attack by slashing and grabbing for her.

The sudden onslaught caught Ellyne off guard. She ducked and dodged its flurry of attacks but was faced with uncertainty. Inexperience and ineptitude hindered her, and she was unable to reliably use whatever abilities she had.

The creature advanced and Ellyne backed up, desperately searching for a way to catch her breath and come up with a form of counterattack. But the Golgolonar was relentless, and it was all Ellyne could do to simply stay out of harm's way.

She wondered, without flocia, if she would've even lasted this long, but her movements didn't feel like they were being affected by it. Had the lines blurred or was she simply thinking too much about it? Either way, she had to devise a way to go on the offensive. She couldn't simply avoid this monster forever.

Distracted by her thoughts, she slipped on the pavement and, though she caught herself, she tumbled forward into the lizard's crushing grasp. It chuckled as it wrapped her in its thick arms and squeezed tightly.

"I don't like you like that," she grunted, trying to mask

her fear when, inside, that was all she felt. "In fact, I don't like you at all. Now if you could just let me go, we can continue to try and kill each other in a civilized manner."

Struggling did her no good but she did anyway. She also tried to use flocia to make herself stronger but was reminded once again how little control she had over it. That fact, coupled with her lack of knowledge, left her vulnerable. She'd originally hoped this encounter would end quickly, but that plan relied on her control over flocia.

"Stop squirming," the Golgolonar grunted, tightening its hold on her. Being this close, she caught the full stench of its breath and gagged. "Let's go for a little ride," it laughed.

Her mind briefly wandered, and she questioned just how these aliens spoke humans' language so well, but magic always seemed to be the answer to those questions. It was silly to question that, given her current situation, but she knew it was a coping mechanism in stressful situations … and possibly put her in more danger.

"I'd rather not," she quipped, trying to regain control of the situation but to no avail.

The oversized lizard leapt into the air, effortlessly taking flight and bringing Ellyne with it. She could only watch as the city fell out from beneath her, the towering buildings quickly diminishing in size as they rose into the air above them.

"Go ahead," the creature laughed, "try struggling now. The fall will save me the trouble of having to kill you myself. I'd prefer to bring you back alive, but I was told dead was almost as good."

Ellyne panicked, suddenly realizing she was in over her head. Her friends—and Marik—had tried to warn her but she didn't listen to either of them. And now, here she was, high above Karnascus in the clutches of an alien she knew nothing about, unable to control her abilities, with no escape.

She'd assumed this fight wouldn't be much more difficult

than a Kithrak patrol and, after she'd decimated the last one, her confidence had sabotaged her.

She tried to breathe calmly, but her enemy was squeezing her tightly enough to make such an endeavor difficult. "Are we going somewhere?" she asked, still trying to project a cool exterior while trying to stay conscious.

"I'm to take you back to the ship. After that, I'm sure the hierarchs would enjoy studying you. They've a lot to learn from someone like you and your unique abilities. They've seen what you've done and … well, that's all I'll say."

Ellyne shivered, now more frightened than she'd ever recalled. She shook uncontrollably at the thought of another prison—another laboratory. Memories of the Kithrak prison came rushing back. She remembered every session with needles and strange devices, strapped to a chair.

Helpless.

"I'm not a lab rat" she screamed, fighting back tears.

"You will be. You have no choice in this matter, human. Either way, we can't have you running about, causing problems."

"So, I'm a threat?"

The Golgonolar remained silent.

Ellyne felt a small fragment of confidence return. If her short time back on Seralune garnered that much attention from these aliens, then they must have seen her as a threat. And if they were even the slightest bit concerned, that had to be worth something.

That did nothing for her in her current predicament, however.

The alien ship got larger as they approached. While the lizard had wings, there was no way such a hulking creature could fly so effortlessly, especially carrying extra weight—and straight upward, no less. She assumed it had to be using magic to achieve such power and grace. She wondered, if she could disrupt its spell somehow, if it would fumble and drop her.

What troubled her, however, was the fact she wasn't absorbing anything from the beast. If it were using magic, shouldn't her ability be disrupting it, even if that wasn't her intention? It must have been channeling straight flocia.

The Golgolonar shrieked as something collided with its back. Ellyne only caught a glimpse, but it looked purple, and was probably powered by magic. Several more followed, originating from somewhere in the city below. Her captor weaved and dodged but, while its ascent was graceful, its clumsy, hulking frame wasn't agile enough to avoid all the projectiles. It screamed in pain and shouted in a language Ellyne had never heard before.

It also loosened its hold on her and, sensing her opportunity, she wriggled free of its hold but grabbed its foot before she plummeted to the ground.

"Shit!" she spat, "I should've thought that through!"

She fully knew there were no real options, but she would rather die than go back to being an experiment. This time would be different, though. This time, her friends probably wouldn't be able to rescue her. This time, she'd be trapped in the spacecraft above her.

"You have no options here, human," the Golgolonar laughed, quickly regaining its composure. "You either come with me or you fall to your death."

"I'll choose to die free before I go anywhere with you."

Ellyne let go of the creature's leg and closed her eyes, ready for the end to come. Her thoughts turned to Nicole—her friend. It was funny how, if this had happened years ago, she probably would've thought of a glass of squama juice. Now, however, she felt sorrow for Nicole. She hoped her friend would be okay without her.

Marik, though, could go to hell and rot there for eternity.

Maybe the Free People would make her a martyr. Perhaps

her death would help their cause and hasten them to action. Some good could possibly come from her demise, and that at least made her happy.

She heard the Golgolonar scream again. Ellyne suspected it'd been hit by more attacks from below, but she was perplexed by how close the creature sounded.

And, oddly enough, there was no falling sensation. She felt no rush of air.

She opened one eye, then the other. The Golgolonar still hovered several feet above her, trying to dodge the purple darts of light from below.

"What the hell?"

She wasn't falling, that much was readily apparent. The how and why of such a feat escaped her, but there was no time to ponder the cause. Instinct took over and she found herself flying at the creature.

Flying! How was that possible?

Her fist connected with its jaw, knocking spittle everywhere, but she didn't stop there. She rained down blow after blow, savagely pummeling the creature as it struggled and howled beneath her onslaught. She reached for her blade and buried it in the creature's abdomen, silencing her adversary and sending a purple shower into the air. Her rage took over and she stabbed it several more times, shouting obscenities at her now dying opponent.

"Oh shit!" she shouted as they both fell. She maneuvered herself on top of the Golgolonar corpse and prepared for the end, taking a tiny bit of solace that she would at least die free and take one of the alien bastards with her.

Maybe her battle with this monstrosity, if anybody saw it, would rally others to the cause in addition to her death. Perhaps the Free People would realize they could effectively fight back. Instead of running in the face of the Golgolonar, they might rise and take back Karnascus. The Golgolonar could be beaten, and they now knew that.

This was of course just one enemy, but Ellyne was merely one person and she'd defeated one alone. Of course, she was going to die in the process.

"This was a terrible idea!" she shouted to herself, seconds before they collided with the street.

ELLYNE'S VISION was something akin to an abstract painting with vague, blurred shapes that eventually blended as the brush strokes wandered aimlessly across the canvas. Muffled voices mixed with chaotic, unidentifiable sounds added to her confusion as she tried to get her bearings.

She saw motion everywhere. People running, perhaps? Overwhelmed, she shut her eyes and cupped her hands over her ears, trying desperately to shut out the world so she could think. It did little good, however, and the myriad of stimuli threatened to enrage her.

Which was when the thought occurred to her—she was alive! But how? The fall … she thought it impossible to survive, yet here she was. Her body ached but she didn't feel any injuries, nor could she see any cuts, bruises, or missing body parts.

"I guess the lizards really *are* as tough as they appear," she mumbled, the words feeling sluggish on her tongue. She couldn't understand her own voice through her clouded hearing anyway but then, there was no one around to hear it. "Nothing like cushioning your fall with a reptile corpse, I guess. If it knew it'd saved my life, I bet it wouldn't be happy."

Slowly, she opened her eyes and removed her hands from her ears, resisting the urge to shut out the world again. It almost hurt, everything happening around her. If she could just lie on the ground in silence and rest … if everyone could've simply left her alone, it would've been wonderful.

Something in Ellyne's back popped as she slowly sat up, leaning forward, and brushing blond hair out of her face. "I'd prefer not to do any of that again," she mused, hearing her voice clearer, but still distorted. "What about you, lizard face?"

A black blob approached, and Ellyne tried to stand in case she needed to fight, but her arms and legs failed to support her, and she faltered. "Fine," she sighed. "If you want to kill me then just go ahead. I'm too tired for this shit. Just do it quickly because I don't want to wait around."

She didn't want to die, but Ellyne knew she couldn't fight right now, no matter how dire the circumstances. But the black shape stopped and, instead, shouted words Ellyne didn't understand. At least she knew, whatever it was, it wasn't looking to kill her—at least, not immediately.

"I don't know what you want," she muttered, "but … just give me a second or two, okay? I've had a rough day."

Barely after she finished her sentence, Ellyne found herself entangled in a tight, almost uncomfortable hug. She gasped, both finding it difficult to breathe while also becoming acutely aware of surfacing pain probably resulting from the impact. Perhaps she hadn't escaped unscathed.

"Nicole," she squeaked, "not so tight, girl. I survived crashing to the ground only to be crushed by you."

Either her words were muddled and unintelligible or Nicole wasn't listening, because the hug continued as did the jumbled noise coming from the girl's mouth. Ellyne decided to ride it out. The girl would eventually release her death grip and then probably say something about having to flee.

Slowly, the blobs became more distinct shapes and muffled, jumbled noises became words, the majority of which, if Ellyne concentrated hard enough, she could largely understand. She felt her faculties return and wriggled free of Nicole's embrace to finally stand on shaky legs.

"… ridiculous! I've never seen anything like it before!" Nicole laughed and shouted. "That was so intense and cool and holy cow I'm so glad you're all right, Ellyne! I mean, I *hope* you're all right, but it looks like you are and—"

"Nicole?"

"What?"

"Take a breath."

Ellyne inspected herself, noting the numerous holes in her clothes that showed no evidence of underlying injuries—not even dried blood to indicate a past wound. She flexed her arms and stretched, expecting to feel some sort of pain but, aside from a little stiffness, she felt nothing out of the ordinary.

"And I can't believe what you did! It was amazing! First you were up there flying and fighting the Golgolonar and then you came screaming down and, bam, plowed right into the street and I thought you were dead but you're not dead, but you looked like you probably were but anyway the Golgolonar's dead I think!"

The Golgolonar. Where was it? Ellyne looked around her and finally spotted the creature—what little she could see. Only part of a tail and a foot lay outside what appeared to be a crater in the street. As she approached, cautiously watching for any signs of movement, she saw people huddled in alleys and shops, behind vehicles and benches, watching her. They pointed and whispered to one another, obviously captivated.

"I hope they all enjoyed the show," she mused as she

neared the edge. Suddenly, Nicole was next to her, and they both stared down at the scene.

"Nasty," Nicole gagged, turning away. Ellyne could hear the heaving sounds as the girl tried not to vomit.

"I … I did *this*? How the hell did I survive something like that?"

The lumbering lizard's body was barely recognizable, having been partially dismembered, shredded, and lying in a purple pool. The crater itself was a few feet deep and maybe ten feet across which, Ellyne had to admit, was impressive.

"Of all the things I've accomplished during my time on this rock, this must be the most impressive yet. You know what this means, don't you?"

Nicole returned a confused look.

"Ellyne Thandaral, golden gunslinger, mage breaker and now, dragon slayer!"

"Also, possible meteorite," Nicole giggled, but the levity quickly died. "Don't get ahead of yourself," she said. "You could've died, you know."

"How did I not end up like *that*?" Ellyne asked, mouth agape and eyes wide. She pointed to the scattered bits of the Golgolonar. "Even using its body as a weird kind of shield … I should be dead, too. At the very least, I should be injured, but I'm neither."

Nicole laughed nervously, trying to both look away but also staring at the carnage. "You were … sort of glowing when you descended."

"Glowing?"

"Yeah. My guess is you were protected in a way by flocia —channeling it somehow."

"I'm cursed," Ellyne spat.

"I don't understand. What you did was amazing! It's never been done! I don't think anyone knew it was even possible!"

"All my life, I've avoided magic. I can't use it. I don't *want* to use it. I was perfectly happy without it but now, not only can I use magic, but I *am* magic. I can't escape it. I can't even control it!"

"Well, I mean, that's not really accurate—" Nicole's words trailed off, obviously discouraged by the glare Ellyne sent her way.

"Magic is … a prison. It corrupts and creates disasters and pain."

"But it also creates wondrous things!" Nicole argued. "We've come so far since we discovered magic. People live longer, healthier lives and new discoveries are made all the time. None of that would've been possible without it."

"Or it might have been possible, and simply taken longer. There are probably entire civilizations on other planets somewhere that have never touched magic and are probably doing just fine without it."

Nicole frowned. "Okay, so, we should probably get to safety. Just one of those guys was tough enough to take down, we don't want to be hanging around when its friends show, wondering what happened."

"Good idea. I guess, let's get Marik and get back to my apartment. Wait, where *is* Marik?"

Nicole tugged Ellyne's arm. "There's no time to talk about it, come on."

"What exactly is that supposed to mean?"

"It means we need to leave, and we'll discuss it when we're not fleeing a murder scene."

Ellyne didn't budge.

"Nicole … what aren't you telling me?"

The girl sighed, defeated. "I'll explain on the way, but we need to get out of here first."

Ellyne looked up at the massive ship floating high above. "Yeah," she muttered, keeping her gaze upward, "I think you're probably right. Let's go."

Like rats when the lights are turned on, they scurried into

the alley, dodging trash and debris, until they were a few blocks away when they stopped to catch their breath.

"Well, that—"

Ellyne held her finger up to Nicole's face. "Shh," she whispered. "Do you hear that?"

"It sounds like a fight."

"Exactly." Ellyne badly wanted to go back to the scene and watch whatever had transpired. She nearly suggested to Nicole that they return but resisted the urge.

"I wonder who's fighting?"

"No idea, but I'm pretty sure none of them are friendlies, so if they wipe one another out, I'm okay with that." Ellyne chuckled. "Just as long as we're not caught up in it, of course. Maybe the Kithrak and the Golgolonar got into it."

"They *do* seem to dislike each other."

"Maybe we can turn them against each other and mop up the survivors. Either that, or I'm going to need a whole lot more bullets."

TWENTY

"WAIT," Ellyne growled, "he did *what*?" She paced her living room, trying with all her might not to break anything out of rage.

"He … kind of ran away."

"What the hell?" Ellyne clenched her fists at her sides and kicked at a bit of fuzz on the carpet. "That coward!"

"He said he couldn't be seen with us. I tried to get him to stick around, but he teleported away before I could even try to convince him."

"He's a damned coward and if I ever see him again, I'll—"

"Ellyne, he was scared. I mean, he was *really* scared. I've never seen him rattled like that. He's usually just a confident, pompous jerk."

Ellyne laughed, staring out the window. "Good! I want him to be scared—of the Golgolonar, the Kithrak, the Ilserate, and … me. Mostly of me."

"Well, he saw what happened between you and the Golgolonar, so I guess there's a good chance he is."

Ellyne moved to the kitchen and searched the cupboards for snacks, grabbing the first bag of chips she saw.

"He's been helping us, Ellyne. I couldn't have come to

rescue you if he hadn't been part of it. You wouldn't be here without him."

"And thank you for once again reminding me I owe him." Ellyne ripped open the bag, sending a shower of salty snacks into the air. "Damn it! I blame Marik for this, too."

Nicole quietly snickered and flourished her hand once in front of her as the chips rose off the carpet and deposited themselves back into the bag. "I know you hate magic, but it *is* good for some things!" she giggled.

"Well, if I ever need to lob salty snacks at my enemies, you'll be the first person I think of." A smile briefly broke through Ellyne's scowl as she shoved a handful of chips in her mouth. "Okay, maybe," she said, her words muffled as she ate, "but magicking some chips into a bag is a tiny justification for all the harm magic has done."

"Magic has done more than feed your face," Nicole laughed.

Elyne sat on the couch, spewing chip crumbs from her mouth. "Need I remind you of the grika?"

"That blame is misplaced, though. The grika are strictly human and Kithrak creations."

"The grika are a byproduct of not using a T-helm which, before I liberated everyone from the burden of magic, was a requirement for every human ... except you, of course. And, now, nobody need wear one."

"Yeah, because magic is all messed up and wonky. People don't need to use T-Helms because there's barely any flow of magic to begin with. I'm not sure that's a really great trade."

"It is for me," Ellyne beamed.

"Says the cranky gunslinger who can't use magic at all."

"And never wants to."

"Yeah, that too. My point is magic isn't itself inherently bad. It's been twisted by those who wish to control it. Whether the T-Helms are evil remains to be seen. We know what happens without them though. Magic is just a tool—Magic isn't fallible, but humans and Kithrak are."

"And golgarglenor."

"Yes," Nicole laughed, "the Golgolonar too. My point is a wrench is also just a tool—not evil or good. It can be used to help build things or, well, you can hit someone with it."

"The world is filling up with people and aliens who still want to control magic," Ellyne groused. "I thought I'd solved that problem by taking it away, but I apparently didn't do a good enough job."

"What if you can't though? What if you can't take away magic? What if magic is as natural as the air we breathe and you simply … I don't know … concealed it?"

Ellyne scowled but she knew the girl might be right. She was trying not to feel anger toward everything and everyone, but Marik's actions coupled with feeling helpless to enact any kind of meaningful change left her feeling empty.

She had to admit, however, that having a nice, rational conversation with Nicole was refreshing. The girl was usually so bubbly and vivacious, Ellyne had trouble getting a word in at all. She wondered what had happened to her during the two years Ellyne was absent. She thought about asking but, instead, munched on some more chips, unsure how to approach the subject. If Nicole wished to divulge that information, Ellyne knew she would—and probably wouldn't shut up about it.

The two sat in silence for a spell, Ellyne crunching loudly and Nicole appearing lost in thought. Perhaps their conversation had given them each something to think about, or perhaps they were both processing the events that had transpired earlier. Ellyne figured she would be thinking about that for a long time to come.

"So," Ellyne finally said, "you said I was … glowing?"

Nicole's eyes instantly lit up and she shifted to face Ellyne on the couch. "Oh goodness, yes! I've never seen anything like it! It was like you were on fire, but you weren't actually on fire, of course. At least, I don't think you were."

"How is that possible? What happened?"

"Well, I've been thinking about it. You know how you can sometimes see flocia—like, actual flocia?"

"I vaguely remember that, yes."

"Well, I think you were harnessing so much power that I, too, was finally able to see it like you can. Ellyne, it was radiant and beautiful! I swear I could actually *feel* it! To produce effects like that … well, you might be the most powerful creature anywhere!"

"But … how? I didn't *try* to channel it. In fact, I tried earlier, and it didn't work. If it *had*, then I would've avoided being that high up in the first place."

"I think you … you *are* flocia. You're the source now! You didn't actually take it away from us; you merely became the Teranyne, and you simply don't know how to share." Nicole pretended to pout but eventually laughed. "This is, I think, why magic is so unreliable—because you're unreliable!"

"Gee, thanks."

"Oh, sorry! I didn't mean to—"

"Kidding. I'm kidding, Nicole."

"Anyway, if you knew how to control the power within you, then mages could draw their power directly from you. You'd be like a mobile flocia power source!"

"That sounds … kind of creepy and a bit disgusting."

"It's wonderful!"

"No, it's not!" Ellyne jumped from the couch, throwing the bag of chips to the floor. "You're telling me I'm the source now. I'm the Teranyne—me! I'm having a difficult time understanding what's wonderful about this. I don't want to use flocia. I certainly don't want to *be* flocia! This isn't great. This is the exact opposite of great."

The chips inside the bag crunched under her foot as Ellyne nervously moved about the room, unsure of where to go or even what to do. She punched the couch, unable to think of a solution. This wasn't an enemy she could simply shoot.

"What am I supposed to do with this?" she continued. "Wait, no, I've got it!"

"Got what? Ellyne, you're all over the place."

"Says the girl who's always all over the place," Ellyne smirked. "No, I've got a solution. We go back to the Sistix and climb that damned hill and put flocia back where we found it! Surely, I can just return it to its home and it'll be all happy and it'll leave me alone."

"I don't know, Ellyne."

Nicole nearly bounced off the couch from the force of Ellyne dropping back onto it. "Why not? It's perfect! I took flocia from the source, right? I can put it back!"

"This is new territory, and something tells me it's not going to work. Besides, we'd have to get back into the Sistix, which is a problem in and of itself."

"We got in once before; we can do it again. It'll be easy!"

Ellyne was certain this idea would work. It made complete sense to her, and her spirits lifted to a height they hadn't reached in a long time. She could finally rid herself of this power she never wanted.

"And how do you suggest we do that?"

"We'll just pay Iksillix another visit and—"

"Ellyne, I don't think he's going to help us. In fact, I'd be surprised if he didn't try to kill us instead."

"Okay, okay. So, we'll have to convince him."

"I'm pretty sure he'll never speak to you again. How on Seralune do you think you'll convince him?"

Ellyne fluttered her eyelashes and grinned. "I can be charming."

Nicole laughed but Ellyne got the sarcasm loud and clear. "Oh really?"

"Absolutely. I can turn on the charm and be persuasive. Trust me."

"You dug out one of his eyeballs with a spoon last time, Ellyne. I don't think he's going to cooperate. No amount of charm is going to make him come around."

"It ultimately worked, though, didn't it? That was just one way I can be persuasive!"

Nicole sighed. It was her turn to get off the couch and pace nervously. "I don't think you can just put flocia back, Ellyne. I already pondered this option, should the need arise."

"You said this is new territory. It's worth a shot, right?"

Ellyne felt hope fading. Nicole may not have been the utmost scholar on flocia and magic, but she had more intuition and natural talent than probably everyone on Seralune combined. She knew things nobody else could glean from books and Ellyne trusted her opinion over other people's facts.

Nicole stared at the carpet, her hands fussing with her pantlegs. "I'm sorry, Ellyne. It's really not worth a shot. I'm almost certain it won't work. Flocia ... flocia *chose* you. You don't think just anyone could've simply waltzed into the Teranyne and absorbed it, do you? That would be certain death."

"Then what?" Ellye shrieked. "What the hell am I supposed to do? I'm a walking bomb that could go off randomly. I have this power and I don't know how to use it or what to do with it. And I sure as hell don't even want it!"

"I'm sorry."

"And you tell me I'm the source and mages can draw power from me so, what does that mean? Do I just hang around Seralune, providing them with power like a damned battery?"

"No," Marik said, appearing out of nowhere.

"You damned coward!" Ellyne roared, lunging at the man, and wrapping her hands around his throat.

Marik gagged and sputtered, struggling to free himself from her grasp but all attempts failed as she pinned him against the wall, her rage fully in control. Whatever the man was trying to say came out only as grunts.

"Ellyne, no!" Nicole yelled, rushing to his aid, and trying to pry her hands free of his neck. "Let him go!"

"Why should I? He abandoned us. I told you, he's only looking out for himself, and it was only a matter of time before he betrayed us."

"Ellyne, if he betrayed us, then why did he come back?"

A moment passed when nobody moved. Ellyne stared at both Nicole and Marik, frozen by indecision, rage, and fear. She needed answers and nobody could give her any. But killing Marik would at least accomplish something.

Her hands around Marik's throat felt wonderful, and she wasn't going to let that go.

"Ellyne!" Nicole shouted, her voice seemingly muted—a mere backdrop to Ellyne's overwhelming rage and frustration.

She persisted, resolute in Marik's punishment. Her grip around his neck tightened and she clenched her jaw, growling, and channeling her rage through her fingertips.

Nicole continued pleading but Ellyne paid her no attention. The girl's lips moved, and she continued trying to loosen Ellyne's hands until something snapped.

Ellyne was thrust violently backward. She collided with the couch, tumbled over the back, and hit the wall, just inches from the window, staring up at the ceiling.

Without hesitation, she was on her feet and about to lunge at Marik who collapsed on the floor, but something stopped her. She couldn't advance.

"Let me go, Nicole," Ellyne spat, struggling against an intangible force produced by the girl's outstretched palm."

"No. You don't want to kill him. That's not like you."

Ellyne pushed against the spell, taking a labored step forward. "How do you know what I want?"

"He didn't betray us. He came back to help! He's not our enemy, Ellyne!"

"I'd forgotten you're powerful enough to affect me with magic, but things are different than before, aren't they? And you can't stop me now! You've seen what I can do."

Ellyne felt the spell against her. She could almost taste it. It was powerful—far more powerful than any other spell she felt. She couldn't fight Nicole's magic—it was too strong—so she needed a different method to circumvent the girl's power. Instead of struggling against it, she embraced the magic and let it soak into her—seeping into every pore.

And then she forced it back out.

Nicole slammed into the wall and slumped to the carpet, moaning.

"I told you, you can't stop me. Nobody can! And I'll do whatever the hell I want. If that means killing this piece of shit traitor, then so be it."

"Ellyne, don't do this." Nicole pleaded meekly. She tried to move but slumped back against the wall.

Ellyne looked at Marik who still breathed but lay motionless, also slumped against the wall. She wasn't sure how long she stood, staring at them, growling and balling her fists. Her anger urged her to act—to kill the man once and for all. He deserved nothing less.

They didn't understand. Nobody did. How could they? She was on her own again, fighting alone with undisputed, incomprehensible power but without control. It was power she didn't ask for and was now burdened with, crushed under its immense weight. She was the source and everyone relied on her for their magic.

And she wanted nobody to have it.

What good were her friends who stood in her way? They had no solutions yet they diminished her potential. If she couldn't be rid of flocia then she would embrace it. She would set everything right, no matter what the consequences. The world would burn if it was necessary.

Whatever it took.

She suddenly snapped to as her thumb slowly pulled back her revolver's hammer, her gun pointed squarely at Nicole.

Then she pulled the trigger.

THE BULLET MADE it only a foot out of the chamber before Ellyne, using flocia, deflected it into a nearby wall where it embedded itself. She lowered the gun slowly, panting with rage, and gently holstered the weapon, never taking her eyes off Nicole who remained largely motionless.

"No," she whispered, "you can still be useful to me. You can't stop me. *Nobody* can stop me."

She stomped into her bedroom and traded her bloody torn clothes for an untarnished outfit, inspecting the myriad of holes and tears she'd accumulated. Judging by how damaged they were, she probably should've been dead. It was another testament to the power she commanded. If a fall that high couldn't kill her, could anything?

"But I also can't have you standing in my way," she continued, emerging into the living room. "A traitor, and the friend of a traitor. I'll take care of this myself if I must personally send every last one of those lizard things back to where they came from. Should you try and stop me, I won't hesitate to cut you down."

She slammed the door behind her. Normally, she escaped

covertly through her window, but now she felt no reason for that. She could go wherever she pleased, whenever she liked.

"Who's gonna stop me?" she mused. "I'd like to see someone try."

She almost *wished* someone would challenge her. She needed an excuse to further explore her new abilities and stretch her legs a bit. She barely understood how these powers functioned, and there was no way to learn but through experience. If someone should happen to anger her, well, she just might let loose.

Ellyne made her way through the throng of people on the sidewalk as usual. What was unusual, however, was hearing the muted gasps and whispers from some individuals in the crowd as she passed by. Had they seen? Were they there when she defeated that monster? Did they know who she was?

She tried to ignore the scattered reactions while simultaneously keeping an eye on everyone through the corners of her vision. The Technos would absolutely position themselves against her and the Teranynes would probably try to coerce her to join them—a complete reversal from the way things used to be. She had always walked that line—potential ally to one, hated enemy to another.

The Ilserate had surely seen the spectacle. They probably saw everything—the Kithrak, too. Not only had Ellyne challenged a new enemy, but she'd inadvertently sent a message to all her old enemies. She'd done more in a few minutes than the Ilserate had done in two years.

"Good," she growled. Several people took notice of her, hearing her voice. "Nobody before had the power to clean up Karnascus," she whispered, "so I guess it falls on me."

She'd never felt such confidence or such a drive to fight back. It was as if all her frustration and anger over magic bubbled up all at once because, now ... now she could actually do something about it, and neither Marik nor Nicole could stop her.

And how dare Nicole try to save Marik! "Trying to save a traitor … only a traitor's ally would do such a thing. If Nicole stands with Marik, then she doesn't stand with me. And to think she had me believing we were friends!"

She stood alone—probably hunted by literally everyone in Karnascus. But would anyone make a move against her? Surely even the Ilserate had to feel some level of fear. Both the Technos and the Teranynes would be foolish enough to confront her, that much was certain. But the Kithrak and the Ilserate … they'd most likely bide their time and watch for weakness.

Surely, they'd have a plan eventually, though. They would either have to neutralize her or somehow coerce her to join them. Such a thing would put them in control. Where, before, they fought over Nicole they would now fight over Ellyne. The very thought made her laugh.

She eventually stopped outside a familiar storefront and stared at the hanging sign. The letters, once dormant, sprang to illuminated life on her approach.

She pushed open the door to Victor's bar and slipped inside. "A drink is what I need right now."

Upon entering, the screens on the walls flickered and popped, finally springing to life, but the rest of the room fell silent. Even Victor paused his conversation with someone at the bar and stared at her. He looked almost as if he were gazing at a stranger.

"Ellyne," he stammered, "uh hi! The … uh, usual, I suppose?"

"Yes, please, and make it a triple if you don't mind."

She approached the bar, feeling every pair of eyes in the room follow her as no one uttered a word. Had news of what happened gotten out this quickly, or had everyone here seen what she did?

She didn't like it. There was no danger, but there was tension in the air and frustration rose within her. Being the center of attention like this made her uncomfortable—exposed and out in the open. She made it to a stool and pulled it out.

"I would appreciate it," she growled, turning to the crowd, "if you assholes all minded your own damned business and maybe stopped staring at me like I'm some freak exhibit at the museum."

She heard several gasps and the stunned crowd stared blankly at her for a moment before most of them averted their gaze, trying without success to act naturally. Ellyne stared at them all, realizing her fingers toyed with the gun at her side.

A gun that suddenly seemed so clumsy and ... archaic when compared to her newfound abilities. Did she even really need it anymore? Once she had control over her abilities, maybe she'd ditch it.

She finally turned from the crowd and sat on the bar stool, now immediately aware of the man sitting next to her and whose eyes appeared fixed in her direction.

She turned to him and scowled. "And what are you staring at?" Her hand rested on her gun again. The urge to draw it was strong. If she put a bullet in this man, who would stop her? The urge to find out nagged at her. She'd started many bar fights in the past. Would this be any different?

"Oh, uh, nothing!" the man stuttered, falling over his own words. "I'm just going to ... go ... over there now."

"Good," she replied as the man grabbed his drink and hustled over to an empty table where he promptly sat and kept his gaze pointed down at the drink he clutched in shaky hands.

"What the hell is wrong with everyone, Victor? It's like I'm on fire or something. I don't like everyone staring at me."

Victor grunted and mumbled something she couldn't understand as he filled a glass with squama juice. "Welcome back. I assume you enjoyed your time in prison?"

"Thank you. Wait, how did—"

"Your friends—the girl and that bald guy—filled me in some time ago, as they were making plans to break you out. I don't know why they trusted me with any of that information, to be honest."

"Who else knows?"

"Just me."

He mumbled something more, but Ellyne's attention was already elsewhere as she stared into the alluring blue liquid she swirled about in the glass.

Once again, she found herself with motivation and absolutely no plan of action. The only difference, now, was the overwhelming advantage she held. But she couldn't just fly up to the alien spaceship and take them on, could she?

"Wait," she mused, "can I fly? Maybe I *can* just zip on up there and break their stuff."

Maybe, if she defeated enough of them, they would leave, fleeing like cowards. How many of them were there, anyway? Their ships were huge, sometimes blocking out the sun's light entirely, so there had to be plenty of them.

And the Kithrak were obviously afraid of them, but why? Were these Golgolothings that powerful?

If she could gain control of her abilities and rely on them, then she doubted their numbers even mattered. She'd take them all one if she had to.

Ellyne felt certain something was missing from the equation, but she wasn't sure it mattered. She would dismantle everything and everyone all the same and then she would figure out how to rid herself of flocia permanently.

"Or not. Maybe I should keep it. After all, I took it. I seized flocia when nobody else could. It's mine. Maybe I should hang onto it. I bet I could keep humans free and peaceful. I mean, we all know the Ilserate can't seem to do shit about that anyway. If I continued to be the Teranyne, then I could dictate who could use magic and when ... assuming I learn how to control it."

"I'm sorry," Victor said, "were you talking to me? I was busy."

"Just talking to myself."

"Well, if you need anything, just … just let me know, okay?"

"Wait," she said, looking up at the man. "What's with everyone in here? Staring at me and whispering? People on the street were doing it too and you … you're acting pretty weird, yourself."

Victor leaned in, propping himself on the bar with his elbows. "Word gets around, Ellyne. You created quite a scene out there. Besides that, nobody's ever killed a Golgolonar, let alone taken one on in plain view of everyone. Nobody's successfully fought them since the day they arrived. All confrontations ended poorly for us. Even the Kithrak folded without a fight."

"Yeah, but it *just* happened. How is it—"

Victor turned his gaze upward to the screen above him.

"This is Gabrielle Simms, reporting once again from Karnascus-15, on location of what was a brutal and deadly fight between a woman and one of the alien Golgolonar."

"Well, shit," Ellyne spat, downing her drink in one gulp. The blue liquid's familiar burn as she swallowed was like seeing an old friend after many years apart. "That explains it, I guess. I often forget people watch screens."

"Don't you ever watch the news?" Victor laughed nervously.

Ellyne gently slid the glass toward Victor. "You know I don't."

"Oh, right. I don't even know why you have a screen in your apartment."

"It came with the place. I'd yank it off the wall but then I'd have to stare at empty holes and probably pay for the damage eventually."

Victor poured another drink and set the bottle down next

to the glass. He knew her well enough to know that bottle would be empty soon.

She grinned. But she also braced herself for the question she knew was coming.

"As you can see from this recorded footage," the reporter continued, "this woman, now identified as Ellyne Thandaral, is bathed in radiant orange light as she plummets back to the street and collides with the pavement, only to be ejected at least thirty feet away."

Apparently, she channeled enough flocia to allow *everyone* to see—not just Nicole. Nothing like being a beacon of illumination, plummeting from the sky for everyone to see.

"What happened out there, Ellyne?"

There it was.

"I'm going to kill them, Victor. I'm going to hunt down and kill every Golgolo asshole until they flee Seralune with their tails between their legs."

"You can't be serious," Victor gasped. "Ellyne, they're really powerful, and tough to kill."

"And, yet ya girl killed one."

"One, yes. But there are thousands more where that one came from. And I hear there are far worse monsters— additional arms, legs, tails, whatever."

"Ilserate authorities are unsure of the golden gunslinger's whereabouts at this time," the lady on the screen continued, "but they urge extreme caution to the public."

"I guess I'm not anonymous anymore," she muttered under her breath, taking a swig of squama juice. "That's unfortunate."

Her thoughts were already calmer and more whimsical as the alcohol quickly got to work. Her muscles relaxed a little, but she was still focused and resolute.

"Okay, so," Victor stammered, looking a little uneasy, "how are you going to do this? Just call each one out and work through the ranks?"

"I haven't thought that far ahead yet. But if that's what I must do, then I will. And I'll kill anyone who gets in my way. We're prisoners, Victor. First to the Ilserate, then the Kithrak and, now, these lizard things. It's got to stop. It's going to get bloody—alien and human alike."

Her friend took a step back, shock written all over his face. "Ellyne, you can't … you can't mean that."

"If you're not working with me then you're my enemy, Victor. We've been prisoners for too long. Nobody else has the courage or the power to free us."

She guzzled the rest of her drink and slammed the glass down.

"But I do."

"Are you absolutely sure of that, Ellyne? You're talking about taking on literally *everyone* in Karnascus. And you can't tell me you want to harm other people. I know you, Ellyne. You're not a cold-blooded killer of innocents."

"Old Ellyne wasn't, Victor."

She offered her tik card to the worried man.

He grinned nervously but didn't move to take the card from her. "Since when did you start paying for your drinks?"

"… and there are many who question the golden gunslinger's mysterious two-year absence, only to reappear suddenly." The reporter paused for a moment. "After what transpired here—after she left this massive crater in the street, killing a Golgolonar, there are rumors that squads have been dispatched to neutralize her."

"Since I became a celebrity, of course. I mean since I became one … again," Ellyne grinned.

"And since this encounter," the reporter continued, "magic itself appears to be more stable—an element which both Kithrak and Ilserate scientists are investigating, with the permission from the Golgolonar of course."

"So, what will you do now?" he continued, waving off her

attempt to pay. "I wouldn't even know where to start. I don't glow orange and fall from the sky though," he chuckled.

She returned the card to her pocket and rose from the stool, cracking her knuckles. "I'm gonna find one of these neutralization squads and … neutralize them."

"Then what?"

"Find another. Then another."

She headed to the door.

"You can't fight the Golgolonar alone, Ellyne," Victor called out behind her.

"Watch me," she muttered.

CHAPTER
TWENTY-TWO

SEVERAL PEDESTRIANS GASPED and jumped out of Ellyne's way as she exited the bar. For a moment, they shared glances, with nobody sure what to say or do. Not even during the height of the war, when she was both a most feared enemy and a lauded hero, did she receive this much attention.

"Word travels fast," she mumbled, muscling past the forming crowd and leaving them behind even as she heard several claps and cheers. "Fools," she spat. "They have no idea."

She sensed the irony—about how she herself was always clueless, building the bridge as she crossed the chasm. This was no different, except she knew some information very few others knew, which provided confidence for a change.

She carefully watched those around her riding on hoversticks, driving in vehicles, or simply loitering nearby. It wasn't as if she didn't trust them but ... no, she didn't trust them. And they were all sheep, submitting to the Ilserate or whoever currently wielded the largest weapon, all the while being grateful for the scraps of magic they were fed so they could live their lives in relative comfort and convenience.

And, apparently, magic was indeed more reliable, as there were more people about, making liberal use of it.

At this point, she wasn't sure what she wanted to do—take magic away from everyone, give magic back to everyone … or just tell everyone what to do and kill those who got in her way. The third option was the most palatable.

She was probably the most powerful being on Seralune—a title Nicole once held. She could do what she wanted and go where she wanted. Who could stop her? Everyone feared her. True, some revered her, but she was certain there was fear, too.

"It's the mage breaker!" a man nearby shouted, pointing to Ellyne. "Hey, everyone! It's the mage breaker! We love you!"

Using flocia, Ellyne pulled the man to her and grabbed him by the throat. She scowled, mere inches from his face, feeling nothing but anger inside. The man gasped and sputtered, trying to loosen her grip. Such a thing would get him nowhere, however, as she channeled flocia to enhance her strength without effort or thought.

She could kill him and there was nothing anyone could do. Sure, they could try to apprehend her or maybe mark her as a wanted fugitive but that would all be for show. They couldn't stop her.

His eyes pleaded with her. "Please," he gurgled. "I'm sorry."

She released him, dropping him to the sidewalk, coughing and gasping. He clutched his throat and stared up at her, dumbfounded and confused.

"I'm sorry, "he sputtered meekly, lowering his gaze to the ground. "I didn't mean to—"

She ignored him, leaving him behind both physically and in her thoughts, wondering if she should've killed him.

For the first time ever, she felt unrestricted. There was freedom in power, and she had plenty of both. No longer did she have to live life always looking over her shoulder. The Ilserate couldn't control her and the Kithrak couldn't touch her. Oh, they'd both probably try but she was confident it would go poorly for them.

No, her fear was gone, replaced with confidence, and she welcomed the opportunity to send everyone fleeing from her. The Technicians and the Teranyne Order hadn't even attempted to pester her. It was, however, only a matter of time before one of those groups attempted to manipulate the situation and perhaps try to use her. The very thought excited her and made her giddy. Let them try.

Was this why the Kithrak and the Ilserate subjugated the people of Karnascus? Because they could? Certainly, they had other reasons, but she wasn't sure they needed any. No, the more she thought about it, the more believable it became that they simply wanted control. The T-helm experiments— turning people into ravenous grika—proved that well enough.

She wanted answers but, more than that, she wanted to be rid of all of them—the Kithrak, the Ilserate, and the flying lizards. Since nobody else seemed equipped or motivated to perform this service, it appeared the task fell to her alone.

And she still wanted to be rid of flocia more than anything —no matter how much she loved the power. It was unnatural and it corrupted everything it touched. It was a cancer she needed to cut out. She would get rid of it completely... somehow. However, not before she overthrew the oppressors and placed herself in a position of power.

But she was getting ahead of herself. First, she needed to expel the lizards from Seralune. That seemed the easiest part of the whole thing. If she fought them hard enough, they'd leave, wouldn't they?

Having time to think it through more, doubt began to creep in, and she began to wonder just what it would take to force them to leave. She knew next to nothing about them except they were tough and persistent. But would they remain if she relentlessly attacked them?

And then she'd deal with the Kithrak … and then the Ilserate. Those two seemed like they'd be easier after getting rid of the lizards. Ellyne's task list appeared to be getting longer.

Suddenly, the mission felt insurmountable. These were wars fought by armies, not one person. And wars lasted years. But she was more than just one person, wasn't she? It wouldn't be easy, and it may take some time, but she could do it. She'd already sent a message to not only the lizards, but to *everyone* on the planet.

A Kithrak patrol approached. Three bots conspicuously stuck out in a sea of people as they tried to navigate the busy street. Ordinarily, they would glide around or over people but the new bots—those with legs—had a tough time getting around in crowds. People tried moving to avoid the patrol, but such an action was difficult when there was nowhere to go.

Ellyne confidently strutted toward the approaching bots. She was curious as to how they would react to her presence once they identified her. Her confidence swelled. And though she knew she needn't hide or flee, she still felt the urge. After so many years of trying to fly under the radar, this was a new world for her.

"Old habits," she mused. "Come on, let's see what you do once you notice me. I'm right here."

She didn't have to wait long. It was obvious the moment the patrol detected her. She saw the bots stop and two Kithrak conferred while the crowd flowed around them.

Ellyne, however, didn't stop, and the two Kithrak noticed immediately. She could see concern in each of their three eyes. That concern quickly turned to fear.

"They're sending out higher-ranking mages," she mumbled. "Not even trying to blend in anymore, as if they want everyone to see them. They must be trying to appear in control, but I bet they're worried about something. Probably me. Good."

The patrol abruptly changed course, heading toward a nearby alley. The bots made no effort to avoid people and the mages shoved pedestrians out of their way using magic.

"You're running?" Ellyne laughed, hurrying after them. "Oh no, you won't get away that easily."

She hurried after the patrol, having an easier time with the people around her than the bots were having. While the Kithrak and bots had to work and muscle through the crowd, Ellyne found everyone willingly moved out of her way. Some shouted, some gasped and pointed, and others simply gave her a wide berth.

"Go get 'em, mage breaker!" someone shouted.

"The mage breaker? Where?" she heard a woman say.

"Over there!" someone replied. "She's chasing the patrol! Hell yeah!"

Ellyne paid them no mind. She was fixed on her targets and followed them into the alley. There, she saw them scurrying away from her and a grin crossed her lips.

The two Kithrak spotted her and immediately began casting their spells with fear in their eyes as they tried backing away. She cackled and watched them as both their spells fizzled.

The bots awkwardly lumbered on mechanical legs, moving between her and the mages, obviously trying to block her. Ellyne laughed some more, feeling the two mages tugging on flocia, attempting more spells, but she somehow kept it away from them as if it belonged to her only. She was unsure how this worked, but there was no time to ponder the situation.

Her first urge was to draw her weapon, but she stayed her hand and instead slashed the air in front of her with her finger, sending a radiant wave of blue energy at the bots. The blast collided with two of the machines, sending various sparking scrap and shrapnel in several directions.

"That's new," she mused, inspecting her hands. "Wonder how I did it."

The two Kithrak muttered to each other with shaky voices, pointing at Ellyne as they slowly backed up. The remaining bot raised its gun, but Ellyne was already too close for it to adjust its aim. Another bolt of energy flew from her hand, tearing through its armor and leaving a smoking husk.

She felt the Kithrak tug at flocia as they again tried to cast their spells, but it refused their commands, remaining with Ellyne instead. If only she knew how she was making that happen, she could literally bend the entire planet to her.

"It's okay guys," she sneered, "performance anxiety's an actual thing, and it probably happens to everyone. But you never really had a chance in the first place."

She raised her palms and bathed the two mages in blazing energy.

"Get out of my city," she muttered before she turned and strutted out of the alley. "And get off my planet." A sizable crowd gathered to witness the spectacle and stood in stark silence as she moved through them. They gave her room to pass, gasping and whispering as she exited the alley.

Observers in the street scurried to move out of her way, saying nothing and letting her pass unmolested as the sea of onlookers literally parted for her. Pride and confidence swelled within Ellyne. She was invincible—a beacon to the people of Karnascus—and she would rid the city of anyone and anything that stood against her.

"We love you, mage breaker!" a man from the crowd shouted.

Ellyne stopped briefly, clenching her fists. The urge to turn and yell at the crowd was overwhelming, but she resisted. How dare they speak to her!

"I've been fighting for you urchins," she whispered to

herself, "and you still sit on your asses, gobbling up magic and letting everyone control you. You're pathetic. Get up and do something for yourselves."

"You're our hero!" another man shouted.

"No," she shouted back, "That I'm not."

Her pace quickened and she wanted nothing more than to escape the throng of worthless sycophants that clung to whatever shreds of magic they had. They would pledge their undying allegiance to anyone who showed immense power. Right now, it just happened to be her but tomorrow it could be someone or something else.

"Now move out of my way," she shouted, her hands suddenly glowing with red energy.

The air around her crackled and her arms tingled as she threw a bolt of raw flocia into the air. "I said MOVE!" she shrieked.

People scattered. Some screamed, others gasped, and a few were trampled in the panic, but none of this concerned her. She hated them for being subservient, for using magic and, most importantly, for being in her way. They should've been thankful she didn't turn her flocia on them. They got to live today, and that was their gift for leaving the area.

"That's right," she mumbled, "flee. You'd just be cannon fodder for what comes next."

Ellyne sauntered out of the alley and into the street where many of the onlookers had fled. Most of them scattered or tried to hide when she emerged, but it appeared they were still captivated by her and couldn't completely pry themselves away.

"Free yourselves!" she shouted. "Stop being servants of the Kithrak or whatever other power comes along! Magic is a prison! The sooner you accept it, the sooner you'll be free!"

Her voice echoed through the street. The people she spotted in the area remained, watching her, but nobody spoke, and nobody moved. They looked at one another and then back at her.

"It's time for us to rise up," she continued, "and take back our city! The Kithrak are not the peaceful magic stewards you think they are! They're using you! The Ilserate is using you."

Ellyne stared up at the sky, watching the hulking ship hovering high overhead, waiting for any sign of activity. "Any second now," she mumbled.

CHAPTER
TWENTY-THREE

ELLYNE SAT ON A BENCH, tapping her fingers on the gun at her hip, shifting her gaze to the sky, hoping to see some action. She sighed and picked a bit of dirt from under a fingernail while the city's inhabitants slowly emerged and resumed their activities. Some stared at her, and others paid her no mind, but those who knew made sure to give her a wide berth.

They had a look of terror mixed with curiosity as they passed her. She chuckled, comfortable with her status. They were prisoners and didn't know it. She would free them since they couldn't free themselves and, once that was sorted, she could finally address the whole magic thing and determine what was best.

Ellyne didn't see them at first. The ship floating high above masked them in its shadow as they descended—speeding to the ground before they spread their wings and circled, rotating slowly until they dropped to the street nearby.

Eight hulking Golgolonar snarled at Ellyne, baring their fangs in what was either a grin or a growl. She couldn't tell which it was, but it made no difference. Three appeared to be the same caste as the one she'd previously fought. She assumed these were basic warriors. The other five, however, surprised her.

"Two heads, two tails, and four arms," she said, getting up from the bench and yawning. She stretched for a moment and smiled. "Are you two lizards sewn together or something? I mean, whoever your tailor is… they're really good. I can't even see the seams! Exquisite work all around. Bravo!"

These new Golgolonar were smaller in size but appeared just as menacing as the other three. They stood behind their warriors, however, which Ellyne took to mean they might have been spell casters of some kind. The Kithrak's powers and stature supposedly increased in proportion to the number of eyes they possessed. The same could hold true with respect to the lizards' arms, legs, tails, heads … whatever.

Did *anyone* actually know a damned thing about these aliens?

"So, what?" she continued. "You guys sent your supervisors down here just to fight me? Do I get to speak to a manager or something?"

"You will come with us," one of the two-headed creatures growled.

"That's no way to speak to a lady—especially one who just kicked your ass in front of the entire city. I have a counter proposition for you."

"You are in no position to—"

"You will leave Seralune. You'll leave and never return … or I will destroy all of you. That's my proposal. Take it or leave it."

Several Golgolonar laughed. At least, that's what Ellyne thought it was. She couldn't read them well with their vague facial expressions and guttural growls. They could be smiling or snarling, and she wouldn't know the difference. Not that she cared.

Whether they laughed or growled, the outcome was going to be the same—their annihilation.

She laughed with them for a moment before unleashing a blast of energy from her open palms. It hit one of the warriors squarely in the chest, searing a sizeable hole through its body. The alien had barely enough time to look shocked before it fell to the ground, smoke rising from its corpse.

"Wait, what? I don't hear you laughing anymore. Was it something I said?"

The Golgolonar exchanged glances which, again, she couldn't read, but she surmised there was probably some concern involved.

"I have no time for insipid conversation and threats. So, let's get to the part where you fly back up to your little ship, pack your asses up, and leave Seralune. Nobody wants you here."

"This changed nothing," the one lizard scowled, regaining its composure. "You will come with us, or you will die."

"As I said before, I—"

Ellyne was interrupted by a blast of energy from one of the smaller Golgolonar. She felt her strength drain away and collapsed to one knee, gasping for breath.

She struggled to stand, finally rising to her feet, barely able to support herself. "Okay, that was a freebie, but one's all you get."

Three of the smaller Golgolonar raised their arms and fired several bolts of multicolored light. Ellyne gasped, but instinct took over and she, too, stretched out her hands.

The projectiles impacted something mere inches from her palms which shimmered with each colliding bolt. The Golgolonar fired more but those, too, dissipated harmlessly.

"See?" she laughed, inspecting her hands as if there was something to see. "I told you! You've got no idea how badass I am. You should really take me up on my offer."

"I only wish I knew how I did that," she thought. *"Hopefully I can keep it up."*

There was little time to ponder, however, as they renewed their attack with crackling, shimmering rods of energy appearing in each one's hand.

"Well, that's new," she mused. "Look, I can see you're having fun … uh, gripping your rods and all, so I'll just say this one more time and you can go on enjoying yourselves. Leave this city and this planet. Don't come back."

The two Golgolonar attacked in unison, one stepping over its comrade's corpse. They swung together in a coordinated effort, but Ellyne ducked and rolled backward, feeling her strength gradually return. When she got back to her feet, crouching, she thrust out her hands again so they could join their fallen ally.

There was no blast of energy this time.

The Golgolonar paused briefly, expecting an onslaught, but recovered quickly once they realized there was no danger. Ellyne swore one of them actually laughed this time.

Confused, she tried again and failed. "What the—", she growled, having no time to continue her thought as she jumped backward to avoid the Golgolonars' attacks.

She felt the crackling energy swing past her, narrowly avoiding both attacks. "What's the problem here?" She tried again and was met with disappointment. "What good is this garbage if it only works randomly? Come on, flocia, do your job, you piece of crap!"

Ellyne jumped behind a bench, trying to hide her concern from her attackers. Fear and doubt began to replace her confidence, but she hid that, too. Surely, with enough persistence, she'd be able to command flocia properly.

"Hey, listen," she quipped, "how about we talk about this? I mean, you still need to leave but maybe we can help pay for your fuel on the way out? I know a place that has some badass snacks—perfect for a road trip."

One Golgolonar growled while the other sneered and swung at her, its energy baton colliding with the bench, sending a shower of sparks into the air. Ellyne could feel the heat and her arms tingled.

"No? Okay, then, how about this instead?"

She grabbed her gun and emptied all eight bullets into the enemy on her right, pleasantly surprised when she saw purple blood.

"At least *some* things are still reliable," she muttered, dodging more attacks. The bench shattered into flinders and twisted metal, so she backed up, not only keeping her eyes on her attackers, but trying to determine what the other five Golgolonar were doing. As far as she could tell, they hadn't moved.

They simply stood in the distance, apparently observing. She thought it foolish to stand by and watch when they had greater numbers and could easily press that advantage, but maybe they were all big, dumb lizards who brute forced everything. For what it was worth, she was happy with their lack of strategy. It was an easier fight if they didn't join in.

Her two adversaries pressed their attacks, and she danced around the street, trying to keep away from them until she thought of a plan. They were relentless, allowing Ellyne no time to reload her revolver. She didn't dare try to channel a flocia attack that, if it failed, would leave her vulnerable.

The injured Golgolonar slowed and struggled with its attacks, trying to gulp air through raspy breaths that sometimes produced purple spittle. Ellyne holstered her gun and drew her blade, unsure of how effective it would be against them. It was all she had, however, and she was struggling to devise a counterattack. She could at least outlast one of them. If it fell, then it was much more of a fair fight.

It wasn't long before the injured Golgolonar's energy rod winked out of existence, and it sputtered. The other lizard, however, paid it no mind and continued pressing the attack as its ally died in the street behind it.

"Don't you want to check on your friend?" she asked wryly as the lizard swung and missed. "No? I mean, that's pretty rude, don't you think? I guess you two weren't close? Maybe he owed you money or something and never paid it back?"

Her opponent merely growled, showing its teeth, and hefting its energy rod, preparing for another assault.

"You can't beat me," she laughed. "I'm the most powerful being on Seralune and you're just another scaley asshole with an overbite … holding a magic rod. If this is the best you guys got, then I'm sorry to say your existence here is going to be brief."

The Golgolonar lunged with incredible speed, catching Ellyne off guard. Indecision took over and she tried to dodge and defend at the same time but lost her balance and fell to the curb. Before she could react, the beast was on her, striking with its baton.

She convulsed, cutting her scream short as every nerve ignited in a paralyzing fire. The lizard grinned as it stood over her, watching her shake and obviously enjoying its handiwork.

It attacked her again.

She coughed spittle into the air and tried desperately not to bite her tongue as pain wracked every part of her body. She writhed on the ground until it pulled back the baton, laughing at her pain.

"Is that all you got?" she asked, trying to laugh but mostly just gasping for air and trying not to show the fear building up within her. Why was flocia not doing what she wanted?

She questioned her abilities, wondering if she'd miscalculated. Maybe she wasn't as powerful as she'd thought? Had she walked willingly into a trap? Her fear threatened to overcome her, and, for a moment, surrender seemed like a valid option. If she surrendered now, she'd at least have more time to devise an escape strategy.

But that fear, as strong as it may have been, was mixed with anger. Fear was a relatively new emotion for Ellyne, but anger … anger was an old, familiar friend she wrapped around her—always with her, whether helpful or not.

The Golgolonar struck her with the rod again, sending her into painful convulsions. Either it believed this was the only way to fully incapacitate her or it simply wanted to cause her pain. Either way, it seemed to enjoy its actions and didn't appear to want to stop.

Ellyne's fear increased, along with her rage as her vision blurred. She would have her revenge on her attacker, even if it meant forfeiting her own life in the process. Her mind focused on her enemy, funneling hatred and fury at it as if they were a laser.

If she died here today, would she become a martyr?

She balled her shaky fists and grunted through clenched teeth, trying to regain control of her limbs as the Golgolonar readied for another strike. She knew this might be her last opportunity before she eventually blacked out, and that determination was all she needed.

The lizard struck.

With monumental effort, Ellyne rolled to the side and knelt on the pavement, still gasping for air. The energy rod crackled and sparked as it collided with the ground. The lizard looked at her, its face unreadable, but she hoped it was surprised.

It lunged at her, swinging the rod wildly and missing as she again rolled to the side, coming up in a kneel. Though it felt as if she were moving through water, she was still able to dodge, but she wasn't sure for how long. The urge to draw her gun was overwhelming, but it was still unloaded and there simply wasn't enough time to reload with her shaky, sluggish fingers. Her blade might have been ineffective, but it was the only weapon she had.

It swung again and, this time, she instinctively countered with an uppercut. Using the full force of her body as she stood, she leapt upward and connected her fist with the lizard's chin.

But there was more behind it. She knew it was flocia this time. For a moment, she felt powerful again—invincible—and she embraced it fully. She wanted more.

The creature's neck snapped with a sick, audible crackling sound and it crumpled immediately, its glowing rod disappearing as it collapsed in a heap on the pavement.

"Ha!" she yelled, looking down at the body. "I told you, I'm the most powerful person on Seralune." She lightly kicked the corpse and then threw her glance to the other five Golgolonar—each with two heads, four arms, and two tails.

Any ill effects from the Golgolonars' weapons dissipated, replaced by unnatural strength and energy. If flocia cooperated for just a minute or two longer, this fight would be over easily.

"Your turn," she shouted, pointing at them. If they had any emotion, they didn't show it. In fact, they didn't even move. She couldn't tell if they were observing her or waiting for her to challenge them. They may as well have been statues.

Ellyne ejected the empty cartridge from her revolver, slid another in its place, and slapped the cylinder in shut.

Except for the six of them and three Golgolonar bodies, the area was empty, though Ellyne could see curious bystanders huddling in alleys and behind buildings, unable to turn their gazes from this conflict. Curiosity mixed with fear—it was a strange combination, but the more people who saw this fight, the better.

She approached the five Golgolonar and, as she got closer,

they slowly fanned out. She knew her reckless approach wasn't the best strategy, but she wasn't about to back down. Even when they formed a circle around her, she stood her ground. The urge to panic was strong, but she suppressed it, instead tapping into her confidence and strength. This was new territory to her.

She fired off all eight bullets, choosing multiple targets and hoping to drop at least one of them. But each bullet harmlessly bounced off something—whether it was their thick, scaly hide or some kind of barrier, she wasn't sure. She'd seen mages with magical protections before, so it wasn't a surprise.

"Okay, fine," she groused, reloading her weapon again and shoving it back in its holster. "Don't bring a gun to a magic fight, Ellyne. I get it." She drew her blade and extended it.

The Golgolonar didn't budge. Even when her bullets threatened them, they stood steadfast and motionless, completely undaunted. They thought they were in control. Ellyne hoped to prove them wrong.

"Did you not see what I did to your goons back there? Do you actually think you can do any better simply because there are more of you? Or is it because you have more arms and shit?"

There was no response.

"No? Nothing? You must be super fun at parties."

They merely glared at her, making no move to attack or defend themselves. Were they that confident? Or maybe this was a stall tactic until reinforcements arrived. She looked up at the ship floating high above but saw no additional enemies approaching.

"Well," she growled, "okay, then, I guess let's do this already."

She made a move toward the nearest enemy with her blade in hand but, before she could take more than a few steps, weakness overcame her, and she struggled to remain standing.

She felt drained and exhausted. This couldn't be a natural consequence of flocia given how often she'd tapped into it before and never felt this way. Had she finally found her limits? Had she somehow channeled more than she could handle?

She took a labored step forward and dropped to one knee, staring up at her adversaries through clouded vision. The lizards remained motionless with their clawed hands outstretched in her direction.

"What are you doing to me?" she asked, her voice shaky and quiet. The Golgolonar ignored her, focused on whatever it was they were doing. Ellyne's rage subsided, now replaced with fear and exhaustion. No, this had to be their doing—either a spell or something else.

Fighting to stay conscious was all she could manage. Standing upright or walking were out of the question, let alone mounting any kind of attack. Whatever was happening to her, there was no way to counter it.

She tried with one last effort to channel flocia, grasping desperately for any shred of power and strength, but there was none. Her vision dimmed and she gasped for air, feeling as if walls were closing in. Her blade clattered to the ground.

"Sonofa," she muttered before she collapsed.

CHAPTER
TWENTY-FOUR

ELLYNE'S EYES SNAPPED OPEN, and she struggled to move, immediately recalling prior events. She stared at the ceiling, unable to see much else except for the two Golgolonar nearby, each in front of her. Judging from the sounds in the room, her suspicions led her to believe there were two more behind her, maybe even more than that.

Her head was restrained, which kept her from getting any kind of decent view of her surroundings, though she didn't need to see everything to realize where she most likely was.

"Where am I? And what exactly happened?"

The second question felt more important, and she played back what she remembered before she ended up … wherever here was. Of course, "here" was probably just another room where she could be poked and prodded like the lab rat everyone believed she was. What little she could see fit that bill so far.

It did feel eerily familiar, though she tried to convince herself otherwise. She couldn't be positive, but she believed she was lying in a fully reclined chair—just like a medical chair from a hospital or … like the chair from the Kithrak prison.

But she obviously couldn't be back in the prison for obvious reasons so, where was she? Her mind scrambled, trying to deny the facts. Try as she might, she couldn't ignore the signs and she panicked.

Struggling against the wrist and ankle restraints, she thrashed and tried to pull herself free. She first tried breaking them and, when that didn't work, she attempted to slide out of them. Her efforts were fruitless, and reality began to set in —she was trapped. Whatever restraint was around her head appeared just as sturdy as the others.

"No," she muttered under her breath as a tear slid down her temple, "not this again. What the hell do you want with me now?"

There was no reaction from the two hulking lizards she could see, even when she tried to break her bonds. She still felt unnaturally weak and the brief struggle against her restraints left her winded and shaky.

She heard movement from somewhere in the room— possibly from behind her. It was impossible to see most of her surroundings, so she had to rely on what little information she could gather. She only caught fuzzy glimpses of the other two lizards from the far corners of her vision, but they hadn't moved. There must have been someone else in the room.

"Get a grip, Ellyne," she whispered to herself. "You'll get out of here … wherever here is. Just be patient and wait for the opportunity. Just … breathe or some shit."

She tried to relax, feeling her muscles loosen and her breathing slow. In doing so, she felt the flocia within her, like an old friend, except she still wasn't on good terms with it and, try as she might, she couldn't embrace the power within her. She reached for it, but it was always just slightly out of her grasp. It almost felt like it was moving away from her, and she was chasing it. But moving where? How? For once she wished she knew something about magic and flocia and how either worked. Her hatred of the Golgolonar and her captivity was possibly stronger than her hatred of magic.

But there was plenty of anger and hatred to go around, and her captors would discover this fact once she was free of her restraints—once she figured out where she was and whose asses she had to kick.

"Let me out of here," she growled through clenched teeth while continuing to struggle against her bindings. "Let me go now, or—"

"The last time you got free," a voice from behind her said, "you caused major destruction to an expensive prison facility. I think it's best you stay put for now, lest you repeat that performance."

"Wait, I know that voice." She felt like throwing up, now her rage now mixed with fear. "You're that asshole doctor—"

"Scientist," the voice hissed, "and I tend to think I'm rather cordial—at least that's what I'm told. My fellows don't seem to have any problem with me, anyway. It only appears to be you who has issues. And you do have plenty of issues, now, don't you?"

Ellyne heard him moving around behind her, making noise with his metallic instruments and whatever other implements of torture he had on the counter. On the edge of panic, she desperately fought back tears, gritting her teeth, and digging her fingernails into her palms.

She wished for rage to overtake her. Anger was something she could cope with but sadness—the hopelessness of Kithrak captivity—was overwhelming. She finally broke and the tears flowed freely down her cheeks.

"What do you even want with me?" she sobbed. "What can you possibly discover that you haven't already found?"

The Kithrak appeared in her field of view, inspecting several shiny, dangerous-looking implements. Whether he was going to use them on her, or his display was simply to instill fear, she wasn't sure, but she suspected both.

His face was scarred from what appeared to be severe burns.

"Nice face," Ellyne quipped, momentarily chuckling, but her mirth was brief, and sadness quickly returned.

"Oh, we're largely past the discovery phase," the Kithrak laughed, poking her playfully with one of the sharp instruments. "I have it on good authority that you think you're the most powerful being on the planet. You certainly made that message quite clear. For a while, I was beginning to believe the rhetoric. After all, that was quite a show you put on for us all."

"Let me loose and I'd be more than happy to confirm it for you."

"Not likely," he chuckled. "You are, in fact, quite powerful, I'll give you that. But you're a fool to take on the Golgolonar—even with the Free People's meager help. You could have a vast, well-equipped army and you would still taste terrible defeat."

Ellyne perked up, still fighting back tears and failing. But she couldn't ignore what the Kithrak had just said. "You sound like you're familiar with the situation and—wait a minute. You seem to know a lot about me. Who's been spilling my secrets?"

"I believe you're familiar with him," the Kithrak laughed. "He's a close colleague of mine, actually."

Marik appeared from behind her and stood next to the Kithrak. "Hello, Ellyne," he said, his voice devoid of any emotion. The look on his face matched his demeanor. "How nice to see you here. I'd say it's a pleasant surprise, but it's neither pleasant nor a surprise."

Ellyne winced as fine spittle droplets landed on her face.

"Asshole!" Ellyne shouted. "I knew you were playing us! Nicole trusted you but I told her—wait, where's Nicole? If you hurt her I will—"

"Relax," he chuckled. "I'm sure she's just fine. But if

you're asking if she's also a captive, the answer is no. She's not a prisoner. Honestly, though, I didn't figure you to be the caring sort, given how you blasted the crap out of her."

"And you."

"Yes, and me. Pain I'm sure will be returned to you."

Ellyne winced as spittle droplets flew from the man's mouth again with his over pronunciation. The tears had stopped and the anger within her began to surface. "It felt pretty good," she laughed.

"Anyway," he continued, "your ability is quite impressive. You put the most powerful mage in her place with a simple thought. I merely told Kisternes here how impressive you were. His eyes lit up when I mentioned you, and he wanted you brought to him which, I must say, you cooperated rather willingly. You basically gave yourself up."

"I'm not your damned lab rat."

"From where I stand," Marik laughed, "that's precisely what you are. But none of this is really my concern now, as I've got more important work to do than babysitting a ... lab rat. She's all yours, Kisternes. I've got a few individuals to discuss things with."

"I commend you on your efforts. You've done a fantastic job of pissing me off yet again."

The bald man flourished his purple robes and exited the room, leaving Ellyne alone with Kisternes, the two lizards in front of her, and the two behind her she could occasionally hear but could barely see.

"Just lie still, Elleene." Kisternes inspected one of the instruments and then disappeared behind her. "This is a delicate process, and it could take a while. I wouldn't want a sharp instrument to accidentally slip on account of your annoying squirming."

"My name is Ell-een-ya. With all the time we've spent together, I'm surprised your brain can't comprehend that fact."

"Oh, it's not that I can't understand what your pitiful name is, human, but I simply don't care. You're nothing more than a toy at this point. An annoying, mouthy toy that will soon no longer be a problem."

"You're lying."

"Maybe," Kisternes chuckled, reappearing next to her. He leaned in close, grinning. "But now that you're tied down in a chair and, thanks to my colleagues here, helpless, it doesn't much matter does it? Now be a good girl and lie still. I need a blood sample."

"So, the lizards are definitely part of this. They're more than just brutes sent here to protect this asshole from me."

"Ow. Are you sticking the whole syringe in there?" Ellyne winced, feeling the needle penetrate her skin. She'd had blood drawn before and it was never this painful, so the Kithrak was either lousy at his job or he was doing it deliberately. Of course, he'd drawn her blood countless times so she knew he was doing it deliberately.

"You know," he continued, "if I thought you would give honest answers, I would simply ask you some questions, and this could all be over both quickly and painlessly."

"I wouldn't tell you if I knew."

"That's the spirit." The Kithrak once again leaned in closer, his face now inches away from Ellyne's. "Quite honestly, It's more fun this way. Even if you answered all my questions, I'd still run these tests on you because it's enjoyable for me. I'm not even sure what I hope to find, and I doubt the results will be conclusive."

"How very psycho of you."

Ellyne felt more impending tears which she fought back successfully this time, focusing more on her anger and trying to plan her escape. There was only one door she saw, and it was on her left—where Marik had exited the room. But it wasn't an escape route, that was the problem. She'd have to evade four Golgolonar and a Kithrak, and who even knew what lay beyond that door? She could've been in another asteroid prison, far removed from Seralune.

"What are you even looking for?" she asked. If she couldn't immediately escape, maybe she could distract him long enough to find her opportunity. "I'm just a human."

"A human immune to magic. A human who can channel flocia."

"Well, okay … yeah, there's that."

"And, just recently, a human who has proven she can not only control flocia but can also keep it from other magic users. To say these are not common traits is a tragic understatement, since not even my kind can perform these feats. In fact, nobody but—well, let's just say it's exceedingly rare in the first place."

There it was. Kisternes may have calmly said the words, but she was certain her abilities were a major cause of worry among the Kithrak and Golgolonar ranks. Until he said them, she wasn't even sure that's what was happening, but his candor confirmed it. The Kithrak would never let her be free. The Ilserate wouldn't either, and they would try to control her just as they had Nicole.

She had powerful abilities. Controlling those abilities, on the other hand, was proving difficult at best. She wondered how much the Kithrak knew about her control, and she decided to prod further.

"What's so special about that? It seems to me the Golgowhatevers did the same thing to me before I was brought here."

She was bluffing, having no real idea if that's what had really happened. All she knew was she had been surrounded and felt strange … as if something or someone were pulling energy directly out of her, not only preventing her from retaliating, but causing her to collapse.

"And, if that's what they were doing, then what's the big deal? Does this mean I'm really a lizard and I just don't know it? Ooh! Do I get a membership card to their little club or something?"

Kisternes disappeared behind her, making noise with his equipment. "You're very perceptive. But it's one thing for the Golgolonar to do it. It's entirely unheard of for another species to have that ability—especially in an individual who can't use magic in the first place. Like I said, it's unheard of in any species but the Golgolonar to exhibit such ability. And, whereas all Kithrak are attuned to magic, not all Golgolonar are capable of commanding flocia."

"That's it, keep talking," she whispered.

"Besides, it's currently taking five Golgolonar to siphon enough flocia from you to keep it from your grasp. You alone managed to lock flocia away from hundreds of thousands of people at once and I would like to know how you did that. So, yes, if you're not going to tell me then I will find out on my own."

"Five, huh?" she laughed, satisfied with the information Kisternes had leaked to her. She'd only seen four, so this was good information. "Sounds to me like they're not as powerful as they think they are, then."

"Oh, it's not that," Kisternes continued. "You're more powerful than they thought."

Ellyne smiled, trying to remain calm. She'd gained priceless information through the Kithrak's overconfidence. When she finally escaped, she would spread the knowledge to the Free People. Hopefully it would help them in some way. Maybe she would be able to finally control her ability better but, to do that, she first had to actually escape.

"Okay, look," she relented. "I ... I do know a couple of things and I can tell you if you promise to ease up on the doctor of pain persona. Because, damn, that needle is painful, and your hands are super cold."

She was improvising with every passing second, unsure of what an escape opportunity would even look like if one presented itself. If there was something she did well other than shooting people, it was bullshitting and stalling.

"Ah," he replied, the surprise in his voice readily apparent. "So, you remember our last sessions, do you? They were truly a lot of fun, as is what I have in store for you now. However … I might skip a couple of tests if you were to divulge what you know."

"Please don't hurt me," she said meekly. She wasn't used to the role but hoped to use her internal fear to her advantage. "Yes, I remember. But I didn't know what you wanted back then. I wasn't aware of my abilities or my potential."

"My dear," he chuckled, "neither did I. That didn't make it any less enjoyable for me."

"You're a damned monster." Her tears were real, but only because she let them flow. She used her very real fear to complete the ruse. "Please, just … listen to what I have to say before you go cutting me open."

"Very well. You may speak. I guarantee nothing, however."

"I need you to lean in closely, though. I don't want *them* to hear." She motioned to the Golgolonar with her head. "And you also probably won't. This is most likely information you're going to want to keep to yourself."

Kisternes hesitated, obviously considering the opportunity, but Ellyne could see the skepticism on his face.

"Or if you'd rather these boys learn the secret … and no longer require your services, I—"

The Kithrak perked up and appeared at her side. "Very well," he whispered, "you've got my attention."

"They might use it against you," she whispered back.

"What makes you think that?"

"It doesn't take a genius to notice you guys aren't exactly fast friends. What is it, more of an employer-employee relationship? Do they pay you?"

She was far out on a limb, making up whatever she could

and hoping there was a shred of truth behind it. Kisternes' facial expression did nothing to shoot down her theory and, for that much, she was relieved. She might have been touching on some truth.

He smiled and leaned in, apparently eager to hear the juicy information Ellyne had to share with him.

"I'm not entirely sure how it works," she whispered, completely making up everything as she went.

"Okay, yes?"

"But when I concentrate and I'm able to reach inner peace," she continued, barely able to comprehend her own lies. "It's sort of a placid pool and, when I touch flocia, that pool ripples and I can shape it into whatever I want."

This was prime bullshit, and she was impressed with her own lies. The urge to include a joke about his mother was strong.

"Yes?"

She motioned for Kisternes to lean in closer, and he obliged.

CHAPTER
TWENTY-FIVE

"HOLY CRAP THAT HURTS!" Ellyne screamed.

Her vision clouded and she saw stars. As far as she could remember, she'd never headbutted anyone before and now she knew why. This was not something she wanted to do ever again.

"Damned human!" Kisternes shouted, reeling from the blow and stumbling backward with his head in his hands. Ellyne's view of him was sketchy, but she was sure she saw blood.

"Gotcha!" she laughed, trying to hide the excruciating pain. It felt as if her skull would explode, but she beamed with accomplishment. If only she knew what to do next. It was difficult to concentrate through the pain mixed with elation.

Ellyne was surprised the Kithrak fell for her ruse when she herself saw only a slim chance of success. She underestimated how badly he wanted information—information she honestly lacked. Additionally, she learned a valuable bit of information herself—the Kithrak obviously didn't trust the Golgolonar.

The Golgolonar moved to protect the stunned Kithrak, but

he motioned them away with his hand. The moment was brief, but it felt like an eternity to Ellyne who sensed the momentary ripple in flocia and felt her strength return. Instinct kicked in and she acted, supposing she must have surprised them and disrupted whatever they'd been doing to keep her docile.

Seizing on the opportunity, she reached out and connected with the power, allowing it to rise inside her. There was no effort this time—a key difference from past events—and the power threatened to overcome her. Whatever flocia was, it was quite clear it, not she, was in control and she acquiesced, allowing it to guide her.

The window was brief, but it was ample time for her to act, and the result was not only spectacular, but also deadly. She broke her bonds and leapt from the chair, simultaneously blasting the room with force that shattered both glass and bones.

Everything in the room flew in random directions, slamming into walls, the ceiling, and the Golgolonar. The chair crumpled, creaking as it twisted and ultimately flattened against the floor. The cabinets exploded and the various instruments and tools buried deep into the walls.

Kisternes yelped as his body twisted in unnatural ways, finally colliding with a wall. Though their physiques were far more durable, the Golgolonar in the room succumbed to the force. They made various grunts and squeals as they collapsed to the floor and lay motionless and shattered.

For a moment, Ellyne stood, dumbfounded, and stared at the scene before her. The room was in shambles, and the walls had buckled in several spots. But she knew there was no time to pause. Using flocia, she grabbed Kisternes and pulled him close, leaving him floating in the air before her.

He was alive and conscious, but only barely on both accounts. She scrutinized him, squinting and staring, inspecting his broken body, and listening to his raspy breaths.

Blood dribbled from his mouth and only one of his eyes was open.

"It appears this is the end of our … relationship," she laughed. "I've always been really bad at breakups."

"You're … dangerous," he sputtered, coughing up blood. "They fear you. They won't let you live. You'll have not one moment's peace."

"They? Who's they? Your superiors? Who are they and I'll give them more reasons to fear me."

"Yes," he muttered, "but not as much as *they* do." More blood dripped from the Kithrak's mouth as he weakly pointed to the Golgolonar bodies. His arm fell to his side as he exhaled his last breath.

"Son of a bitch!" Ellyne yelled, throwing his corpse across the room. "You give me a tiny bit of information, then you just up and die? What the hell? I didn't even get to finish you off myself."

She found her gun and blade on the floor, wrapped in her jacket and lying amidst shattered glass and twisted metal. After equipping herself, she stepped over a dead Golgolonar and kicked the mangled door several times before it finally collapsed, hitting the ground with a crash.

A crowd of curious Kithrak scattered when she emerged. She watched them flee—like rats when the lights turned on. The urge to go after them was strong. She wanted to hunt each and every one of them down and put a bullet in them, but she resisted, realizing her escape was more important.

She did, however, pause long enough to load a fresh cartridge in her weapon, grinning as she swung the cylinder shut. "I thank you for the wonderful accommodations," she shouted to the empty corridor, "but I'll be leaving now!"

"There isn't even anyone around to hear your wit. Typical."

She expected swarms of mages and soldiers to eventually oppose her as she strutted through the deserted passages, but she moved about completely unchallenged. This was eerily reminiscent of the Kithrak prison, and for a moment she was back there, a prisoner, and felt sadness.

"I swear, if I'm back out in space on another damned asteroid, I'll tear this place down." She gazed at her surroundings, hoping to spot any hint of where to go. There were indeed signs scattered about, indicating directions with arrows and text, but the words were illegible—probably Kithrak scrawling. The Kithrak alphabet wasn't something humans normally saw, so she could only assume this was the case.

"Maybe I'll just tear it down anyway," she growled, slamming her fist into one of the signs, knocking it from the wall and sending it clattering to the floor. She swore and kicked it down the hallway and watched as it embedded itself in one of the walls ahead.

"Where the hell *is* everyone?" she shouted. "I've got some complaints and I want to speak to your manager!"

For being such an asset to study, it was eerie that nobody had been sent to apprehend her. Where were the guards and lizard brutes? It stood to reason they wouldn't want their prized lab rat to escape. Surely, they didn't want her roaming unchecked among them.

"Unless," she mumbled, "they're all afraid of me. Kisternes did indeed say I was feared. Maybe they're all cowering and hiding."

A wry grin crossed her lips and her angry stomps turned to struts as she gleefully pranced through the empty corridors, unchallenged. She danced and skipped, humming and laughing while kicking open random doors in hopes of finding an enemy to exterminate.

"Anyone in here?" she asked after kicking open the nearest door. Ellyne continued, breaking down each door she found. "How about here? No? Maybe *this* one! I can't exact revenge if I can't find any of you. And I *will* find you."

The next door shattered and broke loose from the wall

from the force of Ellyne's flocia-powered kick. Channeling it was unintentional, but she was pleased with the results, nonetheless. Flocia appeared to be on autopilot now, and she embraced it.

"Well, hello, what is that?" she asked herself, staring at the shimmering circle on the floor of the otherwise dark, empty room. A low susurrus of voices whispered to her, though she couldn't understand what they were saying. Ordinarily, she would have thought this was strange and been concerned but she was flooded with power and a thirst for revenge. A few supposed voices in her head were nothing to worry about.

"The Kithrak have some really messed-up secrets in their basement," she muttered, slowly approaching. "Hello? Who's there? Anyone? No? You guys live in a boring place with … intriguing artwork on your floors, apparently."

The voices continued, almost inaudible, as she approached the shimmering area. "This could be a trap," she whispered, pausing. "I step in there and end up incinerated."

"But," she continued, "it seems senseless to have some random trap just sitting here behind a locked door. And besides, I doubt it can harm me anyway. You know what? Screw it."

She jumped inside the circle and braced for something bad to happen. To her dismay, but entirely expected, nothing happened. Her entire body tingled, and the circle dimmed almost completely.

"Of course," she spat. "Why would this be any different? Because it's magic and it won't affect me. Why am I not surprised?"

Ellyne closed her eyes and relaxed, exhaling a deep breath, and hoping to somehow bypass her magic immunity. This shimmery circle was different—far different than anything she'd seen before, and she was certain it held a clue. Aside from that, she had nothing better to do and nowhere else to go. If she could somehow use this circle to either escape or destroy something, she felt she had to try.

"Okay, flocia, do your stuff … or something. Can you just, you know, work this once? Maybe help a girl out?"

Her limbs still tingled but the soft voices stopped their whispers—either that or she just wasn't paying close enough attention. She wasn't accustomed to letting go—to relaxing. Was she doing it right? Would it even work? Without any real understanding of flocia or her unique abilities, this was like trying to fire her gun without a trigger.

"Come on," she shouted. "Seriously, can you work for me just this one time? How can I be able to both channel flocia but also not be affected by it? What nimrod thought this was a good idea? Either give it all to me or none of it."

She reached out again, feeling the sensation within her, like a reservoir behind a fragile dam. It felt as if flocia recoiled every time she reached for it—almost as if this were some kind of elaborate game it played.

"Seriously? If I get out of this alive, you and I are going to have a little chat—woman to … mystical force thingy."

The tingling in her limbs subsided but she could feel the well of flocia within her. Had she figured something out? Could she truly control this ability? "Just … please work and I'll be your best friend."

She heard grunts and guttural noises shortly after her body stopped tingling. "Oh, that's not good … or maybe it is."

Her hand went to her gun the moment her eyes opened, and she fired three bullets, instantly dropping two Kithrak and a Golgolonar.

Her gaze immediately scanned the room for any more potential enemies. "I guess I'm not *your* best friend," she laughed, prodding the Golgolonar corpse with her boot. "Okay, then, where the hell am I?"

She found herself in a room vastly different than the one

she'd left. Panels and holographic screens crowded every wall. While they resembled the controls she watched Derek use countless times, they also looked far more … alien, if such a thing was possible.

Illegible symbols cycled and scrolled on various screens while panels of all kinds beeped and alternated flashing lights.

The two Kithrak corpses lay against their panels, slumped lifelessly in their chairs where she'd shot them. They almost looked as if they were merely sleeping on the job until one noticed the blood pooling on the floor beneath them.

"What the hell?" she gasped, inspecting the bodies further. She saw multiple wounds on their backs. Some appeared to have healed over while others looked recent. "That's interesting," she mused, "and gross. Looks like everyone got what they deserved. Now I just need to find out where I am and where I'm going … and maybe just tear everything down in the process."

The door quietly slid open on its own when she stepped up to it, revealing a larger room beyond where everything was a stark contrast to the empty rooms and corridors she'd just left. More panels and controls were scattered about— some against the wall and some on freestanding consoles. Ellyne would've found it wondrous if she wasn't so intensely focused on escaping. She guessed she was seeing sights few humans were privy to.

She was about ready to move on when something outside one of the windows caught her eye. She holstered her gun and moved to get a closer look, gasping when she realized what she was seeing.

"That's … Karnascus," she muttered, putting her hand against the window's energy field. Of course, there wouldn't be glass on a spaceship, but she was somehow still taken aback when she realized this fact.

"Holy crap, they brought me aboard one of their ships!"

she laughed. "I guess that complicates things a bit, but at least I'm not on some dead rock in the middle of the galaxy somewhere. And I've got a rather unique view of the city."

Ellyne wasn't sure how long she stared out the window, gazing down at the buildings which seemed so small from up high. It was truly a beautiful sight, but this was a situation she wasn't expecting, and it complicated her escape somewhat. It was never easy—they couldn't have tucked her away in some moldy Ilserate building somewhere.

"Okay," she muttered, "time to pivot then. I can escape from a lizard ship. I'm the mage breaker. I'm ridiculously powerful and everyone's afraid of me, right? It's time to leave."

She turned from the window and drew her weapon, but she paused a moment, lost in thought as a grin escaped her lips.

"Or…" she continued, "I can stay."

The various panels flashed with bright, multicolored lights, emitting beeps and various other sounds. Ellyne looked around her and focused, feeling flocia in everything around her, including herself.

The lights on every panel simultaneously turned green.

"I'm gonna steal myself a lizard ship."

CHAPTER
TWENTY-SIX

ELLYNE GAZED out the ship's window, staring at the ground below, the clouds above, and another massive Golgolonar ship floating nearby. She wasn't sure how the craft she was on compared to the size of the other ship, but she surmised it was much smaller. Maybe the one she saw out the window was their capital ship … if they had one. It certainly was enormous. To her, it seemed like overkill.

"How could anyone possibly fight against something so large? How many dragon people are in that thing? And how many are in *this* ship?"

As always, she had an idea but no plan. She loaded her gun and slipped it back in its holster at her hip. There had been little resistance thus far, but she suspected that was about to change. Certainly, the lizard beasts and Kithrak wouldn't let her simply roam around their ship and escape without a fight. After all, they'd worked hard to capture her in the first place.

"I need to find the bridge," she muttered, turning to the door. "Or the control room or whatever they want to call it and kill everyone and everything on this floating monstrosity. Surely, they've got some master control thing where they all stand around and issue commands or something."

She turned from the window and slowly approached the door, inspecting the various panels and consoles as she passed. For perhaps the first time, she was almost glad not to have a plan of any kind. Sure, she wanted to make her way to the main control center, but she also wanted to hunt down and slaughter every last Kithrak and smelly lizard thing she could find. Her thirst for revenge was great.

And she was fairly confident nobody could stop her. By bringing her to their ship, they'd brought about their downfall.

Two Golgolonar looked shocked as the door opened, apparently unprepared to find Ellyne standing on the other side. Instinct took over and she put a bullet in each one, dropping them before they could act.

"Time to move," she grunted, leaping over the bodies and charging down the corridor with her gun gripped tightly in her right hand. "No idea where I'm going, but I can't sit around."

She briefly wondered if Marik was still aboard somewhere and, if he was, if she should seek him out. The urge to tear the entire ship apart to find him was strong and she believed she could do it—if flocia cooperated, of course. Something told her, however, if he knew what was happening, the coward would've already jumped ship. That may have been the only smart thing the man had ever done.

She startled five Kithrak as she rounded a corner, nearly colliding with them. They jumped back and thrust their hands in front of their faces. Ellyne braced for the barrage of spells to collide with her but gave pause when she saw them cowering. Though she couldn't understand what they said, she knew pleas when she heard them.

"You're ... afraid?"

At first, Ellyne kept her weapon pointed at the floor,

watching the Kithrak as they slowly backed away. Two of them shook their heads and sobbed, tears streaming from their multiple eyes.

"You *are* afraid!" she laughed, grinning madly. "Good. You should be."

She gunned them down, emptying the remaining six chambers and sliding in a new cartridge immediately thereafter. There was no witty catchphrase or gloating. She spat on one of them as she ran past, unsure of where she was going.

She ducked into a room, waiting for a sizeable group of Golgolonar and Kithrak to pass, then continued her journey, remorsefully letting them go unscathed. They all deserved death, but she had now set her sights on the larger prize, believing she might have just devised a plan to kill them all without having to hunt for them one by one.

A plan!

Several times she encountered groups of Kithrak and, each time, the result was no different. The few Golgolonar she fought met the same fate. If she had to kill every last one of them, she would. And she would enjoy every moment. But, right now, she only cared about those who stood in her way.

"Focus, Ellyne," she whispered to herself, picking a random direction. For all she knew, she was traveling in circles, but the lack of bodies in the corridors convinced her otherwise.

Each encounter ended the same—with Ellyne wandering the corridors and leaving a trail of bodies in her wake. She almost felt like she was once again fighting in the Flocia Wars. The two circumstances weren't much different except, this time, she knew which side she was on.

"Why the hell do the golgolowhatevers need such large ships? And why can't they have clear signage pointing me where I need to go?" She turned down a corridor and caught sight of at least two Kithrak as they fled around a corner. "It's like they don't want me to kill all of them or something."

Ellyne sprinted until she caught up with her quarry, ending their lives without hesitation or remorse. She left the bodies behind, turned a corner, and channeled flocia as several spells pelted her. She staggered forward, letting the effects wash over her, and unleashed a stream of energy from her fingertips, striking the three Kithrak mages. Their screams were brief—cut short as their bodies were partially incinerated by the blast.

Ellyne laughed, kicking one of the partial corpses as she moved on. She fully expected to hear alarms by this point and was surprised by not only the lack of flashing lights and ear-piercing sounds, but also by the relative emptiness of the ship. She wondered if there was some sort of silent signal based off magic that only they could detect. It seemed feasible but it didn't matter to her whether they were alerted. She would fight through as many Kithrak and lizards as she had to.

The ship's corridors were sleek and smooth, and Ellyne noticed few doors during her rampage, which was why she gave pause when she found herself standing outside a closed door at the end of a hallway.

Like all the doors on the ship, it was a sliding mechanism but, unlike all the others, this one stubbornly remained closed.

"Really?" she laughed. "A locked door? I guess it's a good sign—maybe I'm finally in the right place. It's about damn time."

Using flocia, she poked and prodded the door. The metal creaked and groaned as she pressed harder until, finally, the door gave way and fell inward, slamming onto the floor.

The room beyond was filled with panels, screens, and several odd-looking chairs, all situated in front of large windows that offered a full panoramic view of the sky, the city below and, fortunately, the massive spacecraft ahead.

Four Golgolonar and ten Kithrak stood between her and the ship's bridge. The hulking scaled brutes each held a crackling stun baton, ready for combat. Drool dripped from the fangs of one of them as it grinned and pointed to Ellyne, grunting and snorting. It motioned for the Kithrak to attack.

The Kithrak paused, however, looking at one another. It appeared none of them wanted to be the first to act. Ellyne could read the fear on their faces as clearly as a screen on the Karnascus streets. She herself hesitated, curious to see how it played out.

Several Kithrak muttered to one another while a few others appeared to back up—slowly retreating or at least looking for cover. All four Golgolonar grunted, pointed, and growled but the Kithrak apparently refused to act.

The Golgolonar didn't appear to be in a hurry to start a fight either, but the Kithrak's refusal to engage left them in an even more awkward position.

For several moments, nobody acted or reacted. Ellyne wasn't sure what the aliens were planning, but she herself was determining the best and most efficient way to kill them all, preferably without damaging the equipment in the room. She stayed her hand, however, still gripping her gun but making no move.

One of the Kithrak fled—running for a door to Ellyne's left but, before it got far, a Golgolonar lashed out with its baton, knocking the convulsing alien to the floor. The brute shouted something, then pointed at Ellyne again.

Another Kithrak made a run for it but it, too, didn't make it far and was grappled by another of the hulking lizards. This time, however, its punishment was a broken neck.

Ellyne emptied her gun into the four Golgolonar—two bullets for each. They must not have had any defenses because that was enough to drop all of them. Even their thick hides couldn't stop her bullets this time.

The remaining eight living, conscious Kithrak were stunned and confused—both frightened and grateful at the same time. They murmured in their alien tongue both to one another and to Ellyne. The moment she thought they were going to attack her, she found herself embraced by several sobbing Kithrak with at least two others trying to get in on the hug.

"Oh," she said, unsure of what was happening, "hey, you're welcome … I guess?"

Using flocia, she violently ejected them, smashing them into the walls repeatedly. When she was sure they were all dead, she dropped them to the floor.

"Okay, now to do what I came here for."

With flocia, she reached out to the ship's controls and felt them acquiesce. Once again, all the lights in the room went from red to green as she connected and brought them under her command.

She sifted through a myriad of different functions, quickly scanning until she found the door controls. With barely a thought, she used flocia to create a barrier sealing off the bridge since she'd quite obviously destroyed that particular door.

"That should keep out unwanted guests," she muttered, activating the locks on all the ship's doors. "And keep everyone on board. At least for a little while. Now, then, how about weapons? Surely this monster ship's got some."

She searched again until she found the ship's weapon systems and brought them online. "The two main cannons ought to suffice," she mumbled, activating them. "I just hope they're beefy enough to take down that monstrosity."

She brought both cannons to bear, aiming them at the massive Golgolonar ship ahead of her, waiting impatiently as they spun up or heated or whatever. She didn't know what they were doing, just that they were taking their sweet time.

"Twenty percent … come on, can't you go any faster? It's tough to gain the element of surprise when it takes an hour and a half just to activate a couple of weapons."

As the two massive cannons warmed up, Ellyne thought she could feel them drawing flocia—like a massive fan in front of her, sucking the air past her and threatening to take her with it. It felt like an enormous amount being drawn and Ellyne couldn't help but grin, eager to witness the result.

"Thirty-five percent. At this rate, I'll be here all day just waiting. I seriously thought Golgolowhosit technology would be better than this." She tapped her foot and approached the front window, staring at the larger ship in the near distance. "I wonder…"

Ellyne focused on the flocia pouring into the weapons. Instead of letting them pull it, she pushed power into them, adding to the flow. "That's more like it," she laughed, sensing the power level jump to fifty percent.

She pushed harder, forcing more power into the guns and sensing the energy levels rise even further. As she powered the guns, however, she noticed the larger ship start to move.

"Oh no you don't," she laughed, forcing even more flocia into the cannons until they were at one hundred percent charge.

But she didn't stop there.

She pushed more flocia into the weapons systems, apparently overcharging the cannons but, as she did so, she sensed alarms and warnings from the ship. She ignored them, completely unconcerned about possible repercussions.

"Good," she spat. "I'll damage two of their ships at the same time."

Just as the cannons signaled a critical failure, she fired them. The ship rocked and groaned, violently shaking and knocking Ellyne to the floor as dual explosions filled her ears.

"That was awesome!" she shouted, getting to her feet in time to witness two explosions tear into the other Golgolonar ship. "That's right! You want some more? No? Tough shit!"

She focused again, intent on powering up the cannons but was met with crushing disappointment. In her elation and thirst for more power, she'd indeed damaged the weapons and they ignored her commands.

"Damn it," she swore, bringing her fist down on one of the consoles. "Even your ship can't handle me. Fine, then, I don't need weapons. I can still end this."

She powered up the ship's engines, urging it forward at maximum velocity.

CHAPTER
TWENTY-SEVEN

THE SPACECRAFT JOLTED SUDDENLY, nearly sending Ellyne to the floor. She steadied herself, leaning on one of the consoles as the ship lurched forward. Through her flocia link, she connected with the onboard computers and used the controls to force more power into the engines, unconcerned with any damage that might cause.

She chuckled, recalling how much trouble Marik had controlling their tiny ship as they fled the disintegrating asteroid prison. He'd be red with rage if he knew what she was doing.

The irony was not lost on her—how she'd damaged the ship's weapons by doing this very same thing—but none of that mattered. The larger Golgolonar ship was on the move, and this was her one chance to strike back.

"This is much more convenient than fighting every alien one by one," she laughed. "Go ahead, try and run. I'd run from me, too."

She checked the weapons systems again, but they remained inoperable. It didn't hurt to make sure. After all, she had no functional knowledge of their technology. For all she knew, they could repair themselves or simply come back online after they cooled down. For a moment, she considered using flocia to attempt repairs—if that were even possible—but quickly scrapped that idea, afraid of making things worse.

"Can't this thing go any faster?"

Ellyne searched the controls but found nothing helpful. She couldn't explain how she knew what they all did except she simply *felt* them, and instinct took over. She simultaneously reveled in the power she had while she also disgusted herself with the methods she'd used to gain it. Soon, however, none of that would matter.

"You can't run from me," she cackled, presenting her middle finger to the ship ahead. "You're a slow-ass, giant ship and I'm a slightly less slow, tinier … um, ship."

She felt her own spacecraft gaining speed. It appeared acceleration wasn't its strong suit, but it had eventually picked up some momentum. The other ship, however, was accelerating as well.

It was also injured.

Ellyne wasn't sure how much damage she'd done with the ship's weapons, but the larger ship was shedding debris and plumes of smoke rose from the two points of impact.

As her target slowly gained speed, she adjusted course, continuing to fly straight toward it.

"What are you going to do now, lizards?" she shouted. "I'm coming for you—all of you! You couldn't stop me before, and now I have one of your ships!"

She laughed. They were obviously afraid of her, fleeing like cowards. They apparently weren't as powerful and intimidating as everyone thought.

But she was more powerful than anyone imagined. And she was about to show the entire city just how true that was.

Even if it was a one-way ticket.

Ellyne noticed something happening ahead. It began as a

tiny sparkling, shimmering light on the ship's surface but quickly grew into a radiant orb.

"Well, shit," she muttered. "Looks like they have weapons, too. I probably should've thought about that." She searched the ship's functions for anything that might help but came up empty. "Uh, c'mon ship, turn or something!"

A blinding orb of energy launched from the spacecraft, and Ellyne knew it was going to impact her ship. She braced herself even as she still tried to steer the craft out of harm's way. But such a bulky object wasn't nimble enough to avert the collision and the impact knocked her to the floor.

"Okay, so that presents a small problem," she spat, getting to her feet. Using flocia, she reached out to the ship's systems and found, ironically, only the weapons systems were damaged in the blast. They must not have known the cannons were already inoperable.

"You guys clearly suck at this," she teased over an open communication channel. They most likely wouldn't understand her words if they received the message at all, but she felt the taunt was absolutely necessary. "You can't stop me. I'm going to kill every one of you—on your ship and mine!"

Her craft continued to accelerate, still aimed directly at the other ship which appeared to be charging its weapon again.

Ellyne regretted damaging her own weapons so early. She also wished she'd targeted their cannons first.

Another orb of energy slammed into her ship, causing a shower of sparks from the ceiling and several of the control consoles blinked off and on before stabilizing. Her knowledge was limited, but the damage apparently hadn't affected any flight systems. She continued her course, getting closer to the monstrous ship ahead.

Suddenly, warnings flashed on the consoles, and they emitted a hideous, shrieking noise. Ellyne couldn't read the illegible Golgolonar script, but her connection with the ship clearly conveyed the message.

Warning: Collision Imminent.

"That's the idea, genius."

Despite the repeated warnings and annoying, ear-piercing cacophony, she urged the ship forward, watching as her target quickly got larger in the front window.

She wasn't afraid—she wanted this. She was about to singlehandedly free her planet from the aliens' tyranny while simultaneously freeing herself from the curse she bore. She could think of no better way to go out.

"Here's to a free Seralune."

The enemy ship started to fire its cannon again, but it was too late.

Ellyne closed her eyes and exhaled.

EPILOGUE

ELLYNE OPENED HER EYES, staring up at rays of sunshine filtering through a canopy of leaves. The familiar, babbling sound of water filled her ears and she sat up, gazing at the familiar sight of the fort she'd built here as a child.

"So," she muttered, "is this what happens when you die? You get sent back to your childhood hideout for eternity?" She stood and dusted herself off, gazing at the serene beauty of the forest with which she was intimately familiar. "I guess I can live with that. Or, well, *not* live with that."

Overhead, a blue wriggler squawked.

"Except for that, of course. I hate that damned bird."

She reached for her gun, hoping to catch a glimpse of the noisemaker, and possibly put a bullet in it, but her hip was bare. Even the holster was missing.

"I guess, then, no weapons in the afterlife? So, I'm obviously in the bad place—cursed to listen to that little shit weasel for eternity? Brilliant."

At least Seralune was free. She was free. Though she still harbored hatred for both the Kithrak and the Golgolonar, she was at peace with her sacrifice.

She walked to the stream to get a drink, relishing the cool, refreshing water. She stared at her reflection in a still pool of water and almost saw herself in a younger version—the girl who routinely retreated to the forest to play, make believe and live out various adventures. Such a thing was appealing back then but now, not so much. Adventures were overrated.

The bird screamed again.

"Shut up already," Ellyne shouted, throwing a rock into the air. She heard it sail through several branches and land somewhere in the distance. Undeterred, the bird yelled in reply.

"Maybe that damned bird's stuck in the bad place and we're here to torment each other for all time."

She sat next to the creek, listening to the water flow, and wondering what to do next. If this truly was the afterlife, it was going to be long, boring, and annoying. She'd never been one to believe in any kind of higher power but then, wasn't that sort of what flocia was? Or maybe magic was simply technology nobody really understood yet.

She heard the flitting of the blue wriggler's wings as it landed next to her. If she wanted to end its life, this was the perfect chance. It was within arm's reach, yet it didn't flee.

"That's odd behavior for a bird," she mused. "I could reach out and snap your neck at any time, and I think you know that but here you are, sitting next to me, fearless."

The bird looked up at her as she stared at it. The animal was beautiful with plumage that ran through many shades of blue. She'd never seen one this close. For as annoying as its squawks were, it was a lovely sight.

She slowly reached out and gently stroked it. To her surprise, it remained steadfast and unafraid. Even more surprising was the fact that it didn't yell at her. "I may have found a way to finally get you to shut up," she laughed. "Is this what 'kill them with kindness' means?"

That was when it opened its mouth but, instead of its shrill cry, it uttered one familiar word.

"Unity."

Acrid smoke filled Ellyne's lungs as she gasped for air. She choked and coughed, opening her eyes but closing them immediately as dust and dirt dropped on her. At first, she could hear nothing, but that nothing eventually became muffled sounds—shrieks and screams, explosions and screeching metal.

She couldn't move. She was pinned under something and, though she tried to squirm, it only seemed to shift whatever was on top of her and make things worse.

"Well, this is fun. I guess no afterlife for me. But how am I even alive? I should have died. I wanted to die. Maybe I still will."

"So, what then?" she shouted, spitting out dirt and chunks of stone, "I'm destined to die here, buried under whatever this shit is? Can I go back to the forest instead?"

She tried connecting with flocia, hoping to blast her way out of whatever was on top of her, but it was difficult to concentrate and impossible to breathe. It appeared she wouldn't have to worry about being buried alive for long.

She felt the end coming with the insatiable desire to gasp for air that simply wasn't there as she began to slip into unconsciousness.

"At least I took them with me. I took them all with me, the bastards. I'll take everyone down if I make it out of here. Whoever's left—if there is anyone left. I'll come for them all."

"I think she's under here!" a muffled voice shouted. "Hang on, this shouldn't be a problem."

Ellyne felt the weight on top of her disappear as the sun tried to penetrate her eyelids. She coughed and gasped for breath, suddenly able to move as she wiped dust from her face and sat up.

Nicole was the first thing she saw which brought glee to her heart. The girl knelt in front of Ellyne, staring at her intently. For the first time in a while, Ellyne felt joy and was happy to be alive.

"Nicole! It's you!"

"How could you?" the girl asked, sadness painted on her face. "You're a monster!"

Nicole's spell was powerful. Ellyne felt her body try to absorb the incoming magic, but it overwhelmed her, and she had only a split second to think about it before she lost consciousness.